FLAMES OF ADVENTURE
DRAGONBLOOD

C. C. MILTON

To my loving daughter,
The day you were born, you stopped crying for a few seconds, and looked at me. Time stood still for me then. I knew from that moment I would always love you, and do everything in my power to be a good father.
Always be the best person that you can be, and remember that I will always be your father.

About the Book

Dragons being hunted for sport caused the race to panic as their numbers dwindled. One dragon discovered that she could use magic to shape-shift into the human form and breed with them. Over the course of a thousand years, a new race emerged: dragonblood. A dragonblood has the looks of a human but the strength of a dragon.

This is a companion novel to *Flames of Adventure: Embers of Darkness*. It is not required to read the first book before reading this one, but reading it at some point would help with understanding some of the chapters. Instead of the same story from another character's point of view, this book consists of new characters for the most part. The events take place at the same time as the previous book, and some of the chapters will overlap with chapters from the first book. I thank you for taking the time to read *Dragonblood and I hope you'll enjoy it*. The next book in the series will be *Ashes of Chaos*.

ABOUT THE AUTHOR

Born and raised in Alaska, I have always loved the art of storytelling. In school, I would always write short stories. Having an active imagination, and also a keen mind that was interested in history also helped me with writing.

Now a father of three, I try my best to find the time to write. I teach creative writing to kids in the school I work at and try to help them if they want to become writers.

I sincerely thank you for taking the time to read this book and I hope you enjoy it.

1. Edition, 2023

Cover designed by MiblArt

Papyrus Author, Inc. - Virginia Beach

c.c.milton99@hotmail.com

❀ Created with Vellum

THE CURSED ISLAND

In the center of the mortal realm where all the oceans touch lies an island where no one dared to live, for the monsters that occupied the waters and the lands are ancient creatures who were created for a war—now with no purpose— killed all who came near it.

A lone ship made its way towards the shore. Waves crashed into its sides, pushing it towards the razor-sharp rocks. The ship carefully made its way towards a small dock made of stones.

A man in a black doublet jumped onto the dock before the gangway was in place. He looked around, making sure no beast would appear and hinder them. He had dark tanned skin, and crimson hair and eyes.

His voice was elegant and soft as he spoke. "I again thank you for shipping this cargo for me. I'm grateful to your family."

"Aye sir, no problem. You saved me great-grandfather, I just be glad I be able to settle the debt," the captain said as he limped towards him, waving at the crew to move the cargo.

"Oy, be careful! We must not damage them," a tall well-built man ordered the men as they moved.

The captain cleared his throat. His voice was a little shaky. "This shipment, these slaves, ya sure no one will miss them? They be mostly younger than ya normal cargo."

The man smiled. "I assure you this will not come back to haunt you. Tell me about your son. Is he doing well?"

The captain cursed under his breath and spat as he spoke, "Bitch of a wife took him. It be the curse of a sailor. Gone too long, she must have been lonely. It be why I be retirin' after this. I know I be able to win her back. Not every day a half-dwarf gets lucky with a half-gnome."

He looked at the people stuffed in the cages and cleared his throat. "I know it be none of me business, but... I be wonderin'—what these people for?"

The man patted him on the shoulder and said, "I will honor you by allowing you to know about this as a retirement gift. You see, my lord needs slaves regardless of their race. He needs their energy so he can escape from his prison. He is to be married to whom we Fallen worship —our master."

Then, a young voice called out to the captain, "Daddy!"

The captain looked around. "I know that voice."

Suddenly, a shadow loomed over the captain. He turned back to look at the man and realized that he was now a towering eight feet tall. His voice had also became deeper. "I never told you my name, that is the least I can do. I Taranis, the general of my lord's army."

The captain stood there frozen. He only found the strength to move when he heard the cry again. This time, he saw where it had come from and ran towards a cage. "Albert! Sir, this is me son," the captain shouted.

His son cried loudly. "Daddy, he killed mommy! That man broke into our house and killed mommy."

"Sir please, I beg of ya. I will supply you with double the shipment free of charge. Allow me to bring me boy home. I swear we won't speak of this to no one." The captain never took his eyes off his son as he spoke. All he could do was hold the boy's hand.

Taranis laughed, "Sir, I know you will not speak of this. I congratulate you on your retirement and your reunion with your son. As I said before, my lord needs the energy."

A loud ripping noise echoed across the sky as cracks formed in it.

Black tar-like vines shot out of the cracks and consumed everyone, even the sailors. Their screams lasted for about an hour before everything became silent.

Taranis kneeled down and lowered his head. "Lord, it is almost time. She has been awakened, and her sister is dead. If you prove yourself this time, I am sure she will return your affections for her."

A dark ominous voice echoed through the sky. "My dear friend and loyal general, you know what must be done next." The opening closed up.

Taranis stood up and walked back on the ship, scoffing. "Shit, I should have left a few alive. How do I operate this thing?"

He looked back at the cage from where he had heard someone crying. With a deep breath, he said, "I spared you two it seems—I do not know why I always spare a person or two each time. Captain, are we able to run the ship with just three? We don't have a lot of time before the Falhex beast arrives to eat what's left of the bodies."

CHAPTER 1
REBECCA

A light breeze blew through the window, gently kissing the cheeks of a sleeping girl. The morning sun shown on her face and forced her out of her slumber. She slowly exposed her yellow eyes to the new day. Her fingers combed through her hair, also a similar yellow, and she stretched with her other arm. She stumbled towards the window with excitement. She took a deep breath which was followed by a shout, "Hello morning! May I find my true love today!"

She rushed down the stairs and sat down at the table with her twelve siblings. Most of them looked the same, yellow eyes and hair. Only a few random ones had black hair with red eyes. Their mother walked around with some maids as they carried large platters of food.

"Rebecca, you are their older sister. Why do you not help around?" Her mother frantically placed the platter down while the kids attacked it like wild dogs. She scoffed, "You are the only one in your brood who is yet to move out. And do not use the excuse of being single again! Half of your brood is still searching for a mate."

Rebecca sighed. "But Mother, you know I need to focus on finding her—my love. I can't be distracted with work and bills."

"I do not understand you not wanting to help spread the bloodline of our clan. We are the smallest clan in the capitol. We are lucky your

father is the finance officer of the king." Her mother sat down and grabbed a roll of bread. She continued, "And talk formally around the house. I do not want any of these pups picking up your bad manners."

"Calm down, my love. We had two large broods with twelve hatchlings each. And none of them died during the hatching. Our bloodline is not going to diminish because of her desire for other women." Rebecca's father smiled at her as he walked towards the study.

"But she is setting a bad example for these pups. Rebecca, you already wasted several mating cycles. Do you wish to stay looking like a whelp for the rest of your life? At least have a single brood so you can be more attractive for the ladies you wish to bed." Her mother eyed her as she stared at the table.

Rebecca slammed her fist on the table. "To hell with this! I'm just going to grab a bite to eat at the market! I may meet my Miss Right at the bar," she grunted and ran off.

"To hell with her and my sisters!" Rebecca laughed as she ran down the street. "What do they know of true love? May today bring me the woman of my dreams."

"Ah, Rebecca. I see you must've had another fight with your mother. Come here and eat with us," the farmer's wife shouted and waved at her.

As Rebecca came closer, her body became paralyzed by an aroma. Some drool escaped the corners of her mouth and she sniffed the air. "Oh my goodness, that smell is heavenly."

The farmer's wife chuckled and held out a bun coated in sugar and spice. "Tomorrow is the big graduation celebration." She let out a sigh, "Oh right, normally your family is usually on vacation during the event. You've never been to one."

Rebecca grabbed the sweet roll and tore through it like a savage beast. "But not this year. My father has decided to retire at the end of this fiscal year and hand over the job of royal accountant to one of my brothers. He has also decided to not take any vacations this year," she said with a full mouth.

Rebecca looked around after she finished eating and quietly asked, "Is Amanda around? I wanted to say I am sorry."

The farmer's wife looked at her with a firm stare. "No, she is now engaged. Look my dear, I don't care what you are into but you need to think before you kiss someone. You've known each other for years so she is not mad at you. She just wishes to not see you for a while. You ruined her first kiss after all. But don't worry, she is planning a big surprise for you when she visits us," the lady chuckled as she patted Rebecca's shoulders.

She handed her a basket full of rolls as she said, "Here you go, young miss. Take this to your father when you get home."

Rebecca grabbed the basket and ran off as she waved. She headed off to her usual spot, the Rustic Dragon Keep, a tavern owned by one of her brothers.

"Had another fight with Mom? You only show up here when you have a fight with her. You need to stop doing that. There is a pub in the poor district that is more suited for you," her brother said snootily but smiled at the same time.

"Just hand me a uniform and I will work for the meal," Rebecca scoffed as she held out her arms.

"I see. So it was that bad. I have no problems with feeding you— we are of the same brood—but I do not have a uniform that would fit you. You refused to mate so you are still stuck as a whelp. I will just tell the people that you will surely offend that you are my younger sister." He said as he pushed his glasses firmly up on his face. He sat her at the table near the back and placed two plates of food on it.

Rebecca played with her food and slouched in her seat. "Marcus, why is Mother like that?" she said, unable to take her eyes off of the meat she was rolling around.

Marcus took in a deep breath and poured her some wine. "You are the runt and were supposed to have died. Just cracking out of your eggshell almost killed you. But you survived. Mother is worried about you but hides her fear with her pride. On the other hand, Father thinks that anything you do is a blessing, which is why he is more under-standing of you." He spoke slowly as he ate, trying not to bite the inside of his cheeks. "And Cassy is a whore, so ignore your sister." Rebecca snorted and giggled.

She handed Marcus the basket of sweet rolls and let out a slow breath, not looking him in the eyes as she talked. "Can you take these to father? They are from Farmer Dutch. I will not be going home tonight."

"Ahh! So you found a—" she shoved her hand over his mouth before he could finish.

"No, I wish. I've never seen the graduation ceremony before. I hear it gets really crowded. I want to make sure I get a good spot." She removed her hand and stood up. With a slight wave, she was out the door before he could protest.

As Rebecca approached the arena, she quickly put away in her pocket anything that gave her away as a noble. The ceremony was taking place in the center of the town and touched all four districts. The surrounding booths sold trinkets for whichever event was being held. It was known that some of them were a front for kidnapping rich children and holding theming for ransom.

As a child, Rebecca had played around the area before and was known by some of the merchants. Because of her size, it was easy for her to help them out by entertaining their kids while they set everything up.

"Aye Rebecca, ya helped us a lot. I thank ya," the dwarf merchant said as he eyed her body. "I don't know why ya remove ya crests and badges. We all know ya be a dragonblood, and they be always nobles. No one takes ya cause ya would kill the lot." Rebecca stood there blushing as he handed her a flask.

"Do you know of any good spots for me to camp at?" Rebecca asked before she took a sip. "This tastes like goat piss."

The dwarf started laughing, almost falling over. "Aye, it be what makes ya grow a beard. Ya can stay with me family if ya wish. Me cousin works for the arena. We will get ya in a good spot."

The following morning, loud music played as people tossed rare herbs in the air to bring about a more festive fragrance. Rebecca headed towards the ticket booth the dwarf had told her to go. She was greeted by a rather short dwarf with a thick accent, making it hard to understand him.

"What you be?" he asked.

She showed him the flask and he scoffed. "Ya be bit young ta be in here."

Rebecca cleared her throat as she pointed at her ear, "I, sir, am a legal adult."

He spat on the ground and grumbled, "Dragonblood!" He waddled instead of walking and waved at her to follow. He took her to a balcony that was halfway in the middle of the arena seating. The privet room connected to it had beautiful decorations that she marveled at.

As Rebecca turned around to thank him, she saw that he had his finger up his nose. "I thank you," she said as she tried not to vomit at the sight.

He pulled out a booger and flicked it off his finger and smiled, showing off his stained teeth. "This room never gets used. It be mine for when me bring in lasses." He chuckled slightly. "I hear ya be inta lasses. I could bring ya one if ya want, on the house."

Rebecca cleared her throat and shuddered a little. "No, I'm good. Take care, and thank you." The dwarf grumbled as he slammed the door.

A few hours went by and the students began to fill the arena ground while the people who came to watch quickly filled up the seats. The view from the vantage point was perfect; it allowed Rebecca to see everything.

As the headmaster gave his speech, one word got stuck in her mind: *the army*. She kept changing it in her head as her mind became more fixated on the idea.

If I enlist as an officer in the army, maybe Mother would stop bothering me about being jobless, she thought as the door behind her burst open.

The dwarf's back was facing her and his pants were around his ankle. He was accompanied by a human female dressed in revealing clothing with the dwarf's cock in her mouth.

The woman opened her eyes and gasped, "There is a little girl here, you moron!"

The dwarf eyed Rebecca and scoffed, "Aye, she be an adult dragonblood. She be inta lasses, me cousin says. I think she be eyeballing ya tits."

"Oh, is that so? I have had female clients before, and they say a woman knows the best way to touch a woman." She looked at Rebecca and smiled slightly. "Hmm…the scent she gives off is also alluring," the female said as she licked her lips.

Rebecca stared at the woman's revealing body and sighed, "Yeah, sorry. You are extremely attractive, so I lost control of my pheromones for a second."

The lady slowly walked towards her and said provocatively, "I hear it is an irresistible aroma and it enhances the sex drive," she leaned down and lightly nibbled on Rebecca's ear.

Rebecca looked towards the door. She could see the dwarf smile. She pushed the girl away and turned her head. "A year ago, I would've been all over you, but I am at the age where I need to find a partner. I also don't trust that dwarf. I think he'd try to touch me with that nub he calls a cock."

Rebecca tried to walk out of the room but the dwarf grabbed her by the arm and snarled. "Ya bitch be a virgin ta cock. I be willin' ta fuck that out of ya."

Just as quickly, he let go of her arm in fear when he saw her eyes glow slightly. "Nevermind, dragon cunt be over rated anyways," he said as he shoved her out the door and slammed it.

Rebecca took a deep breath and wrapped her arms around herself. *I miss being touched, but I need to find a mate. I can't help but think about her—well, too late now.*

She ran out and headed towards her house. She barged into her father's study as soon as she arrived and started talking through her rapid breaths. "Father, I have decided that I will join the army."

Her father cleared his throat and nudged his noise with finger. There was a man sitting in front of him, he said, "Do you remember my daughter, Rebecca, my king?"

The king laughed as he talked, "Ha! The one that almost died, yes. I have not seen her in ages. I do hear stories about her from your other daughter. I am glad to see she is full of life."

Rebecca bowed and quietly said, "I am sorry for—"

The king cut in before she could finish. "It is alright. This is your house, and I am a guest. So, you want to be an officer in my army? I cannot have a noble be a basic soldier, can I? I bet you're smarter than your sister," he said and chuckled. He then stood up and patted her on the shoulder as he walked out the back door.

Rebecca's father cleared his throat and said in a stern tone, "There was an incident in a village over a week ago. An entire family was killed, except for a little girl who went missing. Half of the people that went looking for her ended up dead, covered in some sticky black residue. The king wants our clan to look into the incident." He smiled at her, "I think joining the service would be perfect for you."

CHAPTER 2

FAILED TRAINING

"Father, this is not fair. You have never been this harsh with any of my brothers," Rebecca whined as she sat down on the ground, covered in bruises.

"I told you to call me Lord Crast! Once you join the service of His Majesty, you must address even family members by their last names." Rebecca's father adjusted his glasses and took a deep breath.

"Sorry my lord, Father, Sir Crast. Please punch me some more, and call it training." She scoffed and spit some blood on the ground.

"You are a runt, Rebecca. You are weaker than the rest of the brood. Even your skin is not as thick or tough. Therefore, I must train you to fight. I am the only one that can hold back enough to do so," he said as he smiled in a ready stance.

She replied in a mocking tone. "Sir Crast, my lord, and father," she cleared her throat, "I know that we must never give up, but I am in need of rest. You never allowed me to exercise even once out of fear that I would fall over dead, and now you expect me to instantly become a combat expert immediately."

"You are right. I did spoil you a lot when you were a whelp. But my dear Rebecca, if you truly wish to be in the service, you must endure this. It is rare that a dragonblood even thinks of joining the army because we tip the scales. Legends say that we only join the army when something is going to change, and after the reports I have heard from the village—at the same time you requested for this, I am even more convinced that this is what fate says must be done," he said with his eyes closed.

After a few moments, Rebecca's father noticed it had gotten very quiet. He opened his eyes and saw that his daughter was gone. He ran around looking for her and saw that she was at sitting the table, drinking out of a flask. He mumbled as he went back into his study.

"I'll admit that he does get a bit long-winded, I will admit, but Father is only trying to prepare you for what is to come. You might be unaware, but there has been a war going on with the gnolls, which is why he is worried for you, sis." A young man that looked like her father handed Rebecca an orange as he sat down.

"Reggie, why must you go? Father could have picked anyone else from our clan. If you go, Mother will scold me even more for not having a mate to lay eggs with, and Father will just be harder on me with the training. Also, oranges do not mix well with my drink," Rebecca said as she peeled the skin.

Reggie took the orange from her and snickered. "I know, I handed it to you so you could peel it for me. How can you stand that dwarf crap anyways? They say if you drink enough of it, you can grow a beard."

She chuckled. "I know some good-looking women that love beards. Maybe it will help me find my mate."

Reggie sighed. "Father wants this to be done right. He wanted to do it personally but the king refused, so I am to go in his place. I am a decent detective, and I do need something to take my mind off my wife. You know how hard it is for a male dragonblood when he impregnates a human female. The clan's white dragon says she is alright and has a low chance of dying during the birth…but I need to find this missing girl to help clear my head."

He then snickered and pulled on her chin. "A beard would look bad on you. You have a perfect face—for a runt." He stood up, put on his cap, and walked out the door.

Rebecca watched him leave and sighed. She looked at her father and in a winning tone, said, "Alright Father—I mean, Sir Crast. You may continue to punch me in the face." He smiled at her and rushed back into the yard.

* * *

"Mom, that shit hurts!" Rebecca cried as her mother put ointment on her bruised face.

Her mother's face was red. The wrinkles around her face became more prominent as her eyes scowled at her. "You, and the crazy ideas you have. You have zero combat ability! What did you think was going to happen? Your skin is barely able to stop weak metals." She dabbed more of the liquid into the open sores.

"Stop your crying. This will have you healed up for the most part by morning. Really…a dragonblood from one of my eggs whimpering like a baby. Maybe you should find a real master to train you. All your father knows are some random punches and kicks. We never really needed to know anything more." She placed a cup of water next to the bed as she continued speaking. "And do not think of drinking that horse piss the dwarf gave you. I dumped it out and filled that flask up with medicines." She let out a long breath, "I am a little mad that he used his breath attack. Could have burned down the house."

Rebecca let out a whimper as she cried, "Mom, I only have a few things in life that I enjoy. I promised you I would stop going from bed to bed in order to find someone to be my proper mate. yet you still took away my drink."

"At least I did not demand the mate be a male, despite what I think about it," Rebecca's mother replied as she stood up and walked out.

Rebecca looked out the window next to her bed and touched her lips with her fingers. *Still bleeding, shit. I don't even remember walking into the bed. He must have knocked me out again. I hope the night lasts forever. I'm tired of being punched around.*

The following morning, Rebecca grabbed her flask, took a swig and then quickly spit it out. "Four hells! Mother said my drink tastes like horse piss, but I think this is piss!" She quickly drank some more and swallowed it.

Rebecca slowly walked down the stairs and went straight into the kitchen. The only people there were her parents. Everyone else was gone. She peeked out the window—no sight of her younger siblings. Her mother quietly placed a plate of food on the table. The food was from her brother's restaurant, her favorite dish.

"Last time you guys did this was when you told me my pet snapping turtle died, though I know you had Sister take it to the woods," Rebecca said as she warily sat down.

Her father cleared his throat, and said, "After training you for a few days, I have decided that you must find a master to train you. Even if you managed to hit me, I would not be hindered by it and would not slow down. It is unrealistic since the chances of two dragonbloods fighting are slim at best."

Rebecca stopped eating and stared at him. "You are putting me out in the woods, you bastards!"

Her mother's face turned bright red. "Do not use that word on us! But yes, we have packed you some things for your trip."

"You sent off the whelps to grandma's so you could kick me out and not have them cry. Dad, I know this must have been mother's idea. Why did you agree to this?" She paused for a moment. "She said she will cut you off. You no longer have to worry about having another brood, now it's just for fun."

Rebecca's mother blushed while her father cleared his throat. "Young lady, that is not—I mean, none of the masters in town are willing to train you, so you will have to head to the next town."

"I doubt you even bothered to ask everyone in town. What about some of those dwarfs you always praise as masters of their craft? I heard even the finest weaver among them is a war vet," she cried out.

He shuffled his hair with his hands and tried to speak calmly. "They have no idea how to train brawlers. There is no need for us to lower ourselves to use swords, most—"

Rebecca cut him off. "I need to! As was stated, I am weaker! Even when I use my own element in my attack, it hurts me. Dragons have been killed by the same weapons you claim are beneath us, and a real dragon's scales are much stronger than ours." Rebecca got up as she finished and stormed out the door, running without a direction.

In an instant, she collided into someone. "Oh, I'm very sorry. I hope I didn't hurt you," Rebecca said as she stood up and held out her hand.

The other person was a girl, slightly taller than Rebecca, wearing a brown cloak. One of her eyes was brown and the other was gold. Her hair was also a mixed color, one side was crimson while the other was brown. Her body seemed to be in great shape, and she had dark purple lipstick on.

Her voice was monotonous when she spoke. "It is fine. I was distracted by my thoughts."

"Are you sure you're alright? You sound a bit off," Rebecca said as she tried to get a closer look at the girl.

"My mother said one of the side effects of my creation left me void of expressing emotions." The girl stood there with a blank expression.

Rebecca's eyes lit up as she took a closer look at her. "You're very beautiful. I think the different colors of your eyes add to your allure."

"While creating me, my mother, decided on how I should look. My sister said the same thing." The girl said, still with a blank stare.

The girl then sniffed the air. "You are a dragonblood. Are you trying to attract a mate?"

Rebecca stood there with her jaw open, confused. "I am, but it seems to not work."

The girl blinked a few times. "Do you know how to find Verus?" She took a closer look at Rebecca's face. "Why did you do that to your eyes?"

Rebecca giggled and tried to pretend nothing was wrong, "Oh what do you mean? My eyes are like my sister's and mother's. A very lovely yellow."

The girl came a little closer. " No, you have black eyes. I heard about the new fashion of changing one eye color with that magical device. You have it in your pocket. You also have the lens in your eyes. My mother said lies are what lead to the disaster that leads to your downfall, but she also told me to never tell anyone about myself. So I am confused."

"I am a runt. I was told by my sister that when I show a genetic weakness, I won't be able to attract a mate." Rebecca said, not knowing why. She somehow felt the need to open up to this girl.

A strange noise came from the girl's gut. "Are you hungry?" Rebecca asked as she walked around the girl, looking her up and down. *I've never seen anyone with such a perfect body.*

"Mother provided me with no money. I can eat after I return to her next week." The girl still had a blank expression.

Rebecca laughed. "A week? Your mother must be such a devil."

"How did you know? Mortals are unaware of devils." The first sign of expression the girl showed was shock.

Rebecca rubbed her head and sobered up. "My bother owns a restaurant. It'll be my treat. My name is Rebecca."

The girl placed her hand over her stomach. "I would prefer to eat food that was not off the ground. I am Lilith." Rebecca took her by the arm and led her to the restaurant.

"Rebecca, it is the middle of the day. I cannot give you any food," Marcus said, trying to not get angry.

"I have my wallet. I can pay. This girl needs food. I ran into her, and knocked her over, so I owe her." Rebecca smiled and pointed to Lilith.

"She is really pretty. Are you now injuring people so they would date you?" He snickered as he showed them to a booth.

"I have never eaten food that was freshly made. Mother always gave me what was growing in the garden, or the nearest town would hand us their old bread." Lilith said as she sat there stiffly.

"Here you go, young ladies. I already had some food made for myself to take home, but since my sister has such a lovely date, I am willing to give it up," Marcus said and pulled up a chair.

He smiled at Lilith and began to ask her questions, "So, how old are you?"

Lilith took a small bite and answered, "My body is twenty. Mother used magic to age me, to see if her experiment would work. My sister says it is why I am unable to understand emotions. The food is very good." She ate some more.

Marcus sat there puzzled and asked more questions, "So, what brings you to the city? I have never heard of anyone that looks like you."

Lilith finished her food and looked at them both. She said, "My mother has sent me to gather information about my uncle. He was imprisoned, and she does not want him to escape. I was given two weeks to gather the information. I finished a week ago, so I wanted to see my father, Verus."

Marcus pulled Rebecca slightly away from the girl and whispered to her, "She is homeless and crazy. If someone that important had a daughter, everyone would already know. Did you know she has no feelings? I think I have talked to fish who showed more emotion."

Rebecca looked back and saw that Lilith had started to eat the food from her plate. She sighed. "Look, I know she is crazy, but she does have feelings. I saw her show a hint of excitement when I invited her to eat. Her eyes widened a little. She is so very lovely."

He placed his hand over his face and grunted. "Your pheromones seem to not be working on her. Maybe her brain is damaged, or she is not interested."

They walked back to the table and Marcus cleared his throat, "Look, I am sure you are a smart lady, but I have to tell you this to save my sister the heart trauma." He looked around the room to make sure no one could hear them. "She is looking for a mate."

Lilith stared at him. "Yes, I can smell her pheromones. I hear they are irresistible to the ones they want to allure."

Rebecca blushed as Marcus kept talking. "You see, it only works if the other person is interested. The only people that can see them are other dragonbloods, and the only one that can smell them is the one they are trying to attract."

Lilith finished eating the rest of Rebecca's food. "I do not under-stand why she wishes to mate with me. I have no penis. I also do not have any sperm to aid in her ability to mate. I am sorry, but I also ate your share of food."

Rebecca nodded and smiled. "It's alright. Eat as much as you wish."

Marcus nodded. "We use the term 'mate' for everything that revolves around the bed, even for non-reproductive means. So, you are not interested in her?"

Lilith looked at them both. "You mean sex? I have never thought about sex. The only people I have been around are my mother and sister—on the rare times she visited. I am immune to things like poisons, elixirs, sicknesses, and I guess pheromones. My sister explained all this to me. She has had almost thirty children in her lifetime."

Lilith stood up and walked towards the door. She waved at them. "It is getting late, and I am in need of rest. If I do not hurry, my spot will be taken."

Marcus could not help but to ask her, "Where are you staying?"

She pointed towards the center of the town. "Near the fountain."

Rebecca grabbed her hand and looked her into her eyes. "Look, I have a place. You can stay there for as long as you like."

Marcus cleared his throat as he almost choked on his own saliva. "You still have that place? I thought mom told you to sell it. The flask you carry is already a reminder of that mistake, and you kept the place it happened in!"

Rebecca handed him her wallet. She looked right at him and whimpered, "Please, Brother, do not tell them. They kicked me out of the house, and I have no place to go. Take the money you need to keep quiet. I'll pick up my wallet tomorrow." She gently placed it in his hands.

Rebecca ran off with Lilith before her brother could say anything. A few blocks from the impoverished district was a four-story building. The windows were boarded up and was covered in dust. Rebecca unlocked the door and quickly locked it back up. As soon as they got inside, they headed up some stairs to a single door at the top.

"I bought this building cheap from the dwarf merchant. He helped me make it look like it was a desolate building...cursed or something,"

Rebecca said as she opened the door. It was a large room with a bed that took over half of the floor.

"When I was a bit less sensible, this would be my place to hide my debauchery from my mother. Twenty people could fit in this bed." Rebecca wrapped her arms around herself and shivered. "I should have been smarter. The signs were there, but I ignored them."

Lilith kicked the blanket and a cloud of dust filled the room. "It is filthy. It will do." She laid down and took off her robe. Underneath it, she had on a black skin tight tunic and matching pants. It was hard to see with the hood but her skin was a slightly-tanned complexion.

"Wow, you have a great figure." Rebecca could not take her eyes off Lilith's body.

Lilith yawned as she tried to speak, "My sister says I have the perfect body, but I do not understand what she means by it. I must rest now. I need to sleep."

Rebecca looked out of a small hole where the window would have been and said, "It's still the middle of the day." She turned around, and Lilith was standing right behind her. Their noses touched.

Lilith hummed a little. "I have been awake for three days. I have thought about it and I realized I like honest people." She grabbed the pendant around Rebecca's neck and crushed it with her hand. "Your eye magic is not being honest. The black eyes make you look more interesting. They may help you find a mate." Rebecca blushed as she watched Lilith lie back down and fall asleep.

I'm confused. Is she trying to help me find a mate or is she actually willing to try to be my mate? She thought as she picked up the crushed pendant.

"Who is this girl? I'm going to get bored sitting here. Might as well try to find a master," she quietly said to herself.

Rebecca poured out the medication from her flask, and refilled it with a bottle of her favorite drink that she had stashed away in the house. She took one last look at Lilith and headed out.

Rebecca wandered around aimlessly until she reached the park. It had been built by the elves as a place to relax in when the city life became a hassle. The park spanned over ten acres of dense forest. She was about to sit at a bench just outside of the tree line but was distracted by some shouting.

In a clearing, there were two people with wooden wasters fighting each other. There was a bush nearby and Rebecca hid there to watch them.

That girl is really tall. I've never seen a human that tall before. I wonder what half she is. Rebecca stared at the girl's body.

How does her hair have that effect with the light? Her eyes remind me of Lilith's golden eye. Her chest is a bit on the flat side but she looks amazing overall. God, I need to find a mate. She stared intensely at the girl.

The other person was an old dwarf. He sat down and pulled out a pipe. "Aye, we been at this for almost a week. Ya no getting better," he said as he put tobacco in the pipe.

The girl almost sounded like an angry dog as she yelled at him, "Maybe if you aimed for more than just my ass!"

Rebecca tried to get a better look. *I need to get a better look at her,* she thought as her foot got caught on the bush and made it wiggle a little.

"Aye, we have a wee visitor," the dwarf said as he looked at Rebecca with one eye opened. As Rebecca freed her foot, it made her tumble out.

She stood up and chuckled nervously. "Sorry, master dwarf. I heard some shouting so I had to see who it was."

<h1 style="text-align:center">CHAPTER 3
REGRET</h1>

Rebecca's body shifted from side to side. She felt an emotionless voice whispering in her ear. *Get up* echoed in her mind. Her eyes were barely cracked opened when a blurry figure came into view.

She slowly sat up and yawned. "Lilith, is something wrong?"

Lilith stared at her blankly and cleared her throat. "I am hungry. I want to have more of that food we had before."

Rebecca looked around and licked her lips. "I should have dusted this place," she said as she spit out some saliva mixed with dirt.

She then pointed to a poorly-made bar table in the corner. With a dry throat, she said, "I have some money hidden over there. Just some silver coins. Take three and head to the food cart in the front with the dwarf standing there." She held out her family crest that she usually kept in her breast pocket. "Show this to him and he will deliver some stuff for you to last the day. Then wait for me here. I found someone to train me, so I'll be back later." Lilith took the crest and looked for the hidden coins.

"What makes you think I will return? I have my mission, and I cannot fail my mother." Lilith said as she pulled out a pouch.

Rebecca took a huge sip from her flask and coughed as she tried to speak, "You said you have an extra week and that you said you would help me with my mate issue."

Lilith headed towards the door and looked back at Rebecca. She tried to put some emotion into her words. "I will stay with you for the week and help you, as I promised." It was very off-putting the way she delivered her words. She waved and walked out the door.

I wish I could understand what was going on her head. Rebecca took another swig. *I still don't understand her motives.* She sighed. "Time for me to head out."

* * *

"Aye lass, I cannot train ya in a way, but I can give ya experience. Dragonbloods have no formal combat style, so ya best come up with one of ya own," Ulbrek looked up and down Rebecca's body.

Aluxes scoffed, "How can this really help me? I don't know what's going on in your perverted mind."

"Ya just be mad cause I hit ya tits like ya asked." He chuckled as he grabbed Rebecca's elbow.

"Aluxes, ya be unaware of what these are. Ya see, they call it skin, cause it looks like skin an' acts like skin. But in reality, it be tiny little dragon scales. The density be something ta witness. I've seen them break daggers by stabbing themselves," he said as he examined her closely.

Rebecca started to blush as she pulled away from him. "Yes, I know I'm a runt, but my skin is not that tough. I was hoping I could learn how to use a sword, or a spear."

Ulbrek spit on the ground and grunted. "I will hear nothing of it. Ya still be better off with ya fists."

He waved his hand at Aluxes and she stood in a ready stance. With a few pushes and light kicks, he forced Rebecca into a decent fighting stance.

As he grabbed her waist to move it, he pulled her flask out of her pocket. "What be this? I will hold this till ya done with the wee bout. She hits hard and it may break," he said as he walked away. "I need ta see the whelps' fighting ability, so have a wee bout." He sat down and waved his hand, signaling them to begin.

They both stood there, trying to gauge each other. A few seconds passed with not a single movement from either while they looked for an opening. Rebecca smiled as she darted forward. Aluxes was faster with her swing and hit Rebecca's arm hard enough to break the wooden waster. Unfazed, Rebecca made contact with Aluxes' gut with a right hook that caused her to hunch over and gag slightly.

Aluxes tried to hit her with the pommel of the waster but Rebecca dodged it and countered with a swift kick to her thigh. Rebecca tried to follow up with a left hook but Aluxes grabbed her arm. In an instant Aluxes stepped off to the side, rotated her arm behind her back, and kicked the back of her knee.

Aluxes shouted in pain as Rebecca twisted slightly and elbowed her in the leg. Aluxes kneed her in the back and tried to pin her to the ground but was stopped by Ulbrek.

He picked up Rebecca and gently brushed the dust off her. He gently scolded her, "You be drinking that dwarven horse piss. It be making me mad! I will not allow ya ta disgrace my taste with that filth."

Rebecca rubbed her head in confusion. "I thought it was a popular drink? Every dwarf I know drinks it."

He handed her his flask and grunted. "It be a common drink. It also be no better than horse piss!" Rebecca took a small sip and smiled. She continued to have more of it.

Aluxes tried to stand up but realized she needed to sit down for a bit. "I feel like I got hit by a metal rod," she said as she stared at the mark on her leg.

Ulbrek yanked the flask away before she could finish it all, and said, "It be her scales. If she be not a runt, ya would have broken bones. As I said before, they have no real fightin' style. They have no need for one. I can say she does need to learn one. Ya cut her arm pretty good."

Rebecca looked at where she was hit. Blood trickled down her upper arm. Part of the wooden sword had penetrated her skin and was sticking out like a large splinter. She let out a sharp scream as she pulled it out. "What the hell? What type of wood is that?"

He scoffed and noticed that his flask was mostly empty. "I told ya she hits hard. Ya could have left me a wee swig."

He picked up the broken bits of wood and chuckled as he spoke. "Well, I seen water cut stone and grass get stuck in armor by strong winds. If enough force and speed be added, ya can cut anything. Also, ya in whelp body and a wee runt."

He patted them both on the shoulder and sat down as he softly said, "I do have some wee pointers for ya, but I need ta get more training supplies from me shop. Just so ya know, the dragon won. One more hit, and ya bones be broken."

Aluxes rubbed her bruises as they started to discolor. She cursed under her breath as they shook hands. Rebecca waved as she headed back home.

When Rebecca arrived at the house, she noticed that the interior had been cleaned. The bed that had taken up most of the space was now replaced with a queen size one, the bar counter had been repaired, and there was an entire dining set present. She dropped to her knees in shock and screamed.

Lilith came running out of a side room, holding a box full of trash. "What is wrong? Do you not like it?"

Rebecca looked at her and cried, "My giant bed? Where is my giant bed?"

Lilith put the box down and walked towards her. She gently held her hand and said, "After your brother showed up to return the wallet, we decided to clean up a little bit. The bed had some dead bugs and mice inside the mattress. We also found some coins. He said about three thousands worth? He helped me shop so I would not get ripped off."

Rebecca gagged a little as she tried to speak. "Wha…well…I guess I have not been in here for a while. So he picked all this out?" She pointed at the new additions to the room.

Lilith put the box in a corner where there was more stuff to be thrown away. "No. I picked it all out. I like it, it looks pretty. I was going to replace the bed with another giant one, but he said you need to move on, and to pick what I liked."

She then looked at the bandage around Rebecca's arm with a hint of concern. "What happened to the arm? I can heal it for you."

Rebecca chuckled as she removed the bandage. "Nah. It will heal up in a few days. We had an exercise and I got carried away. First day mistakes."

Lilith touched the wound. A slight glow that emanated from her hand and onto the wound. After a few seconds, she removed her hand and the wound was healed. She went back to finish cleaning the place as Rebecca stood there with her mouth wide open. Her mind was unable to grasp what had happened.

"How did you do that? There were no incantations, no runes—not even a scribble of a charm. The wound also healed up with no marks," she said.

Lilith tried to imitate a smile and spoke in an cheerful tone that was scary to listen to. "Simple spells and minor wounds are easy for me. It is in my blood. I just think of the spell and it happens." Then she went back to her normal tone. "Tell me, what happened to you in this room? Remember, no lies."

Rebecca took a deep breath and smiled as she said, "I guess talking about it is the road to recovery." She sat down on the bed and Lilith sat next to her. Rebecca started talking. "I noticed I was not into guys when I was young. My sisters would talk about kissing guys and seeing them naked. When they were almost old enough to mate, they started talking about sex. Every time, I did not care about how the good-looking boys would look at me. But the girls…As I got older, the girls were who interested me."

She looked at Lilith and winked. "When I hit my first mate cycle, I had to hide myself and self-indulge. Our desires are impossible to ignore during that time. Soon, I noticed that picking up girls in my whelp or adult form was simple enough. However, most girls that enjoyed the sack with other girls also liked guys. From time to time, I had to do groups. The men would understand that I was off limits, and I will admit, I found it all a turn on."

She opened her flask and took a large gulp, and then stared at it. "I fell into a hole of debauchery. During mating season, I would host an orgy here in this house, on that bed. Men, women, whatever got me the girl between my legs. I didn't have to worry about having a brood so I figured it didn't matter. But in this very flask that was handed around to everyone was a very powerful drug."

Rebecca looked down at her feet as tears rolled down her face. "Two of the men wanted to get at me. Even in my adult form, a runt like me can break steel with my hands but they had drugged me so I couldn't fight them. Luckily, one of the other guys who did not want to drink before the party had started noticed it and fought them off before they could stick their little pricks inside me. Since it was my party, their attempted rape was given a light slap on the wrist. It would have never happened if I was not into that lifestyle. If a dragonblood is rapped, father is usually allowed to kill the assailant, but I was only allowed to ask for payment since I had placed myself in that situation. I took this flask to remind me of how stupid I had been. After that, I promised my parents that the next time I took someone to bed, it will be a mate."

Rebecca looked at Lilith and smiled. "Do you have any other questions?"

"Why do they call you a whelp when you are barely shorter than your brother?" she said as she handed Rebecca a cloth for her tears.

"That is a fair question. My brother is as tall as the average human at five four. I am four nine. In my adult form, my height is almost the same as his, but my body plumps out more for my curves and my breasts go from this amazing handful to being robust. I think slightly larger than yours," Rebecca said as she used her hands to measure Lilith's breast.

Lilith laid down on the bed and yawned. "I have to leave tomorrow and report to my mother. She found out I finished early. I promise you, I will return in a week and help you find a mate. Mother said I could have some time off after I report to her," she said as she closed her eyes.

"If you come back, I might think we are a family." She smiled. "So, where are the bedsheets and blankets?" Rebecca asked as she looked around.

There was no reply. Lilith had already fallen asleep. Rebecca combed her fingers through Lilith's hair. An odd fragrance would come from her skin each time she stroked her hair. It was like plum perfume —Rebecca's favorite.

CHAPTER 4
NIGHTMARE

"Aye lasses, today we be fightin' in pairs. When I say we, I mean me and this wee whelp," Ulbrek said as he patted Rebecca on the back. "We need ta get Aluxes here the ability ta fight smart."

"What am I going to learn?" Rebecca asked.

"Ya just need a wee bit experience—ya already a smart fighter. All I can do is tell ya is ta have a good stance, and ta keep ya guard up," he nodded as he finished.

Ulbrek pulled up some padded gear and new wasters. The gear was a little bulky, but soft. The wasters were a mix of short swords, long swords, and spears. The wood was dark and heavy.

He tossed one to Aluxes. "This be iron wood. A type of wood that sinks in water. Very dense, good for practice," he said with a smile.

They trained with set drills and combinations of different types of attacks. The combat portion was to improve Aluxes' ability to adapt to the type of fights she would encounter and to use different weapons. The understanding of the tactics, knowledge of group fighting and how it is properly executed were also for Rebecca.

"Alright lass, I wantcha ta use breath attack," Ulbrek said with some excitement in his voice.

Rebecca paused briefly while trying to execute and jab and was hit by Aluxes as a result. "I can't. I mean, I am able to but I won't."

Ulbrek stood up straight and grunted out, "Ya dragonblood, just do it!"

Rebecca pouted and sat down. "No, I'm a runt. It hurts my insides when I do it. There is a medication my mother gave me but…I just won't use it."

He gently nudged the back of her head with his fist. "Look lass, ya not the first runt I seen. Ya have ta get ya body used ta it. It may be life and death."

"I think," Aluxes said and then paused for a moment, "I don't want to get hit with some sort of breath attack. I may heal fast but it will still hurt."

"Quit being a baby. It is not real breath attack. They be able ta add the element ta their attacks. It surround their body. She be lighting base so more like an eel if ya touch her." Ulbrek snorted as he rubbed his nose. "Ya just get a wee shock, I think. Only seen fire type meself."

"Well, if it's only a weak attack, I guess it would be alright." Aluxes stood in a ready stance.

Rebecca growled like a beast as she made a tight fist. "Never mock our breath attack. I do not care if it kills me, we dragonbloods take pride in it. How dare you mock it as weak!" Her body was emanating a glow, and the static started to affect everyone's hair. She leaped into a blind attack that was fueled with rage.

Scared, Aluxes jumped out of the way. Rebecca's fist collided with a tree and an enormous amount of electricity dispersed, causing the base of the tree to explode.

"Weak, my ass! That would have killed me, you old moron. I thought you were an expert!" Aluxes tried to hit the dwarf but missed.

"I think that might have been a wee much. I told ya I only seen a fire type once. But he did say most have no control over it." Ulbrek took a deep breath as he watched the tree fall over.

Rebecca coughed out some blood and fell to her knees. "I told you to never mock our breath attack." She collapsed onto the ground.

She slowly faded in and out of consciousness. Ulbrek and Aluxes' voices carried in her mind as they talked.

"Ya see, they are stuck in the middle. Lot of their lingo still be dragon lingo, and they mixed in human lingo. They call it a breath attack when really it just be an enhancement," Ulbrek said as she heard him sip something from a mug.

"She seems to be awake now. Maybe she can explain our problem to us," Aluxes said in an annoyed tone.

Rebecca slowly sat up and yawned. "Oh, what seems to be the problem?"

"Ya see, our young lass had ta get some of that medicine ya talked about. We figured we just go ask ya mum." Ulbrek then looked over at Aluxes.

Aluxes looked at Rebecca angrily. "I had to lie for you, you little shit. You never told your parents that the dwarf is training you! They think you are off in some random city." She grabbed her by the shirt. "I may not know much about your race but I do know of their punishments."

Rebecca tried to look her in the eyes but was unable to meet her gaze. "They kicked me out, alright! They figured if I was out of the house, it would push me towards my goal faster."

Aluxes let her go and spat on the ground in front of her. "Where have you been staying?"

"A house I own that my dad told me to sell. I had a roommate but she had to visit her family," Rebecca said.

"Look me in the face and tell me I will not get punished!" Aluxes kept staring at her.

"I can't look at you. You're very attractive, and it makes me blush to look into those magical eyes of yours." Rebecca smiled and looked at her.

Aluxes scoffed and sat back down. "All of you hormone-driven people are the same. You try to use seduction to get out of your problems. I'm going to sleep." She went off behind the trees.

"We been camping here for a wee bit. She used ta sleep out here with me but…well, she has nightmares." He looked over at where Aluxes went.

"Do you have any idea what they are about?" Rebecca tried to catch a glance of Aluxes. Barely visible, she saw her remove her armor and expose her bare back.

Ulbrek cleared his throat. "I wouldn't do that if I was you. I asked about it but she blown me off." He noticed that Rebecca was trying to peek at Aluxes. "And she gets very violent when peeked on."

He set up some red runes with the symbol for fire. "From what I been told, she been abused her entire life. She be half-human but no one knows what the other half be. So out of fear, they punish her."

"That just seems silly. You should fear what you are afraid of, not punish it," Rebecca said.

"Aye, it be an odd thing we mortals do. What I find a bit strange be her memory. She be four when her village was destroyed, yet she has no memory of her father and only knows her mother's voice. Me thinks her memory been tampered, erased. Only thing she can remember is the Ballad of the Unnamed Goddess." He sat there looking at the runes, not activating them.

"You know they won't burn on their own," Rebecca said as she tried to peek at Aluxes again.

"Aye, fire be forbidden here. May catch a tree on fire. Me imagination keeps me warm enough." He poked the runes with a stick as if he was shifting coals.

"It be gettin' late. Shouldn't ya head off home, lass?" he said, still looking at the runes.

"I might as well stay the night here. I don't like staying at my place…alone," She said as she stood up to look some more.

"Almost time for ya breeding. It be dangerous for ya ta stay here. I heard ya hormones be uncontrollable the closer it gets." He poked the runes with another stick.

Rebecca sat down and scowled slightly. "Five more weeks. I haven't been laid in almost a year. I do not want to be without a bed-mate again."

"What about ya roommate ya told about. Is she ya type?" He tossed the stick and ate some dried meat.

"Like that lovely lady over there, she is also immune to my charms. She is a nice person, but her mind is that of a little pup. I guess if I took my time, it might work, but she has no idea how to express emotions." Rebecca scoffed.

"Must be hard. Well, I sure ya be alright. Just remember, she been abused as a child. Noting of a sexual manner that I know of, but she has fear of being touched," he said as he laid down and fell asleep.

Rebecca found a soft patch of grass and tried to relax. She tossed and turned unable to rest. She thought of putting some leaves underneath herself but it would be no good.

Shit, I'm not a peasant. How can they sleep like this? I can feel tiny sharp rocks all over me. She sat up and looked around.

"What's the point? I lose more sleep every day the closer it gets to the season," she said as she looked at her hands. "Am I going to die alone?"

She could hear some moaning from the direction Aluxes was sleeping in. Rebecca could not resist but look.

She is a woman after all, no matter how much she protests. I bet that is the sound of her fulfilling her needs. She snuck up to the sleeping Aluxes who was crying in her sleep.

Aluxes had laid out her padded armor to make a bed and used her armor as a blanket. As she tossed in her sleep, Rebecca could see the white under shirt and shorts she had used as a nightwear, covering all of her bits. She would moan out every few moments as if she were in pain.

Rebecca looked at her exposed legs and mid-section. *Not a single mark or a blemish. Her body is the very image of perfection.*

She walked a little closer. *She said she hated men. Maybe she is confused, like that one girl I went out with. She was confused until I helped her.*

Rebecca kneeled down next to her. *Only the leg—I will just touch the leg, around the knee. She is lovely...smooth skin, wild eyes, perfect hair. Her breasts are a smaller size. They make my whelp bust look big but they fit her perfect body.*

Rebecca slowly moved her fingers towards the exposed knee and gently touched it. Her body shuddered with excitement as she slowly moved her fingers across the skin. Her mind was filled with lust as she smiled.

Right when Rebecca got to the bottom of the shorts, Aluxes jumped up and shoved her to the ground. With one knee on her back, she pinned her down. One hand held Rebecca's head while the other pinned her arm to the ground.

"I told you filth to not touch me while I slept! Mildred told you guys in class to stay out of my room. I hate you!" Aluxes slowly pushed down on her arm and smiled as Rebecca cried out in pain.

"Stop! I'm sorry. I was not going to do anything, I swear! Let me go, I am sorry," she cried as tears blurred her sight.

Aluxes smiled as she kept pushing. "I will fucken' kill you Josh, Scott, Lambert—you are all the same."

"Oh my god, you're still asleep! Wake up bitch and let go!" Rebecca begged over and over until a crunch interrupted her cries.

Rebecca let out a scream that made her other cries seem like whimpers. The pain shot through her body like daggers. She became lightheaded and was about to pass out from the pain. Each breath felt like pushing through a wall. All she could think about was her own death.

"Her legend will be spread across the land. Ending war ta save mortal man. Her sword ended darkness all across the land, paid with her life," Ulbrek started speaking but then paused as he forgot the words.

Aluxes quickly stood up and saw Rebecca crying on the ground. "What's going on?"

Ulbrek ran up to check on Rebecca and said. "Ya be sleep walkin'. Well, sleep killin'. I knew this would happen." He looked at the girl on the ground. "Well miss, let me get ya bandaged up."

Rebecca turned over and sat up. "What the fuck is wrong with her? What did she do to me?"

He wrapped two sticks and a cloth around her arm and talked in a calm voice, "Ya arm just be broken is all."

"Broken! How the fuck is it broken? I am a dragon. I cannot have a broken arm," she cried.

Aluxes tried to take a look. "It's just a broken arm. You will be fine."

Ulbrek looked at them both, and tried to keep his voice down. "Ya ever noticed how that dragon skeleton in the church looks perfect? Well, there only be a few metals stronger than their bones. Even a runt like this lass have bones like diamond. I never heard of one breaking a bone."

He helped Rebecca up and slowly walked with her. "I take ya ta the white dragon, lass. Ya be fine."

"But what the hell is wrong with her? She was smiling as she almost killed me," Rebecca was still whimpering as she talked.

"Aye, I told ya she been bullied. She has much anger in her. Head nun be like a mother ta her. Be the only thing keeping her from killing everyone. I hate ta see the day she lets her anger go," he said.

"So what will happen now?" Rebecca tried to hide her pain but winced as she moved.

"She probably won't remember what happened in her dreams. It be why I stay clear from her when she sleeps. She never remembers her dreams when she awakens. But she cries out ta her mum. Me thinks it be her hidden memories trying ta surface." He looked back and saw Aluxes standing at the same place and looking at her own hands. Even from that distance, he noticed that for a moment, the golden circlet was black.

CHAPTER 5
ANGER

"Seven! Fucken' seven!" Rebecca stared at them in anger.

"The white dragon who has lived a thousand years has only seen one broken bone in her life. And her book of records which has records of ten thousand years only has seven. That includes me!" She pointed to her arm, which was in a sling.

"Well, I told ya I never seen a dragonblood with a broken bone before. Just be glad it be healin'" Ulbrek smiled as he handed her his flask.

"So, what will we do now? She can't spar with a broken arm," Aluxes said.

"Like hell I won't! I am going to be an officer in the army when we are done. If I get hurt in the middle of a battle, I still need to fight in order to survive. Give me one of those blasted wooden swords." Rebecca went towards the barrel of wooden weapons and pulled out a short sword. She took a few swings before Ulbrek grabbed it from her hands.

"Aye, daft bastard. If ya refuse ta listen ta me about swords, might as well show ya how ta hold one," he said.

He took the sword and wrapped her fingers around its grip. A few quick nudges straightened her stance and positioned her arm. He gave a gentle push to her front leg to bend her knee slightly. He held her arm and guided her with a few key swings so she would get a feel of the motions.

"Always remember, lass. Keep the blade pointed at ya target. Keep the wrist loose, and tense up only for a moment before a strike. Mobility is key ta a sword. Swift motions, deflect, pierce, cut," he said softly.

He picked up another short wooden sword and stood in a ready stance in front of Aluxes. "Watch how we move, lass. Study how we hold our blades. Watch the focus in our eyes," he finished.

Ulbrek gave a nod and they both went at it. Rebecca noticed how every block was more of a deflecting motion followed by a counter. Sometimes, they would feint the blade to try and get the upper hand. Not once did their eyes look at the weapon or at the movements of the opponent. They read each other by looking into the other's eyes and reacting. Ulbrek tried to go for a thrust but Aluxes swiped the blade from left to right across her body and twisted her arm around her head, keeping the blades locked. Then she stabbed him in the neck.

"Aye, this be called infighting. I admit, she better than I with a sword, even with a long sword. But she still not defeated me with an ax." He began to chuckle as he walked off to sit down.

Aluxes looked at Rebecca. "So, you are going to keep training with us? I cannot make any promises. I might accidentally hit your arm."

"I will. Even though the dwarf may avoid the problem, I will face it…What the hell was wrong with you? The anger and hate that showed on your face as you broke my arm…it was as if you enjoyed it." Rebecca tried not to shout at her but it came close to it.

"I don't remember!" Aluxes snapped back. She then took a deep breath and started to calm down. "I've been told I have nightmares, but I only remember the dreams about my mother singing to me, and the one I had on my birthday."

Rebecca walked closer to her. "You called out for Josh, Scott, and Lambert. You said you wanted to kill *them* but you almost killed me!" She pointed to her arm again.

Aluxes took another deep breath. The shaking of her body made her anger easy to read. "When I was fourteen, some of the cuter boys started to notice me. Well, some more than others. One day, they snuck into my room when I forgot to lock it and decided to hide there."

Ulbrek laughed. "Boys be boys. I remember spying on me nanny, she had big tits. I later lost me virginity to her. I forget her name but I remember her big tits."

Both girls flushed as Aluxes tried to stay calm and tell her story. "Well, anyways. After practice, I would take a bath. I didn't like it when the other girls would point out my small breasts or point out how I was a monster, so I had my own bucket in my room. So I rushed in and got undressed. One of the boys thought I had seen him, and so he jumped out. Then the other two popped out."

She put her arm over her chest. "They saw my breasts. One of them even touched them in the chaos."

She sat down and Rebecca joined her as she scoffed. "A nun rushed in and saw me mostly naked in a room with three boys while one of them had his finger on my nipple. The next day, people started saying I was a slut, a whore…just like my mother. The three boys told everyone I had forced them into my chamber. I was in hell for over a month. That's how long it took the headmaster and the head nun to clear it all up. I hated them, all of them. I wished every boy would die. I wanted to kill them, but Mildred would talk to me...and I eventually moved on."

She looked into Rebecca's eyes. "Look, I am really sorry. I know I have an issue. What can I do to make it up to you?"

"Just give me a hug, and we will call it even." Rebecca said as she opened her one arm.

Hesitant, Aluxes leaned over and wrapped her arms around her and gently squeezed her. After a moment, she jumped back and stood up.

"Did you just touch my breast with that broken hand?" she shouted.

"Well, you seem to hate men, so maybe give me a chance?" Rebecca fluttered her eyes.

"It's not that I hate men. I did go out with one once. He was really attractive, but he cheated on me with another girl. Look, I am attracted to guys. I always wish a nice one would show up. I'm just not into girls. For the most part, I actually hate them more than men." Aluxes said calmly and walked away.

"Well, I guess I should just come back tomorrow. The white dragon gave me some medicines that I need to take every day to heal properly. Apparently, when we break bones, they do not heal on their own. I will show up bright and early tomorrow," Rebecca said as she stood up.

"Aye lass, you be alright?" Ulbrek asked.

"I'll be fine. I wasn't expecting much from her anyways. Don't worry, I shall return tomorrow," she said as she rubbed a tear from her eye.

Rebecca ran back to her house and found her brother at the door, waiting for her with some food.

"Marcus, it's a surprise to see you!" she said.

"What happened to your arm?" he asked.

"I broke it last night. Please don't tell mom or dad!" she begged him as she hugged him tightly.

He squeezed her back. "Is that why you are crying?"

"No, I just had a minor setback. I'm alright." She wiped her nose with her arm.

Rebecca straightened up and looked into his eyes. "So, why are you here?"

"Before she left, Lilith told me to check on you whenever I can until she gets back. She also paid for food to be delivered to you. You were not home last night so I took it back to keep it from being stolen." He patted her head and smiled.

"Will you stay and eat with me? I hate being alone, and I am too scared to camp," Rebecca said.

"I guess I can take the rest of the day off. Today is not that busy and the staff will be able to handle the place for a day without me," he said as he slowly walked towards the bar counter.

As Marcus was setting up the food, he let out a deep sigh. "It hurts when you are trying to find someone to love, and it hurts when you get rejected."

"It was much easier when I would just go from bed to bed, no feelings involved." Rebecca tried to let out a laugh as she rubbed the snot from her nose.

"So…how did you break your arm?" Marcus asked as he divided the food onto two plates.

Rebecca's face became a shade darker as she stared at the food. "Let's just say…our indestructible bones snap like twigs when staring into the face of true uncontrolled anger."

CHAPTER 6
PROMISE

"I see ya returned, lass. We ready to train?" Ulbrek handed Rebecca a short sword waster.

"Are you actually going to train me in anything? Or should I just swing around like a wild animal?" She poked him with the tip of the blade.

"All I can do is give ya pointers on breathing, stance, and maybe footwork. Me style works for a dwarf. Ya be better off ta find ya own style with experience," he said with a smile.

"All he told me was to focus and breathe. Apparently, my problem is my overconfidence in my strength, which leads me to be reckless and makes me angry when it fails. He keeps hitting my ass so I can manage my anger." Aluxes stood in a ready stance with a two-handed waster.

"I told ya. It be the only target I can hit. Ya ass is as high as me head. I don't mind the view, but makes it hard ta train ya properly," he spoke in a rushed tone as he stood ready.

"I say it how I view it." Aluxes smiled as both Ulbrek and Rebecca went in to attack her.

For three days, they tag-teamed Aluxes. Slowly, both girls improved and developed their own style. Whenever the pain in Rebecca's arm would become too much, they would take breaks. During those times, Ulbrek would talk about his experience as an officer, tell them about proper tactics, and how to set up traps and forage for food. On the rare occasions, he would tell them about other races they may fight, and in a poor manner, about how to deal with them.

At one point, Rebecca interrupted him. "What about how they fight? You talk about orcs, gnolls, goblins, and trolls, but you never really tell us their strategies. All you tell us is to hit them here or there."

Ulbrek cleared his throat. "I never really bothered ta study how they fight. I would kill them and it be enough for me."

Aluxes scoffed. "You are a useless strategist. I guess it's the end of the day. I need to find the public bath now—I know you tried to peek at me when I was in the lake, you old fart!"

Ulbrek quickly replied, "I told ya, it was an elf! They visit here a lot."

Rebecca giggled as she walked off. "I will just use my bath at home. I'll see you tomorrow."

She walked slowly, talking to herself. "Shit, home alone again. Maybe I should just tell Father. I know he would let me back in. But Mother…Drakon, I hate this. May you bless me ol' dragon god."

As she approached her house, she noticed that the front door was busted. With a grunt, she dashed through the door and ran up the stairs. She barged into the room and threw a punch at the cloaked figure that stood in the center, but the figure grabbed her fist, pulled her closer, and embraced her.

In an emotionless feminine voice, it said, "I told you I would come back. I was told by your brother this is how you liked to be greeted by friends."

"Lilith? You said it would be a week before you came back!" Rebecca pulled away. "I do love a good hug from a friend, but why did you break the door? I gave you a key."

"I lost it. It fell off when I was over the ocean. I will pay for a new door. I am sorry," she said.

"Oh, don't bother. I doubt you can afford it. I will just get a fancy new door. One worthy of my birth," Rebecca giggled.

"Mother said I can have extra time off since I delivered a good report, so I flew here as fast as I could. I had promised you." Lilith sat down on the bed and began to lie down after patting the covers.

"Flew? What silliness are you talking about?" Rebecca sat down next to her. "Are you sleeping already?"

The next morning, both of them stretched and yawned as they woke up. Rebecca was slightly faster and left the room for a moment. She returned with a basket full of bread. When Lilith sat up, she noticed there was a new door already installed.

"You sure do sleep like a log. I had a rush order on the door and you were sleeping despite all that racket," Rebecca said as she handed her some bread.

"This bread is good. How was training?" Lilith sat at the table and looked at her.

"It would be better if my arm wasn't broken. The medication that the white dragon gave me is not working fast enough." Rebecca grunted.

Lilith grabbed her broken arm. A light pulsed from her hand and went into the arm.

"You are not human, nor a gnome, so it may take a few heals, but you should be able to move it easier," Lilith said as she kept eating the bread.

"This is amazing! I bet it will be fully healed by the end of the week," Rebecca said excitedly.

"Can you skip training today? I want to take a walk with you." Lilith ate the last bit of her loaf and snatched the one in Rebecca's hand.

"I guess it would be fine. Just let me tell the master dwarf. I never missed a single day." Rebecca stared at the floor and shifted her body around.

"I can tell you're nervous about missing a day. Just meet me here after practice." Lilith held out her palm with a small note. Rebecca blushed a little as she slowly placed her hand onto Lilith's and took the note.

* * *

Rebecca stood next to Lilith on the street. The shadow of the building loomed over them like an evil presence. Lilith was trying to look joyful while Rebecca was sulking and kicking at some loose pebbles.

Rebecca was barely able to look up when she said, "So why are we at this dump? I mean, the drinks are not that bad but this bar is very shady." She looked around and noticed a group of men staring at them. "This place is, well, not somewhere someone like you should go into."

"I was told by your brother that you used to pick up girls here. I promised you I would help you find a mate." Lilith pointed to a pretty girl.

Rebecca giggled slightly as she blushed. "She is a prostitute. The men looking at us are part of a gang that snatches up young girls for sex trade. That is why I stopped coming here. That lovely lady there— her job is to lure in people."

Lilith took her hand and blushed. "Oh. We need to go. I made a mistake."

Rebecca shouted at her as she was being pulled. "Hey, slow down. If I didn't know any better, I would think you are embarrassed. No need to worry. You are innocent to these things. Most people that live here have no idea what this place actually is."

"Tomorrow, we will try another place. He gave me a list." Lilith pulled up a parchment with writing on it.

The following day, they stood in front of a lush building. It was made of white marble and there was a rose garden next to a fountain. Rebecca stood there with her hands covering her face as she turned red.

"Why, out of all places, did you pick this one?" She sighed as she rubbed her forehead.

"While you were training, I decided to look at the places on the list

44

so I would not make the same mistake as yesterday. This place looked the prettiest." Lilith took her hand and pulled her.

"Well, shit. I guess you will have to learn at some point—don't judge a book by the cover." Rebecca reluctantly followed her.

The inside was covered with red silk and beds that were all over the floor. Men and women in their own little groups were having orgies. Lilith blushed and looked away. Rebecca smiled as one of the workers winked at her.

"I have not seen you in a while! I heard you stopped the lifestyle after that nasty bit." The worker had on a bright red silk dress. Her tone was a bit on the snobbish side but she was polite.

"This is Lilith. We just want to eat in the dining area. I no longer wish to partake in such parties. But I'm glad to see business is still booming." Rebecca took the worker's hand and kissed it gently. "You were one of my favorites, but I am at the age now."

The worker blushed. "Yes, I understand. I wish I had the same luck as you. When my father found out, he banished me. So I am stuck here forever, lost in the sea of lust." She smiled as she led them to one of the dining tables.

Lilith stared at her feet and her face was as bright as an apple. The embarrassment was noticeable in her voice. "I am sorry. Why would your brother mention a place like this?" She blushed some more as some of the moaning became louder.

"Well, you see. This place is also an established diner. I would bring home food from here at times. He has never really been to these places, nor has he ever looked into them." Rebecca giggled as she looked at the menu.

"You really used to come here? I knew you said you had a life of debauchery, but I never knew it was so extensive." Lilith covered her face with her hood.

"I would rent out a private room. I'm not proud of where that lifestyle took me but I am glad I got to experience life first." She took a deep breath. "Look, I'm fine. I have already established that I shall be alone forever. The food here is amazing. I will order some for us to take home. Maybe tomorrow we can just go out into the town and have some fun."

Rebecca tried to look at Lilith's face. "I know you've been trying to keep your promise, but I will be alright. I need to do something for you. You wanted to find Verus, right?"

Lilith peeked at her through a small gap in her hood. "I was watching him when you were away. I do not know how to approach him."

"He is your father, right? Just go up and say hi." Rebecca pointed to the menu as the waitress wrote some stuff down.

"He has no idea I was created. It would not work. My mother used magic to create me by using part of his soul and combining it with hers. I am the first perfected homunculus." She covered the gap in her hood with the menu.

They waited for their order before continuing, which was quickly served.

"Well, we've got the food. Let's just eat this someplace nice outside." Rebecca took Lilith's hand and guided her towards a bench near the fountain in front of the building.

"So, I take it you really are a pure twenty-year-old beautiful woman. I cannot imagine someone as gorgeous—well, never mind." Rebecca put some food on Lilith's plate and then her own. They started to eat.

Lilith started talking. "I was created ten years ago. My mother aged me ten years more with magic. My sister said it is why my emotions are stunted. I never really noticed that I was a beautiful woman. My sister said it all the time but I never stopped to ask anyone." She took a bite. "This is really good. If I never ran into you, I would have never talked to you. I am glad I did if I am being honest." Her eyes locked onto Rebecca's.

"A few days ago, you said that you flew? I've never heard of any flying spells." Rebecca said.

"I have wings. One is red and the other is brown. I was told by my mother that I am to never show them to anyone, or they will die."

Lilith smiled. "I like having a person to talk too. I always wanted to tell someone about my wings. They are really lovely."

Rebecca gasped. "Wow, you do have emotions." She giggled as she tried to continue. "Well, you do say some of the strangest things. Tell me, what do you like in a person? Do you like men?" she asked as she gazed into Lilith's eyes.

"I never thought about liking men, but I do think if I was to pick a mate, I would want honesty." Lilith blushed slightly. "My sister told me being honest will keeps the relationship alive."

Rebecca stood up and held out her hand. "I promise you that I will keep nothing from you, alright? And you keep nothing from me."

Lilith took her hand and stood up. "I do not want to help you find a mate. I am not comfortable. Even though I promised, I think you should wait." She said as they walked towards their home, holding hands.

Rebecca noticed how gently Lilith held her hand as they walked, and she felt blissful. *This is probably nothing, but I feel like I can hold this hand for the rest of my life.*

CHAPTER 7
DEATH

"Let's have a party!" Rebecca yelled as she danced around the room while holding Lilith's hand. "Today was the last day of my training. I shall join the army by the end of the week!"

Lilith hopped around stiffly like she was made of wood. "I am happy for you. So I guess tomorrow is our goodbye?"

Rebecca stopped to look into her eyes and kissed her forehead. "As an officer, I can live here. You don't have to go."

Lilith went back to her usual blank stare. "I am sure you will find a mate in the military. You do not need to keep me around," she said as she tried to look at the wall.

"Has your mother contacted you yet? Do you have to go?" Rebecca asked, trying to get back into her sight.

"No, she said I can stay here if I want, but I—" Lilith looked down at her feet.

Rebecca grabbed her hands and held them tightly. She smiled, "I can tell when you are sad, and it's alright. I will always be here for you. If you wish to stay with me, you can."

She then took a deep breath and sighed. "Look, my family is going to have a party today. I want you to meet them."

Lilith smiled, but the blank look in her eyes remained there. They headed out the door, still holding hands. The streets were overcrowded and they had a hard time getting out the door. Everyone was watching the royal guard marching.

Rebecca tapped the shoulder of one of the onlookers and asked, "Sir, what is going on?"

He looked at her, confused. "Didn't ya hear the bells? The war has hit the city of Angarth. I hear gnolls by the thousands will be there soon. We beat their arse in the name of the Unknown Goddess," he said with pride.

Lilith squeezed Rebecca's hand tightly and whispered softly, "Can we go? I wish to leave now. I cannot watch them as they walk by. I can see their deaths, and it bothers me a lot."

"You sure do say the strangest things. Well fine, my little cutie. Let's just head towards my house," Rebecca said as she pulled Lilith's hand.

"So, what do you mean you can see their deaths?" She looked back at her as they walked.

"When I am aware of something bad that is going to happen, I can see who will die and who will live. The only one I saw that was going to live was the red-headed girl." Lilith said, barely paying attention to anything around her. She tripped over a small rock and almost fell over.

"You need to be careful. Stop talking so you can focus on walking. We should get there in a few moments." Rebecca pulled her arm a little harder.

"We are here…my wonderful home. I think you should just hold on to my arm tightly. The whelps can get crazy, and I know you get nervous in this type of environment," Rebecca said as she smiled.

"This house is bigger than our home. I hope they like me," Lilith said as she held on to her arm tightly.

Rebecca pushed open the door and shouted, "I am home!"

Immediately, twelve whelps ran up to her, all shouting at the same time, "Big sis, we missed you!"

"Rebecca, come to my study. Alone!" Her father's voice carried across the house.

"Little ones, this is my friend. Can you show her around?" She looked at Lilith and smiled. "Do not worry, they are kind. I will not be gone long." Lilith let go of her.

Lilith stared at Rebecca. "Why are you speaking like that?" She asked.

"Mother will get mad at me if I speak improperly. You should be fine." Rebecca gave her a half smile as she walked towards her father's study. Lilith followed the kids as they ran off.

"You lied to us! I told you to sell that place." Rebecca's father sat at his desk and stared at her. Her mother stood behind his chair.

Rebecca took a deep breath, placed her hands at her sides, and bowed. "I am deeply sorry Father, Mother. I disobeyed you," she said in the most respectful tone she had ever spoken.

"I talked to Master Ulbrek. I should be angry that you did not go away, but he is one of the finest warriors in the land. I am amazed you convinced him to train you." He paused. "Marcus told me you also found a little friend." He looked out the window and watched the kids play tag with Lilith.

"Look, Rebecca. We are angry that you did not tell us you were still here. Living off of what little you had—and at that house of all places! You must sell it right away," her mother said.

"I am deeply sorry…but I must decline that. Lilith and I have made a wonderful home there. We cleaned it up and decorated it. She even started to clear out the lower levels. I plan to live there while I am in the army. Officers are allowed to live in their own home, and I want to stay there." She bowed lower.

"So you found a mate? She looks rather odd," her father said.

"No, we are just friends. I met her the day you tossed me out. She was homeless and—" Rebecca was interrupted by her mother.

"You brought a street rat into our home? How do we know she won't steal from us? Rebecca, you need to understand that she is beneath us," her mother said as she folded her arms.

"Now, dear. Look how Rebecca is behaving. I think this girl has influenced her. We will see how she is during dinner," her father said with a smile.

As the sun started to lower, everyone gathered. All her brothers and sisters came, even the ones who lived some distance away. Lilith tried to sit next to Rebecca but was surrounded by the whelps. One of the little girls started to braid her hair, mixing the brown and red.

Marcus chuckled. "I see the young ones have taken to you. Father, I told you that Lilith is a very nice person."

"What is with her hair and eyes? They are not natural," a girl shouted out. She resembled Rebecca but had yellow eyes.

"Sasha, that is rude. Apologize to her at once," her mother snapped back at her.

"I just do not understand her taste. It is hard enough, her being into girls, but someone that looks like that? She will stay a whelp forever." Sasha chuckled as she pointed at Rebecca.

"Says the girl who is also a whelp like me!" Rebecca tossed a piece of bread at her.

"I shall be married to the prince next week. Mating season has started. I saved myself for him, my love. Unlike being a wh—" Marcus cleared his throat to stop her from continuing.

Still with her nose in the air, Sasha asked, "Where is Reggie? His wife had her egg and is doing fine. I need to tell him."

"He will be back tomorrow. His mission was of the upmost importance," their father said as he looked at the table, covering his mouth.

"Father, get your elbows off the table. It is bad manners," one of the whelps said as they all giggled.

Lilith spoke in her usual monotonous voice. "I was created this way. My mother had to make a delicate split in order for me to survive. Too much of one or the other would have led to my death. Mother only had one sample, and she had to get it right. I am glad she got it right, I do like learning new things. It is also why my hair is red instead of crimson."

"Love, look. I am not saying you are ugly, just uneasy to look at. I guess only Rebecca could like another runt. That is why she is unable to get a man to love her." Sasha flashed her engagement ring as if to mock Rebecca.

"It is a very lovely ring…and we are just roommates. I do enjoy her being around, and it has made my life have more meaning. It has also forced me to make choices that bother my mother," Lilith said.

After dinner, everyone separated into groups. The younger ones played games while the older girls helped clean up. The boys stood around talking about their achievements.

Lilith grabbed Rebecca's arms and pulled her closer, whispering into her ear. "Your father lied. I always know."

Rebecca cut her off. "Ya ya, I know. You can always tell when a person lies. I will go talk to him."

Rebecca stormed into his office. "Father, what is going on? It bothers Lilith when people lie!" She folded her arms and stared at him.

He looked at her blankly. "I guess that friend of yours can really read emotions. It is like what Marcus had described. Sorry, I had to test it out." Rebecca stared at him in confusion. "When someone lies, they give off a color that she can see or an odor that she can smell." He paused for a moment. "Reggie died over a week ago. 'Father, I found the little girl' was the last thing he said to me. A few hours later, I received a message from someone in his group that he was dead. Some black liquid was slowly devoured him."

An emptiness filled Rebecca's gut and she fell into his guest seat. "His wife needs to kn—"

"His wife was in the delicate state of not surviving the birth. News like that would have sent her over the edge. I will tell her once she is in a more stable condition. Tell no one—I do not want any of what I told you to leave this room," he finished, looking at a small carving that Reggie had made for him when he was a whelp.

"You know I can't hide this from Lilith. I actually like her, and she gets really mad at me when I lie. She broke my flask the last time I lied." Rebecca scoffed as she stood up.

"You can tell her tomorrow after you leave. I do not want the little ones to overhear. Lilith seems to enjoy playing tag with them. She is a good person deep down. I have seen many homunculi in my time, but never like her. They normally die after a week, a month at most. Whosoever her mother is must be a very powerful person. Almost godly power," he said as he looked at her.

Rebecca's father handed her an envelope. His voice was a little shaky. "This is a note from the king. He will have a banquet when the soldiers return. You will be attending, and he will make you an officer in the Elites."

"Alright. But Father, how are you holding up? I am surprised Mother—"

"She does not know yet. There is no way she could have kept it quiet. I will let her know when the time is right." He folded his hands and placed them under his chin.

"How could you lie to Mother? Again, more lies I have to keep from Lilith. You have not spent enough time with her to know how this will affect me. I knew you or Mother would do something to make her angry with me." She stormed out.

Rebecca stood near the yard, trying to hold in her tears. She watched the young children play with Lilith. Her mind was filled with memories of her brother. They would often hang out in the kitchen and talk. When she admitted to her family that she was only interested in girls, he was the first one to accept her. She was the one to introduce him to his wife. She wiped her nose with her arm and ran up the stairs into her room. She cried for what seemed like an eternity until she fell asleep.

She opened her eyes and looked around. *It's still dark. What's in the bed with me?* Curled up next to her was Lilith. She was cuddling her in her sleep.

I don't understand her. What is going on in her mind? She thought as she rubbed her fingers through Lilith's hair.

Lilith moaned slightly as some words escaped her lips. "You were sad earlier, so I thought you needed a hug. Was it about your brother?"

"I wish I could tell you, but my father said I cannot. Why did they not put you in the guest room?" she asked.

"They did, but we have been sleeping in the same bed for weeks so I got lonely. I can leave if you need to be alone." They looked into each other's eyes.

"Please stay." Rebecca kissed her forehead. "You are the sweetest person I have ever met. You remind me of the whelps."

In the morning, the girls got their stuff ready. They walked past the kitchen and towards the main door. Rebecca's mother almost dropped her cup as she tried to cut them off.

"Are you leaving before breakfast? Did I offend your friend yesterday?" She grabbed Lilith's hand. "Dear, I am sorry that I said what I said. I have a lot of pride. Just stay and allow me to get to know you better."

Lilith stood there confused. "I...well...I really did not understand what you said about me. According to my mother, I am beneath no one. I had fun playing with the whelps."

"Then did Father make you mad, Rebecca?" She shouted for Rebecca's father. He came staggering out of his office.

"Mother, no. I have orders from the king. I need to get ready for it." Rebecca bowed to both of them and cleared her throat. "Well, it has been a joyful time. We will head back home now. Father, Mother, I will make you both proud of me." She walked out the door, holding Lilith's hand.

They walked out in a hurry and did not slow down till the house was out of sight. Rebecca couldn't hold back her tears any longer and started to cry again.

"There is a small place to sit and eat over there. Maybe I can treat you to breakfast as you tell me what is bothering you," Lilith said as she pointed to a food cart with some benches nearby.

They sat down and Lilith went to order some food. A few moments later, she came carrying some sweet rolls and water. She started to eat but Rebecca just sat there, not budging at all.

"Tell me, what happened to your brother?" Lilith stared at her.

"I... How? My father told me you can see colors or smell a scent when people lie. Is that how you always know?" Rebecca asked as she played with the cup.

"This bread is good. And yes and no. I am able to see colors but it is more than that. I can hear the heart. When you lie and it bothers you a lot, it makes a sound. It also affects its color. But people that truly believe in their own lie or lack emotions, I cannot read them," Lilith said as she took another bite. "I noticed the color change around your father after he said something about your brother, Reggie."

"How come every time we eat and I ask you something, you always start by saying how good the food is? Even when you dislike it, you give it a compliment." Rebecca started to play with her bread.

"Mother told me that it is polite to say the food is good when you eat. Someone put effort into it and it is not my position to judge their efforts. Why are you avoiding the answer?" They stared into each other's eyes.

"My brother was devoured, some dark liquid got to him. He was sent to find a missing girl. His men found him dead, consumed by that stuff," Rebecca said as she knocked over the cup, spilling the water.

The water poured onto Lilith's lap. "Oh, I'm so sorry. I will get something to dry that up," Rebecca said and jumped up.

However, Lilith just sat there, unaware that her lap had become wet. Her skin was pale, and her mouth was hanging open. "Lilith, what's wrong? I've never seen you like this before." Rebecca looked into her eyes. Lilith's eyes had widened as she made a sound from the back of her throat.

Lilith nodded her head from side to side as she shouted, "No, no. Not this. I beg of you!" Tears rolled down her cheeks.

"What's wrong?" Rebecca held her hand.

All of a sudden, she stopped crying and her expression changed.

"Sorry, it was nothing. Maybe we can go and do more fun things? There is something I have seen that I always wanted to try. I think they called it a 'fair'?" Lilith smiled and tightly squeezed her hand.

"Well, alright, I guess. You're just trying to help me feel better in your own way," Rebecca said.

Lilith took her around the fair, playing games at the stalls, watching stage shows, and eating the special dishes. For three days, they were at every event that was being held.

"Well, the troops are on their way back, so I must attend the ball tonight. Would you like to go with me as my plus one?" Rebecca asked, holding up dresses while looking in the mirror.

"Maybe we should go and travel. We could visit my mother?" Lilith sat down on the bed, bouncing her legs up and down.

"This is an order from the king. I have to go. Can you tell me what this is about?" She stared at Lilith blankly.

"I think we should leave today. You and me," Lilith begged.

"I did everything you wanted. I think we should do what I want now. I even got you a fancy dress." Rebecca reached over and pulled out a light-blue silk dress. "I noticed you looking at it every time we walked by the shop."

Lilith started to cry. "I would love to go, but I think we should leave tonight."

"I think it's funny that you hate it when people lie but you lie when it seems to suit you. I'm going to the party and if you change your mind, I will wait for you at the steps. I don't like people who are self-ish." Rebecca tossed the dress at Lilith and stormed off to her brother's restaurant.

"What has gotten into her? Maybe I was too harsh. No, she needs to learn to trust me. She only cared about herself when I was crying over my brother's death," Rebecca scoffed as she slammed her fist on the table.

"You may be my dear sister but if you damage my tables, I will have to ban you from here." Marcus said as he folded his arms.

He sat down next to her. "Look, I don't know what it is about, but I feel like you and Lilith are in a little bit of a lover's quarrel." He took a deep breath. "Just tell her how you feel."

"I did that once. It just made her help me look for a mate. When I brought it up again, she ran off for almost an entire day. I think it's just a dead end." She folded her arms on the table and rested her head on them.

"You are not giving her credit. I am not sure about her situation but I think she is in a lot of trouble by just being here with you. I overheard her talking on a communication stone when you were training. I think she cares for you deeply. You *have* met her, right? Lilith just has no idea how to show it." He gently rubbed her head, trying to calm her.

"If she shows up to the castle, then it means she loves me. If she runs away... I guess it means we are done," Rebecca said quietly.

"You are going to watch the parade? They will be here in a few moments." He pointed out the window. People had started to line up.

"You know I hate crowds. I will just use your office to change." Rebecca grabbed her dress and slowly walked off.

"That pink dress really matches that blue dress you got her. I hope the money I lent you was not wasted." Marcus laughed as he went back to work.

Rebecca went through the back alleys to reach the castle. Off to the side of the main gate were some stairs that went to a smaller gate. The guard that stood there was checking the invitations of the people that wanted to show up before the crowd. She stood and waited on the steps.

"Miss, may I help you? I see you have an invitation from the king. You may enter whenever you wish." The guard was handsome and very polite.

"I'm waiting for my date. I will stand here until I determine I have been stood up!" She folded her arms and leaned on the gate wall. The guard handed her some wine as she waited.

A few hours went by. The party had started. The sun was barely showing over the walls and the moon had slowly started to peek out. She sighed as she turned around.

"I'm sorry, my lady. I guess he was a fool." The guard smiled as he let her in.

"No, I'm the fool. I should have known it was too much for her," Rebecca said as she slowly stumbled towards the gate.

"Rebecca!" She turned around and saw that Lilith was standing at the bottom of the steps. She was wearing the blue silk dress and had some makeup on.

"You showed up late!" Rebecca gently took her hand, and they walked past the guard as he bowed. "I'm so excited to show you off to everyone. This makes me very happy."

Before they entered the hall, Lilith stopped her. "Rebecca, I am sorry. I am so very sorry. Forgive me. I did not want to lie but I was scared. I do not want to lose you.”

“Wow, you had real emotion in those words. But why do you think you will lose me? I will always be here for you.” She kissed her forehead.

“When you told me about your brother’s death, I had a vision. I saw that you died. I am begging you not to enter this place.” Lilith cried as she pulled Rebecca close and hugged her tightly.

“You said all the troops will die. Most of them are back already. It’s all right. I’ll be safe.” Rebecca smiled as they pulled away.

“No, I was wrong about how soon. I can see someone's death a week away if I am made aware of something. Everyone will die today.” Lilith tugged on her arm, forcing her away from the castle.

She continued, “I will show you everything, even my wings. Just let me take you to a safe place so they will not notice you. I do not want to lose you. I promise I will never hide anything from you. I—” Lilith was not able to finish her sentence.

An explosion from one of the castles’ towers deafened them. The sky ripped apart and monsters fell from the hole it created. Chaos filled the air.

CHAPTER 8
THE FALL

"Lilith, I have to go. My sister lives in that castle." Rebecca pushed her away and ran.

"Rebecca!" Lilith cried as she disappeared through the castle door.

Rebecca tried to make her way into the grand hall but stopped monsters devouring some of the guards. Their tiny black bodies made it hard to see their shape in the dark but their wide smiles exposed the glow of their teeth.

A taller monster that had teeth-like claws swiped at her. Instinctively, she blocked it but let out a scream. Blood dripped from her arm onto the floor. Before she could react, she was surrounded.

"Lilith. I'm sorry, my love." Rebecca closed her eyes as the monster took another swing.

The sound of cutting was the only thing Rebecca could hear. She opened her eyes and saw Lilith standing there with a sword. The metal was a crimson red and had a slight glow to it.

"Where did you get that?" Rebecca lowered her arms and stood upright.

"This is a divine weapon. I had told you that I am half-divine. I can summon this whenever I want. My mother is the queen of the devils. It is why I have crimson hair. Well, red." Lilith's voice was back to being emotionless but she had a smile on her face.

"The only way I can see you staying alive is if I never leave your side. I will protect you, but I have limits because I am half-human." She took Rebecca's hand and held it tightly.

"There is a great evil present with the king and his guests. I do not feel that your sister is there. Do you know where her room is?" she asked.

"I think she told me it was in the fourth tower halfway up. The same tower as the prince," Rebecca said frantically.

Lilith pulled her down the hallway and towards the tower. Every time a monster would leap at them, Lilith would cut it down. Not slowing down for even a moment, they reached the tower. More of the monsters could be seen eating the guards.

Rebecca panted, "Lilith, I can't. My arm." The wound on her arm was still bleeding.

"It is quite deep. They seem to be able to eat metals. I can use my healing power but it will cause my ability to use the blade to diminish faster," Lilith said as a green glow emitted from her hand and into the wound.

She ripped off a part of her dress and wrapped it around the wound. "I only used enough to stop the bleeding. I need you to—" Before she could finish, screams echoed from the tower.

"Sister!" Rebecca yelled as she charged in past the monsters.

She burst into a room and came across a young man with no shirt on, barely managing to defend himself against the monsters. Rebecca grabbed a nearby sword and helped him kill off the rest.

His brown hair were the same shade as his eyes, but his face matched the king's. "You must be Rebecca. I...I am the prince. I..." He collapsed as he started cry.

"Where is Sasha?" Rebecca yelled as she looked around.

The prince placed a disembodied arm on his lap. "We skipped the party to make love. I am only the seventh in line so there was no need for formalities. The white dragon gave her some medication to make her mating cycle come sooner. We could not wait for the wedding. I did not hear the monsters sneak in. It ripped off her arm like it was paper… This is all that remains of my love. Are the gods punishing me for not waiting?" He gently rubbed the arm and wrapped his fingers around the fingers as his eyes welled up.

"My love, I will join you soon," he cried as he kissed the hand.

"Prince, snap out of it! She would want you to survive. Follow me and—" Rebecca tried to console him but he stopped her.

He looked at his sword. "I stole this from my father to show her. It is our family sword. He said to make sure that my uncle never gets it. I know this was his doing." His face started to turn red.

"Take it. After tonight, I am sure no one will be left of the line. Just in case someone does survive, hand it to them. Make sure my uncle never gets his hands on it." He handed her the sword and smiled.

"My love is waiting for me. I will never leave your sister's side. She told me she was sorry for hurting your feelings. I will tell her that I told you." He said as he slowly walked towards the window and jumped out while holding Sasha's arm.

Lilith ran into the room with a bite mark on her leg. "Are you alright?" She asked.

"Lilith, what happened? This is all my fault. If I never ran off, this would have never happened." Rebecca cried as she tried to find something to wrap around Lilith's leg.

"I am fine. It is already healing. Did you find your sister?" Lilith asked as she looked around.

"She is dead! And that no-good prince jumped out the window after handing me this lousy sword." She sat down next to Lilith and sobbed.

Lilith stared at the sword. "This sword—it is made out of god's metal. How did they—" She was interrupted by more screams. "We must go now."

"We must go to my father's house. We need to save them," Rebecca cried. Lilith nodded, and they ran into the city.

They avoided the monsters as much as they could. People all around were being devoured and blood ran like a river down the streets. Screams filled the sky. Soon after, fires started to engulf the houses.

In the distance, they heard the sound of the gate explode and debris scattered across every part of the city, killing the monsters and people alike. They managed to reach Rebecca's family home. It was very dark.

Rebecca let go of Lilith's hand and ran inside. "Mother, Father, Whelps! Everyone?" she shouted as she ran into the kitchen. She stopped for a second and then started crying. The only thing she could see was blood dripping from the edge of the table. One of the smaller monsters was standing on it and was in the middle of licking the blood.

Rebecca charged in and punched the beast. His body popped and his black blood splattered all over her dress.

"Rebecca!" Her father slowly pulled himself towards her. One of his arms and legs were missing.

"Father, where are the—" He grabbed her leg, stopping her from finishing.

"They are all dead. Get out now! Save yourself and find peace with your Lilith." Rebecca's father smiled as his last breath left his lungs.

Another small monster came out and giggled, repeating the screams of Rebecca's family as they died. "Mommy, save me! Children, run away! Rebecca, save yourself!" There was a slight gargle in its voice—the blood of her family was still fresh in his throat.

Its voice became a low growl as it stared at her. "Girl, I am a nal. I shall devour you. Do not worry, your flesh will aid in giving my master power."

More monsters slowly came from behind the creature. They all laughed at Rebecca's sight of despair. She collapsed to the ground, ready to give up in her grief. Suddenly, a hand grabbed her shoulder and shoved her towards the door.

"Lilith is hurt. Go take her out of the city. Survive." Marcuse smiled at her. Before Rebecca could respond, the nal jumped on Marcus and started to eat him.

"Marcus, no!" Unable to produce any more tears, Rebecca's cries became dry. Her brother's last words penetrated her mind. "Lilith!"

She ran outside. In the middle of the street was Lilith. Her leg was impaled by a wooden spike and she was pinned to the ground.

"Lilith! This is all my fault again. I am so sorry." She rushed over to help pull it out of her leg.

"It is part of the gate. I know this is all new to you—death and carnage. I sort of know how you are feeling. My human half is telling me to scream in fear but my divine half is keeping me calm. I am sorry about your family. I should have been able to foresee their deaths. It was all my fault." Tears ran down Lilith's face.

"Drakon will give me his blessing, I know it. I will never leave your side again. I love you, Lilith," Rebecca said as she tried to wrap the wound.

"We must hide while I heal. I have to find Father before we go. Mother had said that he is not allowed to die."

Lilith looked around and pointed to a small guard tower in the center of the district. It seemed abandoned. Nothing was in it, not even weapons. Rebecca carefully helped Lilith into the storage closet and used whatever was inside to block the door.

"Sorry, I told you that I loved you again. I know it bothers you. The last time I said it, you disappeared for a day," Rebecca said as she checked on Lilith's wound.

"I am sorry about that. I still do not understand most emotions. I only know what was told to me by my mother and sister. The weeks we lived together though—I learned about being happy." She took a deep breath and looked into Rebecca's eyes. "I promise you that I will think about this matter. Right now, I am thinking of how we can escape after I find Father."

They waited there for about an hour. Lilith's leg had mostly healed, and they removed the random objects they had used to block the door. Lilith handed the royal sword to Rebecca and they took off.

As they headed towards the town center, a blinding light flashed and a few blocks exploded. Rebecca was knocked off her feet and flew into a wall.

A dwarf grabbed her and pulled her into a building. "Aye lass. Glad to see ya be alright."

"The merchant? I haven't seen you in over a month. Your little ones?" she asked in panic.

"Aye, they be alright. I did not bring them this time. They be home still. So if I die, they be fine." He let out a laugh.

Lilith came running in. "Rebecca, your face is bleeding!"

"Aye, I see ya still with that lovely lass. No worry, she be fine. That be blood from me hand." The dwarf smiled as he took off his glove. He had a deep gash across the middle of his palm.

"I be tryin' to get these people outta here. Sewer be nearby. I use to use it back when I was more of a shady person. Ya welcome to join," he said.

"We have to find her father. If you're still near here when we find him, we will join you. Do not wait for us." Rebecca hugged him and they ran off.

Lilith's head perked up and she looked towards the center of the town. "Father is in trouble. We must hurry."

They found Verus lying in the street. His heart was impaled by a spike made of bone. Lilith froze and tears blocked her sight. "Father, no!" She ran up and hugged his limp body.

"Mother said he is not allowed to die. I failed her… I am a failure. He died because of me." Lilith's voice had an emotion Rebecca had never heard from her before—true sadness.

"This is a dragon bone. Is there is a dragon allied with the monsters?" Rebecca looked at the spike closely.

Verus coughed as air suddenly rushed back into his lungs. Rebecca let out a short scream and jumped back. Lilith quickly pulled the spike out and healed his wound.

"How did he survive? He was dead." Rebecca looked at him in shock.

"As Mother said, he is not allowed to die. She knew something bad might happen." Lilith checked his pockets and pulled out dried clay. "A phoenix doll. If you have it on your body when you die, it can bring you back to life, unless the death is natural."

Lilith picked up Verus and carried him into a nearby building and carefully laid him down. She noticed that one of his fingers was missing. "Looks like it was bitten off. Mother can fix that. We need to get him out of here. The doll only works once. He is still weak and needs to rest. Can we move him?" She started panicking as she checked his chest to make sure the wound had closed.

Suddenly, they heard Verus speak. He sounded drained, and he was barely able to open his eyes. "Who are you two?"

"I am Lilith, daughter of Melania, and this is my mate, Rebecca," Lilith said in her usual tone.

Rebecca blushed. "I thought you said you would think about it?"

Lilith nodded as she helped Verus stand and supported him upright. "I did think about it."

Rebecca placed his other arm over her shoulder, and they slowly made their way back to where they had met the dwarf.

"I remember your mother. I met her ten years ago. I thought her only daughter was the amazon queen." He coughed as he tried to talk.

"I was created afterwards. We will talk more after we leave." She tried to make him walk faster but it caused him to moan in pain.

"You look a little old to be ten, but I do not understand how goddesses age. You remind me of my sister…the hair, and the eye reminds me of her." He still struggled to talked.

They reached the house where the dwarf had been but he had already left. They heard some crying coming from inside. Just as they were considering going in, a woman in a red dress came out.

Rebecca recognized her. "I know her. She is a prostitute I saw with that gimpy dwarf." She waved to the woman. "You can follow us. We are going to get out of here. I will keep you safe."

"He is dead, my love is dead. I cannot go without him! You think of him as a gimpy dwarf but I loved him." The woman's face was covered in claw marks.

"I am pregnant with his child. We were going to leave tomorrow and start a new life. He is gone. I can't do it alone. I will wait for him." The woman's frantic speech and her flowing blood quickly lured in ghouls who surrounded her.

"Rebecca, we must go! If we save her, they will eat Father, and I am slowly losing my ability to function without rest." Lilith forced them to keep going. The woman screamed as the ghouls ripped her to shreds and ate her.

"I see the sewer over there. The ghouls are out in the open so we will be safer down there." Lilith pointed as they slowly walked towards an open cover.

As they climbed down, they found a basket of food with a note: *One of the folks knew ya—the farmer's wife. She left this here for ya just in case. Sorry I could not wait for ya, lass. Ghouls showed up. I hope we meet again.'*

They pushed on until Lilith collapsed on the ground from exhaustion. Rebecca carefully placed Verus down and went to check on her.

"I just need to rest. Healing, using magic, and my blade takes a lot out of me. If I was born naturally, the effects would have been less. Just give me an hour, maybe two," she said softly as she fell asleep.

The ground above them rattled violently as they heard some areas cave in the distance. Ghouls roared and growled above them. The laughter of the other monsters echoed.

"Sounds like the bastards are fighting over what eats who," Verus said as he tried to catch his breath. He looked around and tried to stand up. "We can only rest for less than an hour before we have to leave. You may have to carry her."

"What about you? She refused to leave unless we found you. I can't carry you both." Rebecca said, not taking her gaze off Lilith.

"You are a dragonblood. You look like your mother. I knew her before she was married." He slid his back against the wall and sat back down, "Even afterwards, we would still communicate by letters every once in a while. Which one are—"

Rebecca cut him off as tears started filling her eyes. "She is dead! They are all dead! I am the last of my bloodline. The last of my clan." They sat in silence for some time.

Verus looked around and noticed tunnel markings. Each breath that escaped his lips showed that he was out of breath. "I know where we are. There is a small storage room nearby. I used to do my patrols down here, before it became swarmed with ghouls." Barely managing to stand, he used the wall to help hold his weight as he staggered down the path.

The walk was slow. Lilith was surprisingly heavier than she looked. The rivers of shit and piss started to mix with blood. Rebecca thanked the god Drakon that her clan had worshipped for the footpath along the side so they would not have to walk in the stream.

Near a corner, there was a small door. Verus reached around and removed a fake brick from the wall. Inside it was a key that he used to open the door. The room that they entered was large enough to fit four people. There was a small rack on the back wall that had rusted weapons hanging on it. The extra clothing was full of mildew and smelled of shit. Verus reached his hand under the desk and pulled out a deck of cards. Even though the moisture had mostly ruined them, he smiled when he looked at them.

"Why would the royal guard allow this place to get swarmed by ghouls?" Rebecca asked.

"We always had a problem with smugglers and ghouls. The gates over the exits kept the ghouls out for the most part. However," he tossed the cards on the ground, except for one, "a dwarf had the smart idea to remove the gates. What he didn't know was that the ghouls had formed a camp nearby, and when they saw him remove the gate…well, that's how it started."

"The ghouls are just dumb beasts," Rebecca talked down to him.

"To a dragonblood, yes, it must feel like their world is beneath you. Your kind wouldn't have taken notice of their social structure. They have gods that they worship, and they can even craft stone tools. I also witnessed them doing some form of writing and communication with words. They may be just grunts and growls to us but to them, it is speech." He smiled as he stared at the card.

"What's so funny?" she asked, trying to look around his hand.

"The girl I was courting gave me this set. She always liked this card. I would normally toss it out but she wrote me a love letter on this, so I kept it. We ended up getting married when I was promoted," he said and showed her the card. The moisture had made the ink run and the writing was barely visible.

"Where is she? Maybe we can find her." Verus stopped her from talking by waving his hand to dismiss her. "She died twenty years ago." He tried to sit on the chair but ended up on the ground as the leg broke.

"The last time your mother wrote to me was a month ago. She said you wanted to join the army. You have that look she told me about," he said as he looked up at a corner of the wall.

"The look of someone who is a disappointment? A runt? She kicked me out of the house." Rebecca scoffed.

"It was my idea. I told her that if you were serious, you needed to be tested. I see that you passed. You look strong." He closed his eyes.

"I wanted to join because I wanted to have an adventure, find my own place in this world, and maybe find someone." She looked at Lilith and combed her fingers through her hair. "And it did lead me to her."

Rebecca looked at him and noticed that he had drifted off to sleep. "Like father like daughter, I guess. I wish I could rest too."

She did tell him I was her mate. I wonder if she was serious. She looked at the sword and slid it under a shelf. *It will be safer here.*

CHAPTER 9
DAUGHTER!

A slight nudge on her arm forced Rebecca to open her eyes. Lilith was sitting up with Rebecca's head on her lap. Her face still showed no emotions, but Rebecca knew she was feeling something behind it.

"I guess I fell asleep?" Rebecca sat up and rubbed her eyes.

"We must go now. I see our deaths if we stay here any longer. We must leave before the sun starts rising." Lilith said as she stood up.

"Can we talk first? I mean, you told him I was your mate. Did you really mean that?" Rebecca tried to stand up but realized she had lost some feeling in her legs.

"Yes. That time you told me you loved me and I ran off, it was not because of anything you said. It was because I felt something in my heart. It scared me and I ran, thinking something was going to happen." Lilith paused for a bit. "When I saw your death, I knew."

She blushed a little as she said her next words. "I do not want to be without you in my life. This would be best if we are a couple. When my mother ordered me to return a few days ago, I told her no. I cannot leave your side. I have never said no to Mother before. I hope she forgives me."

She kicked Verus' foot to wake him. "We have about an hour at the

69

most. Can you move on your own? We will not make it out alive if I have to carry you." Lilith's tone changed a little from when she had talked to him Before. There was a hint of concern now.

"I think I can manage. But if you must, you can leave me behind. I am an old soldier." He stood up and slowly walked towards the door.

"Mother said you are not allowed to die, and I love Rebecca. I do not want to make a choice. I can help by holding your arm."

Rebecca blushed as she listened to Lilith. *She said it so easily and without hesitation.*

Verus looked at Rebecca. "Are you alright? You seemed a little shocked."

"It just caught me off guard. I'm not used to her saying that." She tried to hide her cheeks with her hands.

They quickly walked through the sewers. Verus' knowledge of the passage ways made their advance easier. A few areas were blocked off where the streets had collapsed, but he knew some routes around them and hidden doors to lead to other areas.

They reached the gate and found that it had already been opened. Near the bottom, they could see some ghouls eating body parts of the people that couldn't make it out on time. Lilith jumped off the ledge and killed them with her blade. She stumbled a little but still pushed through, leading the other two.

As the sun slowly peeked over the field, Lilith demanded that they drop to the ground. A few moments later, the entire city exploded. Lilith quickly placed her hands on the ground and summoned a protection barrier. It sparkled with all the colors of the rainbow as the debris turned to dust as it hit the barrier. When it was clear, she collapsed as she released the barrier. Her breaths became strained as they exited her lungs.

"I have overdone myself. I need to rest a little." Rebecca lifted her head onto her lap, "Thank you," Lilith said softly said as she drifted off to sleep.

"It's how she has been able to stay alive for so long. Most homunculi live for a week, rarely a month. She is twenty. Sleeping is how she is able to regenerate." Verus managed to find a tree that was still standing and rested against it as he drifted off to sleep.

"I swear, like father like daughter. I think they are both just tired souls." Rebecca kissed Lilith's forehead and combed her hair with her fingers, her mind drifting off to her family.

Rebecca woke up and found Lilith's head still on her lap. Their eyes locked as they starred at each other. They gently intertwined their hands and let them stay that way.

Lilith broke the silence. "I still do not know how this will work. We are both females. I have no penis, so I do not understand how we can be intimate. However, I am happy. I will make it work."

"You are such a blunt person. I just wish you had the ability to express your emotions more," Rebecca said.

"I take it you two are a new couple?" Verus said. Noticing the girls shying away, he quickly moved on to something else. "So, why did your mother say I had to live?"

Lilith stood up and kneeled in front of him like she was trying to bow. "Because I am your daughter. I hope I am not a disappointment to you, Father." Her tone had emotions in it. She wanted his approval of her existence.

Verus tried to speak normally but he was clearly a little shocked. "I met your mother ten years ago and we never...you are at least twenty."

"When you made a deal with her, you agreed to give her half of your soul. She combined it with half of her soul to create me. After I turned five, she used her magic to age me ten years. I am sorry if I am a disappointment to you, Father." Her voice had a hint of sadness to it. "I would understand if you hated me, Father. I am an experimental creation." She lowered her head. Tears slowly came out of her eyes but she did not make a sound.

"Look me in the face, girl," Verus said in a stern voice.

As soon as she looked up, he embraced her in a hug. After the shock wore out, she returned his embrace with her own.

"I have a daughter. A daughter! After my wife and unborn son died, I gave up all hope. I have a daughter," Verus cried as he hugged her tighter.

"I have never felt this happy in twenty years. You are a blessing, my angel. I have a daughter," he repeated to himself.

"You do not care that I was created by magic?" Lilith sobbed.

"I saw you bleed from that wound on your leg, so you have my blood regardless of how you were made," he said happily.

"Does my relationship with Rebecca dishonor you?" She cried some more.

"As long as you are happy, my dear, I do not care. I have a daughter. Now I have a reason to live. I am so glad she gave me that dumb clay doll. That phoenix doll gave me a second chance. You are my daughter…" He kissed her on the forehead.

"Well, I'm a little jealous. When she speaks to me, it's in that weird emotionless tone, but with him, it's full of emotions. Maybe it's something she always had locked away. She did sort of get his permission to be with me, so I guess it's a step forward." Rebecca mumbled to herself as she folded her arms.

"Rebecca, please make sure she stays happy. If you can promise me that you are serious with her, you have my blessing." Verus looked at her and smiled.

"Sir, you have my word. I will do everything in my power to keep her happy. I love her." She bowed to him.

Back to her usual tone, Lilith said, "Rebecca, the reason why it took me so long to meet you at the castle was because I was hiding all of our stuff outside the city. Your brother Marcus had a cabin near a lake. Everything is there."

"All of our stuff? You mean everything?" Rebecca was not expecting that.

"Yes, things I cannot part with. Memories of when we had a happy home. I am sorry the nice dress you got me is ruined, but I will treasure it." Though Lilith's voice was flat, her eyes expressed her emotions.

They followed Lilith for over an hour until they reached the cabin. They stood in disbelief when they saw that part of the city wall had smashed it.

Lilith fell to her knees and cried. "I am so sorry. I ruined all of our memories. Are you mad at me?"

Rebecca gently shook her head. "The memories are what *we made together* with all those things. We can get new things and make better memories." She hugged her and kissed her forehead.

"We need to make camp soon. Maybe we can use what is here to make a decent shelter while we rest," Verus said as he moved things around. "You two find something to change into. My armor may be battered but it is in better condition than your silk dresses. Your under-garments are showing."

The girls looked at each other and noticed that their dresses where tattered and there was more skin than silk showing. Rebecca blushed as Lilith just stood there, looking around. They both quickly dug around, looking for some clothes.

"I must admit, this is the most I have seen of you. Even when we lived alone, you always had on that outfit. I see that tan is your natural skin color," Rebecca said as she chuckled.

"I would wash when you went for training or when you went around town to look for something. Mother always told me to wash in private in case I make a mistake and show my wings. She told me if the Seer or the Watcher witnessed me showing my wings to anyone, that person would be marked for death." Lilith picked up a large box and placed it down.

"So, besides being really strong, what else is different about you?" Rebecca kicked the box. "Sounds like it may be clothing."

"I am about as tall as that tree. I figured out how to change my height so I would blend in easier. And especially after I met you, being of this height made eye contact easier." Lilith broke open the box. Inside it was part of their bar table.

"That tree is almost seven feet! You're telling me you're really that tall? Am I allowed to see it?" Rebecca poked Lilith's shoulder like there was a button.

"This dress would rip apart. It is not in tune for magical change, and I do not think Father would want to see me naked. I will show you when we have a moment, I promise." Lilith held Rebecca's hands.

Verus tossed some clothes he had managed to find. "I found some of your clothes. Is that a bar table?"

"These are Rebecca's outfits. I am already as short as I can be. These may not fit me." Lilith said as she held up a shirt in front of herself to measure.

"Yeah, I had a small bar table in my house. We were going to get rid of it when we decided to remodel, but she insisted we keep it when she broke my flask. I guess she felt guilty," Rebecca said.

"I managed to make this fit." Lilith stood in a fresh shirt and pants. Her ankles showed a little and the pants hugged her legs. The shirt was a tight fit. Her belly was exposed and her breasts used up all the space.

Verus took the damaged things they couldn't use and made a campfire. He managed to use their dresses to make snares and catch small animals for food. He even found some wild herbs to add flavor to the food.

"Tomorrow, we will see if we can find anything we can use from what is left of the city," Verus said as he laid down. "You girls get some rest."

* * *

"So, what do we do now that we are a couple?" Lilith looked at Rebecca.

"Well, let us start off with something small for now. I am way too worn out to do anything else. How about a kiss? People kiss in a relationship," Rebecca said as she got closer to Lilith and held her in her arms.

Lilith leaned forward and kissed her forehead. "That seems like what mothers do with children to comfort them," she said.

"Lilith, you are the sweetest person I have ever met. Allow me." Rebecca pulled her closer.

"Do what you think we—" Lilith was unable to finish as their lips locked.

Lilith's lips were a bit fuller than Rebecca's. It made each kiss feel like she was kissing a soft fruit. After a few moments, Rebecca moved her head away.

"So, how was that? I must admit, you are fun to kiss," Rebecca said.

"I have never kissed like that before. I can feel the blood rush to my face. I enjoyed it. I love you Rebecca, I really do." For the first time, Lilith said it with strong emotion behind her voice .

The overwhelming feelings inside Rebecca made her pull Lilith closer and their lips locked once more. She slowly slid her tongue into her mouth and Lilith followed by sliding in hers. They laid down next to the fire, embracing each other as they made out. They fell asleep without letting go of each other.

CHAPTER 10
A LONG BOAT RIDE

A storm clashed across the ocean. Waves as tall as a castle slammed into the side of the boat, knocking it from side to side. The captain ordered his son to try to steady the ship as he tried to lower the sails to prevent them from tearing.

Taranis walked up to the captain. "Is there anything I can do to help?"

"Aye, help me son. The wind is picking up, and he may lose control," he said through clinched teeth.

As Taranis headed over, a large wave slammed into the deck and knocked the boy over the side. Taranis managed to grab his leg and pull him up.

"Thank you, sir. You saved my life." The boy stared at him.

"I hear death by sea is suffering like no other. I do not wish someone as young as you to suffer slowly. Tell me what I can do to help." His voice still had a deep threatening tone but he was being polite.

The boy pointed to the helm and shouted, "Just move it easy. Do not fight the water, or it will break! Just move it so it snakes across the waves. I will work the pump to get the water out of the lower decks."

After what seemed like an eternity, the storm finally lifted. The son and his father collapsed in the boat, worn out from the hard work.

"I am sorry, my lord, but we be tired. We just simple mortals with limits." The captain said, out of breath.

"It is fine, human. As long as you are able to work to your best. I too feel some tiredness from the endeavor." Taranis sat down next to the boy, "What is your name, runt?"

"Albert. Why did you save me just now when you were trying to kill us before?" The boy asked, trying not to directly look at him.

"I do apologize. I have lived in the realm for decades. I have grown a fondness for humans. I can see why the goddess took a liking to your kind. I am only a servant to my lord's demands. He needs the energy of mortals to free himself from his prison," Taranis said as he patted Albert on the head.

"Then why did you kill my mother?" Albert suddenly cried out.

"She is not dead. She abandoned you. Maybe that is why I spared your life on the island. My mother also abandoned me," Taranis said as he stood up. "I tend to spare someone during every feeding."

He lifted his head and sniffed the air. Without hesitation, he summoned his divine blade and leaped over the boy, cutting what seemed to be air. A large, pale hand popped up over the edge of the boat but was cut instantly. Taranis then pulled the boy closer to him and slowly walked him to his father.

"We must wait inside. The storm has awakened some of the beasts that live in the oceans. They are aiming for you, boy," he said.

They hurried inside the hull of the ship and waited until the next day. For days, they sailed. Each day, they would sit and talk. Taranis would ask them about their home life, the things they liked and enjoyed. After two weeks went by, Albert decided to ask Taranis about himself.

"You said that one time you were…" Albert paused in the middle and held his chin, trying to remember, "also abandoned by your mother."

"Yes. I was born without wings. I was considered weak and was going to die as an infant. My lord found me and took me to his father —the king. I was raised to be my lord's guard." He handed the boy some dried fish that he had just made.

"I will grant you to ask me one personal question a day," Taranis said. He could see that Albert had another one burning in his mind. "I will allow two today."

"Are you a god?" There was a smile in Alberts eyes that excited Taranis.

"No, my kind has been erased from your memories. The books are a lie. But I am a divine being." He made a fist with one hand and placed it in the center of the other one. "This fist is the mortal realm. It is actually round. These fingers are where the gods live—in a world of light. The center of my hand is the dream realm. It is what fills up the space in between. The lower part of my hand is the chaos realm, where the devils live. The war between the gods and demons that is in your history books was actually a war with the devils." He finished in a blank tone.

"What about your thumb? You seem to have it far from the rest on purpose," Albert pointed out.

"This, is the abyss, lad. Only pure darkness. It is where the Fallen came from. They corrupted the divine beings such as my lord and created the Fallen army. And since I am his general, I had to follow." Taranis let out a deep sigh.

From then on, Albert asked him a question every day as they worked on the boat. Each one was about small things like his hobbies and the foods he enjoyed. After a week, he started to ask serious questions.

"Why was your lord imprisoned?" The question was to be expected but Taranis still hesitated.

"He fell in love with someone that was out of his grasp. She was lovely and intelligent, but also extremely dangerous. He decided to abandon his duties as a prince and proclaim himself a king. He did everything for someone who was incapable of feeling love. I never agreed with his actions but I followed as a loyal subject and as his friend. His sister was the one who placed him inside his cage in the dream realm. I hope once I free him, he will see his folly and abandon his lust for this woman. She is the purest of evils. She is from the dark place I told you about." Taranis smiled and patted the child's head.

"Does it bother you that you killed all those people?" Albert asked the next day.

"Do you feel sad when you kill a fly? I may have formed a bond with you, but I see you as a lower life. If you fell over dead right now, it would not bother me in the slightest. I would only wish your death to be quick and painless. I despise suffering. I also dislike meaningless slaughter," he replied and handed the boy a carving of an elf. He had used ash to color the hair and oil mixed with ash to tan the skin.

"This is what you mortals call a dark elf. My mother created them. In return, I feed off of their life energy when they die. It is how we divine beings gain our energy back. We feed from the life energy of our creations or the creations we inherit when our parents die," he said as he sat down and started eating.

As the moon beamed down onto the boat, Taranis woke everyone up. "We are approaching land soon. I need you all to be on full alert. I smell something foul in the air, something I have not smelled in thousands of years. It is her."

The captain stood on the deck and tried to peek but all he could see was the pitch-black darkness. "Are ya sure? I do not see any docking lights."

"We have drifted off course. I see a smuggler's dock. I also smell death." Taranis handed Albert a rope that was tied to his belt.

As they approached the dock, they could see some tiny monsters with huge teeth. The monsters giggled as they leaped at the boat. Some managed to land onto the boat while others hit the water and never came back up.

"These are the nox. The larger ones are the nal. They are the beasts that my lord created for our master's army. They devour everything. Boy, stay near me. While they will not attack me, they also do not obey me," Taranis said as he tried to hide the boy behind him.

The nox spoke in unison with a voice that disturbed the boy's soul. "Taranis, Master has made her move. Allow us to eat these mortals."

"They are under my protection as my slaves," he said as he held up his sword.

"Master wants all to be devoured. This is not a negotiation. We will allow them to live if you can get them past the docks alive." The nox grinned, baring their teeth.

"Captain, I promise you. If you fall, I will make sure that your boy will survive." Taranis picked up Albert and placed him on his shoulders.

"Aye, that be all I ask." The captain grinned as he pulled out his sword.

They made a dash towards the bow, avoiding as many of the monsters as they could. They only attacked the ones that tried to pounce on them. They managed to leap off the boat and land onto the dock. Albert fell off Taranis' shoulders and landed in the water. Taranis quickly yanked on the rope, pulling him back onto the dock.

A nal tried to get at the child with his claws. His father quickly pushed him towards Taranis and the man's arm was ripped off. He screamed in pain as the boy cried out in shock. Taranis sliced the beast in half and placed Albert back on his shoulders.

"Get me boy out of here. I will try to hold 'em off," The captain looked at his son and softly cried out, "Do not turn into a disgrace like me, boy. Be a man, a real man. I love you, my son."

Taranis nodded at him and ran as fast as he could as the child's father leaped at the monsters. There was a small gap as they devoured him, which allowed Taranis to run out safely. Once they reached the end, a nal smiled and talked. "The boy shall live, but it is only borrowed time. Master will learn of him and deal with him accordingly."

After the monsters scurried off, Taranis placed the boy down on the ground. "I shall raise you. If I do it right, Master will allow you to live. If anyone asks, you are my son." He told him as they watched the sun rise.

The ground went through a violent rumble and they could see a large cloud of dust in the distance. Taranis covered Albert with his body to protect him from the bits of rock and brick that landed near them.

"Master has made her move. I must train you quickly." He gently patted the boy's head.

CHAPTER II
NO GOD

Lilith was the first one to wake up. She smiled as she noticed how close Rebecca's face was to hers. She sat up and stretched, a small yawn escaping her lips. Her mind was filled with memories of the previous night and her cheeks turned a bright red.

Lilith parted the hair that fell over Rebecca's lips and kissed her. Rebecca moaned a little as she woke up. The more awake she became, the deeper the kiss got.

Rebecca sat up and stretched. "Good morning, my love. I could get used to being woken up like that." She tried to smile but tears slowly filled her eyes.

Rebecca tried to wipe them away. "Sorry, the weight of it all just started coming to my mind. They are all dead." She closed her eyes tightly and gave Lilith another smile. "I am glad I still have you. I think I would have gone mad if I was alone."

Lilith sat back deep in thought. *Tell her you love her with emotion, she would love that. But what if I say it wrong? Maybe she would think less of me. I have to say it properly.* She smiled and replied in her typical emotionless voice, "I love you as well."

However, Rebecca just stared at her with an odd look on her face.

That is not the right response. Is she still feeling sad? Lilith thought as she sat there, looking into Rebecca's eyes.

Rebecca chuckled and rubbed the back of Lilith's head, "I guess you will always have your little quirks."

You dummy, you made her upset. Emotion—she wants emotion. Lilith looked around.

Verus slowly got up and started to check the traps. He did not say a word, just looked at them and smiled.

Lilith jumped up in excitement when she noticed him. "Father, may I join you?" He nodded and she followed.

"I think your friend wanted you to stay there with her. Is everything alright?" He said as they walked.

"I am worried that I will screw things up. When I talk to you, it seems easy for me to show emotions, but with her, I get scared," she said with her head lowered. "I also do not understand what she feels. I told her I love her but it was not the right thing to say. She was crying."

"The lack of empathy you have comes from your divine half. I think your mother did not care for your emotional state of being." Verus took a deep breath and looked at her.

"Then there is the human half. You are mentally at a stage where you are learning who you are as well as things you always wanted to know about. I am a part of you, therefore you had a strong desire to meet me—to know your other half. And then you met Rebecca, who introduced new feelings and emotions that you had no idea you had within you. You are trying to mentally grasp it all and understand it, and so your mind is naturally trying to maintain a safe distance. Emotions can be scary if you have never felt them before." As he finished, he looked at a trap and noticed a dead rabbit tangled in the snare.

Verus continued. "I think she needs you right now more than I do. She has just lost her entire family and all her friends. You are all that she has left. Go to her." He handed her the rabbit and smiled.

"What about you?" Lilith didn't move.

"I know I have you in my life, and that is all I need." He walked off, leaving her behind.

He is right. I need to be with her. She is alone. Maybe she thinks I abandoned her. She placed her thumb nail on the edge of her lip.

What if she stops loving me? I need to try better. She slowly walked back.

Lilith heard the sound of soft crying. She looked up at Rebecca. Her face was red and her eyes were full of tears. She was holding a golden bracelet. On it was the engraving of a dragon and a man.

Is she upset that I left her alone? Does she hate me now? Lilith stood there staring at her.

Rebecca saw her and jumped up. "Oh shit, I'm sorry. My mother made this. She used to be good at crafting. Before she and my dad got married, she studied to become a jeweler. She loved working with silver and gold," she said as she cried some more.

"What are the engravings?" Lilith placed the rabbit down and looked at it more closely.

"It is Drakon, our god. He was the largest dragon ever born. He was also extremely powerful. Our creator merged his soul into Drakon's body and became a god. The month of Drakka is named after him. Father had a statue of him in his human form on his bookshelf." Rebecca tried to hold back her tears but the snot had plugged her nose. She covered her face with her arm.

Lilith immediately hugged her tightly. "You are allowed to cry on me if you want. I am here for you."

"That sounds like something Verus told you to say, but I still enjoy hearing you say it," Rebecca said softly.

Verus cleared his throat. Like a commanding officer, he said, "After we eat, we shall explore the city to see if we can find anything." He pulled up another dead rabbit and a lizard.

After an hour, they reached the outskirts of whatever was left of the city. They stood in horror as they looked around them. Barely anything was left standing, except for bits of stone walls here and there. The ground was covered in grey and white sand, a mix of destroyed stone and marble. The largest city in the world was now nothing more than a city of death. Bodies could be seen all over, even some of the monsters had been unable to avoid the blast. Verus was speechless at the sight.

"I grew up in a small village that had been destroyed but the buildings still remained standing. This is something I never want to see again," Lilith said as she stood there. Holding herself, she tried to stay warm against the shiver that ran down her body but it was to no effect.

Rebecca scoffed. "I doubt we will find anything of use here."

They heard a moan. Some dirt on the ground started to shift and a hand emerged from underneath.

"A survivor!" Rebecca hurriedly pulled the man out.

"Water, I…I need a drink." He fell into a dry cough as he tried to speak more. He spit out some blood and fell to the ground.

"I will heal him." Lilith rushed over and placed her hands on him.

"Rebecca, go back to the camp and find anything that can hold water and bring it here. I have two water runes. They should give us enough water for forty people. Lilith, you stay here and heal people. I will look for more survivors."

"Father, I can only heal about twenty people before I pass out. I am also limited. I can only recover humans and gnomes instantly," she said as she checked the man. "If I just heal whatever is most crucial, I might be able to last longer."

The man cried as he laid there. Lilith did the best she could to help him relax. She stroked his arm and sang the only song that came to her mind.

"Her legend would be spread across the land, saving mankind with her mighty hand." She looked down and noticed that the man had fallen asleep.

Verus shouted for her to come towards him. He had managed to find six more survivors, all of them unable to speak properly from lack of water, and all of them attempting to cry but unable to form tears.

"How long do you need to rest again before you can heal people?" He asked, out of breath.

"Two hours, maybe three. How many did you find?" She started healing them.

"Maybe sixty or more. These are the only ones that could walk." He collapsed to the ground and shook his head. "I saw babies, dead newborns being eaten by rats. I will never get used to such a sight."

For hours, they helped as many people as they could. It was a nightmare for everyone. Some would die even after healing. Lilith became weaker each time, even after getting some rest.

"Lilith, we need to stop. You might die if you keep going." Rebecca gripped her arm tightly.

"I need to keep going. That baby—that innocent baby died in my arms. He arrived too late and died before I could heal him. I need to keep going. I am a divine being, so why does this bother me? Mother always talked about mortal death like it was insects getting what they deserved. But this—I cannot stand the suffering that these people are going through." Even though her words had no emotion as she spoke, her tears rolled down her cheeks. "Rebecca, I…I think you opened the doors to my heart, flooding me with emotions."

"If you die from casting too many spells, you will be saving no one! If you die, I will be alone. I need you, Lilith." Rebecca kissed her deeply and looked into her eyes. "Rest, and we will heal more tomorrow. We will never be able to save everyone but we can be proud we saved whoever we could."

A voice shouted from nearby, "Aye, somebody…get this off of me. This bastard be heavy."

They rushed over to where the voice had come from and Rebecca gasped. "Ulbrek, you're alive!" She kneeled down and hugged him.

He screamed in pain. "Aye lass, good ta see ya be in good health. Get off me, lass or I may grab ya arse."

She pulled away and noticed that her shirt was covered in blood. Lilith lifted up the large stone that was on Ulbrek's chest and froze.

His whole body bloody and his legs were missing. He had a deep gash across his chest which began to bleed faster.

"Ah, shit. The stone was keeping it closed. I used a fire spell ta stop the bleedin' from me legs but this I cannot fix." He pulled out his flask and took a sip.

Lilith tried to heal him but she was too weak. She couldn't stop the bleeding. She cried as she kept trying to pour more magic into the spell.

"Aye, it be alright. I accepted me fate. I just be glad ta know ya made it out safely. Here, take me flask. I want ya ta have it. That fucken' dragon…he thought I be dead so he left me." He spat and drank some more.

Rebecca stared at him, confused. "What dragon?"

Shouting echoed and a man with crimson hair could be seen in the distance. His dark, tanned skin and his height made him stick out.

"That bitch! I must find her. She has my scale." He shouted as he dug through the dirt.

Verus stood there paralyzed. "I can feel a pain in my chest. I think he is the one that killed me."

Lilith stared at him and shouted, "Who are you?"

The man stopped and stood up. Rebecca gasped as she saw him. She looked at the bracelet her mother had given her. "That's him—Drakon. He looks just like Father's statue. He will help us." She smiled.

Lilith stood in front of her and quietly said, "He smells of death. I think he wants to kill you."

The man sniffed the air and grinned as he spoke, "Ah, a dragonblood. Drakon, you said? Yes, that was the name of the body, I remember from when he agreed to let me take him. I am Aeron, the creator of dragons and their god."

He took a few steps closer and spat on the ground. "My creations were the strongest. Other races decided to make them sport by hunting them down to show their bravery. They almost became wiped out, so I followed that bitch of a goddess down to save them. Some of the smaller clans found out they could breed with humans and made your kind—a filthy stain on my perfection. I have made it my mission to kill you all."

"But we worship you! We also have giant statues of you that we worship. I don't understand. Nothing in the texts says you hated us," Rebecca said in shock.

"In the beginning, I tried to entertain the idea, but I decided to not recognize your filthy, impure kind. Even though you have no god, I will grant you the gift to be killed by me. Be a good follower and allow me to do it." He lowered his stance and leaped at her.

Lilith pushed Rebecca out of the way and used her sword to cut him. But he grabbed Lilith by the arm and pulled her towards him. "You are Melania's daughter. I can smell her blood in you. I see that you are able to summon a divine sword at will. I wonder how much it drains you." His voice had a sadistic undertone. He squeezed harder, pressing her hands while she held the blade.

"If I permanently crush your hands with that blade, will they disappear when you unsummon that blade?" He laughed as he kept squeezing.

Lilith cried out as blood rushed down her arm. She tried to kick him but was too worn out from healing all day. Her life flashed before her eyes and eventually all she could see was Rebecca.

A large hammer flew onto Aeron's back, causing him to drop her. He growled and looked back. Ulbrek had sat himself up and had a large smile across his face.

"Aye, wee bastard. We not done yet. I still able ta cast wind magic. Next, I blow a rock up ya arse." He chuckled as blood slowly escaped from the edges of his lips.

Aeron rushed at him, and with his foot, crushed Ulbrek to death. Rebecca charged at him, glowing. She punched at him with all her might. Lighting exploded out of his back and he fell over.

"You monster, you shit-ass monster. You helped destroy this city, you killed my friend, and you hurt my beloved! I do not want you as my god." She spat on his body.

"Strong words from a filthy beast that does not deserve life. That actually hurt. I forgot your kind can still do that stuff." Aeron stood up, holding his guts in as he healed.

Then faster than her eyes could see, he punched Rebecca on the side of her head. She fell over and her head bounced off the ground. Lilith screamed as blood came out of Rebecca's ears.

He was about to step on her when he growled in pain. He turned around and saw Verus standing behind him holding a sword and what was left of a shield.

"I managed to find these in the wreckage. When you tried to kill me, I was off guard." Verus stood in a ready stance with his shield angled.

Aeron lunged forward. Verus leaned back slightly and used the momentum to toss him over. A few quick jabs with his sword as Aaron flew over caused him to land on his head.

"Not bad, human. I see you have skill." Aeron snarled as he slowly stood up.

Aeron tried for another lunge but it was deflected by the shield with another quick stab into his chest.

Lilith crawled over to Rebecca. She was unable to control her tears as she checked on her.

Her skull is cracked. No please. I have to hurry. Will I able to heal her in time? She cried and placed her hands over Rebecca's head.

A green light pulsated from Lilith's hands, and her muscles began to cramp. Her heart was filled with sorrow. She faded in and out of consciousness, yet she pushed on.

"Rebecca, do not leave me. I love you. I promise I will get better at showing my love. Heal, please!" she cried. Her mangled fingers started to bleed. Her efforts to cast the spell was preventing her body to heal.

The words "I need you," exited from Lilith's lips as she passed out.

* * *

Lilith awakened in the back of a wagon. The torches outside provided the only light. Rebecca was next to her with her head wrapped up in bandages. An old lady in a robe sat in the far corner, chanting. She was speaking a language Lilith was familiar with but had a hard time understanding.

"Child, I must thank you. You casted the healing spell on her at the right time. A moment later and her brain would have been permanently damaged. You stopped the hemorrhage, so I thank you." The old lady smiled and bowed her head.

"Are you a dragon?" Lilith sat up.

"Yes, I am. I am a white dragon. Not from her clan. Her clan's white dragon died in the city." The old lady rubbed Lilith's feet.

"I have a potion that you need to give her. Mix a few drops of it in a cup of water. Do this until the bottle is empty. It will help heal her bones. It is rare for our kind to receive bone damage, but I have treated it before." The old lady handed her the glass bottle.

"Verus—is he alright?" She looked around and saw him riding on a horse near the front of the group.

"He was amazing. If the weapons he used were not damaged, he probably would have killed that monster. I have been alive for eight hundred years. Never have I seen a human fight so well," the old lady said as she smiled. "You must be a proud daughter. You have his face."

"How did we end up here anyways? The last thing I remember is healing Rebecca before I passed out." Lilith looked at Rebecca and rubbed her arm. She noticed that her hands were wrapped in bloody bandages.

"After the city exploded, every nation that had a settlement nearby sent out a group to provide aid to the survivors and to see what had happened. I volunteered since I knew of some dragonbloods that lived in the city, and I thought they might need an extra white dragon. When I saw him, I knew who he was—our lord and god Aeron. He attacked some of the survivors who tried to help you guys. Our archers managed to drive him away," the white dragon said with a distorted look on her face.

"He is no god. He is a monster." Rebecca said without looking at anyone. "He is a monster. He's no god—he's pure evil." The tone of her voice made it easy to read her emotions.

"I have heard stories of how he felt about your kind. It must be hard to have everything you were raised on and had faith in to be destroyed. He killed an entire clan over a hundred years ago. I tried to tell other dragonbloods, but no one believes it unless they see it," the old lady said.

She paused and took a deep breath. "Is there anyone left in your clan?"

Rebecca tried to speak but let out a painful whimper. "No, my entire clan was in the city. I have no kinship. All I have left is my mate here, Lilith here."

"You have a small problem. Do you know what happens when only one member is left?" The old lady leaned over to check on her bandages.

Rebecca scoffed. "It has happened to our clan once before, during the war. My ancient elder was the last. Our tales about her say that she had no interest in breeding. However, her instincts took over, the desire to carry the bloodline. And it forced her to take a mate. At the end of the day…we are still animals." She tightly squeezed Lilith's hand.

"I do not know how your condition will be from a year from now, but in your current state, you must not breed. Even after you take the medicines to heal, you will still be weak. I can tell your mating will be next week, maybe sooner. No broods for at least a year." She nodded and pointed at Lilith. "It will probably be fine if it is just the two of you. Nothing rough, just keep it soft."

Lilith blushed. "How can we? I told you I do not have a—" Rebecca covered her mouth with her hand. "I will teach you everything when mating season comes." She softly stroked Lilith's hand. "I love you, Lilith. You are the only divine being I need in my life."

Lilith leaned over and kissed her softly. Thoughts flooded her mind. *Tell her. Have some feeling in your voice. You need her.*

Lilith looked into her eyes and in an odd but soft tone, said, "I love you, more than anything in this world. I will never leave your side. Even if that means I must disobey Mother."

CHAPTER 12

MOURNING

"Lilith, I think we should go back and help the others bury people. I need to find what is left of them…and also Ulbrek. They need to be laid to rest." Rebecca sat up and drank some water.

"The potion makes this taste like piss." She hesitantly swallowed it.

"You only need to take it three times a day, and at this rate, it will only last for six weeks. If you complain and refuse to take it, I will use my magic to make you." Lilith stared at Rebecca in a way that sent a shiver down her spine.

After a few scouts came back to announce the coast was clear, they all headed out. Halfway there, their group joined other groups, and their numbers of a few hundreds eventually became a few thousands. Humans, elves, dwarfs, gnomes, hill giants, and people from other countries all came together to find their loved ones.

Random trinkets, body parts, and other oddities were being placed together. A crowd would gather to see if anything could be used to identify a person. There was a group of scribes with a wagon full of scrolls. These were names of every registered person who lived there.

Rebecca walked to a bloodied mess on the ground and cried, "Master Ulbrek, I am so sorry I could not find you sooner. If only I had been stronger."

Lilith put a hand on her shoulder. "How do you know it is him?" Rebecca pointed to his belt buckle.

In the distance, she could see a dwarf being pulled on a sled by elves. They were holding an amulet that had a light pointing in a direction.

As they passed by, Rebecca cleared her throat. "Need a hand? I can help."

They stopped and the dwarf looked over at the bloodied mess. He cried, "Uncle Ulbrek! Did ya know him?"

She nodded with tears in her eyes. "He was a good friend."

"Aye, well, he still be here later for us. Elf lass, toss a marker. We must find me brother and Rose." He whipped the line like he was commanding horses on a wagon.

"Lord Onyx, you are our king's honored friend, but if you whip us again, we will leave you here to crawl." One of the elves scowled at him.

"Lass, if ya strong, we may need ya help. This light say one of them be alive this way. They may be buried." He whistled at them and waved his hand.

They rushed in the direction he pointed and saw another half-dwarf digging at the ground like a mad man. His body was bloodied and he had black liquid spewing out of his mouth.

"Me brother, Ugthar, he be alive. Gods be praised." Onyx took a deep breath.

Ugthar looked over his shoulder and went back to digging as he shouted, "My beloved is here. I must dig her out. She needs a proper burial. I must find her, my love."

Everyone grabbed tools from the sled and started to dig, Ugthar fell to the ground. His fingers had been worn down to the point they were more blood than flesh. His face was swollen from crying and he constantly coughed out black liquid.

One of the elves shouted, "I hit something. Looks like a large chest."

Ugthar jumped up and pushed everyone out the way. He slowly rubbed his fingers across the top and then gently rested his head on it.

It was hard to hear his voice but his emotions could be felt by everyone. "This is where I left her. That bitch killed my beloved with her own arrow. My love, I found you."

He slowly lifted the lid and gasped as he fell over. Rebecca took a quick peek and goosebumps developed on her entire body. Her eyes filled with tears as she became pale. She took a shaky breath and covered her mouth.

Rose's body was mostly mummified. The decay made it look like she died months ago. Most of her body was covered in a residue that was like tar.

"Don't touch the stuff. It will consume you!" Ugthar shouted as he coughed up more liquid.

Rose's body twitched and raised up into the air, supported by the tar. Her lips moved and let out a laugh that pierced Rebecca's soul.

"I hope I left you enough to bury her. I only consumed what I needed. I am generous to you, Sir Dwarf. I will allow you to be buried with your beloved elf princess." The voice was made of nightmares. Lilith grabbed onto Rebecca's arm and squeezed.

"That voice is the bitch that killed my beloved. I will kill you! I will find you and end you before I die!" His shout slowly became a cry.

"Her last remaining thought was how much she loved you. It is the only good news you will have as you will die a slow and painful death." Rose smiled, "To add to the joy, I'll tell you that you both will never be reunited in death."

The tar vanished and the body fell. Ugthar caught her before she landed on the ground. He cradled her corpse and kissed her lips before falling over. He let out a hellish scream as more liquid poured from the corner of his mouth.

"Brother, why do you not come and help me? I think I am dying," he cried out.

"Ya daft bastard. I got one leg and hand. Ya need to crawl over here," Onyx cried back.

Another elf showed up with a horse pulling a small wagon. "We will place the princess in here so no one will see her and take her back home to her family."

They walked up to Ugthar and tried to pull Rose's body away from him. He screamed and cursed at them.

"I don't understand, why can't they just put him in the wagon with her?" Rebecca asked.

"We want to erase the fact that she married a filthy dwarf. Her shame shall never be known!" an elf replied as he kicked Ugthar in the face and pulled Rose away.

"He be blessed by your king. He oversaw their marriage. He ordered ya bastards to bring us back." Onyx smiled. "Ya forgot he told me that."

Ugthar stood up. He gently pulled Rose away from them and held her. He slowly walked her to the back of the wagon and placed her in gently.

"I'll get in myself. If any of you bastards try to take her away from me again, I swear by the gods, I will kill you with my dying breath." He climbed in and laid down next to her.

"I thank ya lasses for helping. I be back for me Uncle Ulbrek." He smiled and nodded his head.

"Rebecca, I have to report this to Mother. That dwarf has been infected by the Fallen. I must find a way to contact her. She needs to know." Lilith tightly squeezed Rebecca's arm.

"It's alright. You can go to her. The last time it only took you a few days, right? Just fly to her and I will wait for you." Rebecca smiled and nodded.

"I am too weak to fly. But I promised to never leave your side. I am worried if I go, I will never be allowed to see you again, or you might die." She buried her face in Rebecca shoulder.

"She looks like someone I know," Onyx gasped as he watched a woman with black hair, red eyes, and a full of plate armor that was painted black walk by.

Rebecca looked at her and said quietly, "She sort of looks like Aluxes."

Onyx whipped the ropes to the sled again. "Elf wench, follow that lass, please."

The elf looked at him and spit at his foot, shouting, "I am not a horse, nor am I your wench! If you want to follow her, do it yourself."

Lilith took the rope. "I can pull it. Your uncle was important to Rebecca, so I can help him rest by helping you," she said as she nodded.

"Ya voice a bit scary. But well, I never said no to a lovely lass." He smiled.

"The elves aiding you speak differently than most. I have also never seen any have on robes like that," Rebecca said.

"Aye, they belong to the church of the Unnamed Goddess. They grew up in human settlements, so they speak common." Onyx grunted a little and swayed.

"Are you alright?"

Lilith explained, "The drugs that he is on are wearing off. I think the elves gave him something to calm down his emotions. They use it so they can still function while being depressed."

As they followed her, they noticed that there was a single building still standing. Two of the walls were missing, and one of the walls had an old nun pinned to it with half of her body missing.

"So, elves also worship the goddess?" Rebecca asked.

"Aye, but there be a difference. Ya see, humans take a vow to remain pure as the goddess, but the dwarf and elf followers allowed to have sex." He grinned as he spoke but his speech had started to waver.

"She was no virgin, same as the goddess." The lady they had followed spoke with anger as she stared at the body.

"Aye, that be right. Wait what?" He asked in confusion.

"This is the head nun, Mildred. I am here to take her back home to be buried." She gently removed the bone spikes that nailed the nun to the wall.

"Aye, which means she be a virgin." Onyx explained.

"Aluxes told me she treated her like the daughter she was never allowed to have," Rebecca added.

"Yes, that bitch. I am the daughter she was never allowed to have.

She gave that orphan the life I was meant to have." She looked at them and scoffed.

"How she be selected as head nun if she had you?" Onyx sat there, baffled.

"You see, she fell in love with a man and had sex. Nine months later, I was born. When she was offered the spot, she gave me up to be raised by my grandparents. For a dwarf, you are slow in understanding how it works." She gently pulled the nun off the wall.

"It is obvious that you love your mother, so why call her a bitch?" Lilith asked.

"I was talking about Aluxes. She stole my mother from me. Mother would write to me from time to time. She even came to visit me with that runt. But she never told her I was her real daughter." There was still anger in her tone, but she cradled her mother's dead body gently.

"She told me if anything were to happen, she would hide in here. This was part of the original castle that the goddess built. I guess the protection spell was shit. She still died." Her voice broke a little and a tear rolled out.

"Aye, I...I lost me love as well. About to lose me brother. I...I must go, me brother needs me." Onyx looked over and noticed that the elf girl was behind him. She nodded and pulled him away.

"Why do they not get a wagon or something?" Rebecca stood there, watching them leave.

"They are punishing themselves for helping a dwarf. The elves hate dwarfs more than the dwarfs hate elves" The lady stood up. "She is heavier than I would have thought."

"I can help. I can carry her." Lilith gently took the body and carried her.

"I thank you. It must be the burden I carry that makes her feel heavy. I thought she would have survived. I was hoping she would be in there, alive and waiting for me." She started to cry more and sat down.

Rebecca sat down next to her. They sat in silence for a few moments. Then, Rebecca spoke. "So, why do you look like Aluxes?"

"What do you know of her?" The lady's voice was now soft as she rubbed the tears from her eyes.

"We trained together. She told me a little about her life," Rebecca said with a large grin on her face.

"I look like her because I am her older half-sister, Jill." Jill looked right into her eyes. "My father is her father."

They started to walk towards what used to be the outer wall. Lilith walked behind them as Rebecca and Jill walked next to each other.

"Tell me about my sister. I only saw her once when she was eight. She punched a wild boar and killed it," Jill said and chuckled.

"She is tall, probably the tallest person I have ever met that is not a giant. You both have the same face, and you both have anger in your voice when you speak. She joined the elite army, and Verus told me she won an award for saving a lot of people," Rebecca said.

"Yes, our father's blood runs in us. I am the king's personal guard to the Kingdom of Alstat." Jill looked around. "Father was always angry as well."

Surprised, Lilith shouted, "Alstat is over a month's ride from here on horse. How did you get here so fast."

"Mother sent me a letter saying Aluxes was graduating. She wanted to retire and come home so we could make up for lost time." She looked at the dead body. "I guess it was supposed to be just another disappointment in my life."

As they reached the edge of the wasteland, Jill whistled and a horse came galloping out. She took her mother's body and placed it on the horse.

"I thank you for your help. If you ever come to the capitol of Alstat, you will be welcomed as honored guests." She stood there for a moment. "If she survived this, and if you find her, she is not allowed to know about me. Not yet at least."

"Does it have to do with her missing memories?" Rebecca asked.

"Yes," she replied.

"You are welcomed to stay with us for a while. Maybe it will help to grieve a little before you go," Rebecca added.

"No, I must return. I have a husband and son waiting for me back home. He never got to meet his grandmother," she yelled to them as she rode off.

Rebecca took a deep breath and noticed the piles of body parts had grown into a hill. She saw Onyx holding a wooden box with tears rolling down his face.

She walked towards him and touched his shoulder. "Are you alright?"

The slight cheer in his voice was gone. All that was left was his pain. "All they found was her wee head, my beloved." He looked into her eyes. "I think the drug wore off, and I think I prefer it this way."

CHAPTER 13

CHANGE OF PLANS

"**M**aster, there are too many mortals. Things have changed since your slumber. They no longer stay away from obvious danger. It is an influence that your sister spread among them," Aeron said as he kneeled down in front of a little doll.

The doll walked around, rubbing her chin. "Did our puppet survive?"

"Yes, master. He fled and the nal-nox obeyed for once." He lowered his head even more.

"I noticed some changes in the world during my slumber, but I did not expect it to be to this extent. They used to never return to a place that had so much death. I should have waited. It looks like I'll have to wait to retrieve my body." She hovered over a tree branch.

"So, I guess it is true that my sister is dead. Who is this Lord Azaroth? The puppet tried to tell me but all he did was complain." She tried to peek as far as she could.

"He is the child of the Watcher and the Seer. Every so often, the devils and the gods reunite their peace treaty by creating an offspring. They then send them down to the mortal realm to die. He is one of the few who survived to adulthood. To me, he is no problem." He grinned.

"That scar on your face says otherwise. Your body is dying. You need to find that scale." She turned and looked at him. "If you are sure that girl had it, then she ran off. I saw her escape."

She broke a stem off the tree and with anger in her voice, she said, "That stunt you pulled will make things harder. We need to find another way. If only the blasted beasts had more usefulness than eating."

"I hear Taranis is working on getting Apophis free from his prison. Maybe we—"

She cut him off. "The only thing good about Apophis was that his lust for me created an army. Taranis is an intelligent officer. If he wants to free his lord, I will allow him to do as he wishes."

She put her hand under her chin. "I must learn more about this world. Asking you is pointless. Find the general and give him a communication stone. I will play the long game and see if our puppet can teach me anything."

"But Master, he is just a worthless human. Allow me to kill him. It is not worth giving him even the honor of devouring," he begged.

"This is why asking you is pointless! Like the gods, you are blinded by your own ambitions. Was it not you who was defeated by a lowly human? You allowed that cursed god to put a spell on you. And what I saw from your fight earlier, that human would have bested you yesterday if he had proper equipment. No, your only value is that you are loyal and uncorrupted by me. You joined me by your own free will to save your dragons. Prince Loux at least has some intelligence about him."

She leaped off the tree and onto Aeron's shoulder. "I also need to think of a less direct approach. I need to find a human who will join me like you." She smiled.

"Master, a filthy human in your ranks—" She cut him off again by piercing his shoulder with her vine.

"I did not ask, and I did not seek your approval. You will follow my orders, or the first thing I will do is consume you and all your drag-ons." She smiled as she pushed him to the ground, digging the vine in deeper.

"I am sorry, Master. I did not mean to question your plan." He tried to not to show his pain but his whimper gave it away.

She pulled out her vine, walked up to his ear, and whispered, "You are the only one I can trust. I need you to follow my orders without question. If you fall, I am doomed to fail. And our direct approach that you are so fond of will also fail."

He stood up, brushed the dirt off of his body, and bowed. He then immediately turned around and walked off.

"Tell the general I will speak to him soon, I have changed my plans. Make sure you are not seen!"

She watched him walk off and took a deep breath. "I need to have a plan for when he fails. If I learned one thing when Sister defeated me, it is that Father's plan is flawed." She looked around and saw some birds. With a slight movement, she snagged them with her tar-like vines and devoured them instantly.

She hovered low, barely above the ground. *Where is that blundering human, Loux? For a man that needed me, he has done nothing to find me.*

For an hour, she headed towards the city of Angarth. She stayed in the tree line and studied the town. Much of the Holy City landed in Angarth, and almost the entire southern half was destroyed. She watched the people as they tried to cleaned up the mess to start rebuilding.

There is that moron. He is surrounded by too many people. His house is probably the biggest one, how annoying. She punched a tree with her tiny stuffed hand.

She circled the outskirts until she found a large secluded estate. The entire property was guarded by a thick stone wall, wide enough for guards to walk along the top.

She floated off towards the main gate when the guard was distracted. She placed herself under the street lamp and laid down on the ground.

The guard noticed her laying there. "What do we have here? Sam, look at this."

He walked over to the doll and picked it up. "How did you get here? Did you notice this doll before?" He looked at the other guard.

"I don't know. Just throw it out. Probably festered with maggots," he said as he turned his face and waved his hand.

"Nah, this is a pretty doll. I bet some kid wandered too close, got scared, and ran off. My daughter has a doll like this. I will just put it in the office. Some little girl might come back to claim it," he said and smiled.

"You're too nice to be a guard, you fool. Just toss it out, and if the little girl returns, just kick her to teach her a lesson," the other guard said bitterly.

"That's why you can never get a girl to marry you. You hate kids. Women love it when their man plants his seed in her. That's what my wife told me when we met." He laughed as he walked into a small office on the other side of the gate.

The doll stood up when the guard walked off and patted the dust off herself as she grunted. *That guard is filthy but the other one wanted to throw me away like trash. I shall consume him the first chance I get.*

She slowly waddled off, avoiding the guards. There was maid was shaking out a rug. She left the window open. As soon as she disappeared from site, the doll flew in.

Mortals and their fancy giant homes. How do they manage to find their way around? "His blasted room should be obvious to find!" she shouted in a low voice.

"Hey, did you hear something?" A maid walked in, and another one followed behind.

"I think you're going crazy. I heard nothing," the other maid said with a deep breath.

"Oh, look here. Wow, this is one of the cutest dolls I have ever seen." The first maid sounded as giddy as a child.

"What is a doll doing here?" The second maid sat down in a chair.

"I bet it's from that cute guard at the gate. He's been trying to court me. I told him I like dolls." She picked up the doll and hugged it.

"You mean the one that hates kids? You would be perfect for him since you also despise them," the other maid said, trying to hold back her laughter.

"It is because I would have to share my dolls if I had a girl. I think I have seen this doll before." She looked at it closely.

"I think this is the doll that the little girl gave the prince, the one that died. He showed it to me while I was cleaning his room when he was staying at the inn." She smiled and danced around with the doll.

"I'm telling you, if you keep up that secret little affair with the prince, it will end badly for you when he becomes the king. A scandal like that is something he cannot afford," she scoffed at her.

"I shall just place this in his room. He said it was important. Maybe he will reward me again tonight. I think what you don't understand is that a man like him would be glad to keep me in his bed while having another be his queen in public. Lords do it all the time." She smiled and walked off into the hall.

Minutes went by but seemed like hours before the maid reached the prince's room. She silently opened the door and placed the doll on a bookshelf.

"My, are you a little cutie," the maid said as she dusted off an old pillow. "I will fix you up a nice spot here by the window."

She cleared off a spot and gently placed the doll down. She went off and came back with some flowers and doll clothing.

"The lord will be happy to know that I kept you all nice and safe." She looked at her hand and noticed a little black dot on her finger. "I think you got some dirt on ya. I guess I shall clean you up next time I see you." She blew a kiss at the doll as she closed the door.

"Foolish mortals are such a waste of time. Only good to feed from. Yet, I cannot help but think I am just the same, to be consumed by father." The doll looked out the window and watched the maid talk to one of the guards.

When these humans are joyful, they seem to have more life force in them to consume. I shall not consume her yet. I can use her body for more research as I explore. She closed her eyes and watched from the essence she had left on the maid.

Loux burst into the room, shouting. "This is going to cost more than I expected! Telling me to tax more. This is the problem with rich people. They do not understand that numbers are real power. If only I could just remove the rich non-humans and steal their wealth."

Suddenly, there was a giggle in the room. "Prince, did you forget about me and our deal?" The doll said.

The prince leaped back and screamed. "How...how did you get in here?"

"You said you will find my body. Yet here you are, rebuilding a mostly destroyed city." She folded her tiny arms. "To make matter worse, you left me thinking I was—what? Killed off by my own spell? By our contract, I am allowed to devour you and everything you hold dear." She grinned and slowly walked towards him.

He fell to his knees and begged. "Look, it was not like that. I knew you would find me. But I had no choice. The most important parts of my plans have a time limit. It is expected of me to rebuild a capitol. And because I already have an estate here undamaged, it would make more sense to move it here. If I take too long, people might think I have other plans and may sniff around. Finding your body will only work if I keep the nobles busy."

"I overheard you mention something about defying the other nobles to keep the poor happy? If I find value in what you say, I shall keep our deal." She hovered onto his shoulders.

"Well, you see, the poor outnumber the rich. Even if I send my entire army to deal with them, they would be outnumbered and eventually destroyed. The proper balance is to know when to make the masses follow you." Sweat poured from his brow as he talked.

"So you are saying that in order to get more work done, you make the workers happier, and this gives them more energy?" She rubbed her chin.

"Yes, if they are happy, they are willing to die for your cause. Humans in general tend to be more energetic when happy." He stood up and looked out the window.

"I have noticed something similar when I devoured mortals." She rubbed his ear and said softly, "I will keep you alive. I feel I can learn something from you."

She hopped off and watched the prince as he left. She placed her hand slowly into the pouches stitched into her dress and pulled out a communication stone.

I cannot trust my minions without me guiding them every step of the way. I have to change my plans. I do not want Father to devour me. She placed her hands over her eyes.

"I have a part of my essence still alive all the way over there? How is that so? Who has been keeping it alive?" She watched as a man with no lips and eyelids fed a rabbit to the essence.

She used her essence to take control of the tiny animal. "Dumas, I can see that my kiss has left an impression on you that is still there."

He let out an empty laugh. "I see you are finally awake." He folded his arms and said in a low tone, "I kept this part of you alive, knowing you may return. Shall we chat for a bit? In exchange, I will give you the item you need to free your body."

CHAPTER 14

THE CITY OF GRAVES

A week went by as tents surrounded the once Holy Capitol. Any person who had any knowledge of working with stones recycled what they could to make gravestones. Large wagons full of dirt came nonstop day and night from the elf kingdom. The people gathered the dirt in the center and built a hill.

Lilith helped tend to the wounded while Rebecca stayed in their tent as she recovered. Many gladly gave them supplies to pay for the aid and even managed to help make Lilith a new outfit. It was similar to the outfit she had when she first met Rebecca, except that it was a bright blue.

"Rebecca, you need to get fresh air every day. The white dragon taught me how to care for you. She even gave me a copy of her medical book." Lilith popped her head in and gasped. "What happened to you?"

"I matured, shit! I knew my luck was bad, but this is the worst." Rebecca's voice sounded more mature and was muffled by her shirt which got stuck as she tried to put it on.

"You grew more than I expected. You told me many times but I was not prepared for this." She walked over and helped Rebecca get her shirt off.

"Looks like I will have to get you some new clothes. You can borrow some of my extra ones. Only your belly should be exposed. Your body is curvier than mine, so maybe a dress?" Lilith gently placed some clothes next to her.

"This sucks, I'm still not fully healed and I'm horny as hell. I was hoping we could do a lot of fun activities." Rebecca pouted and folded her arms.

"We will have many more times of doing that. You need to first heal completely. The white dragon told me any action during this time can—" Rebecca kissed her.

"You talk too much. I know, and it's fine. None of these skirts fit me. My hips are bigger. Remember that I lay eggs so I have bigger hips than most." She pointed at them and giggled.

Lilith wrapped a small blanket around Rebecca's waist and took her hand. "There is a tailor nearby. We will get you something that will fit properly."

As they exited the tent, people stopped and stared at them. Some of the men had drool dripping from the corner of their lips. One whistled at Rebecca and winked. Lilith held her hand tightly and pulled her closer.

"Hey, it's fine. This is normal when we mature. You are actually hurting my hand," Rebecca said cheerfully.

"I will kill anyone that touches you," Lilith whispered.

"Oh my, a dragonblood. I have never made clothing for a lord before." The tailor tried to tidy herself up as they came into her tent.

"Pardon my mess, noble lady. What can I do ya for?" She started to pick up some linen from the chair.

"As you can see, I am in my mature cycle. I am in need of clothing that will fit for a month at most." Rebecca tried to speak in a snobbish accent but failed to do so.

"Sorry, I'm not much of a lord. Just a runt. My mate Lilith said you are really good, so please make my clothes. I have some coins." She put her hands together and stared at the lady with her starry-eyed face.

"Ah, so you are the one the lady been talkin' about." She waved her hand. "No need, if it weren't for her, my son woulda' lost his arm. I make ya something fancy."

Lilith gave Rebecca a deep kiss and said softly, "I will go to work now. Wait here until I come back. It would be around two hours."

"She must be jealous. Women only kisses like that when they is worried their lover might do something with others." The tailor smiled and giggled.

"How can you be sure? It's rare for her to express any emotion in her voice," Rebecca asked.

"Her eyes tells ya how she feelin'. I can tell she has a lot of conflict inside of her. Oh, to be young and in love." The tailor measured her and started to cut fabric.

After a few short hours, Lilith came back holding a plate. "I was paid in food today. How is your outfit?"

It was an ashy gray outfit. The top was a little baggy and the bottoms were a bit loose. "I made it how she asked, not to attract any eyes. She also wanted it a color that would not matter if it got dirty." The tailor was cleaning up.

"I want to help. I know I cannot do anything big but maybe u can help with other things. It's not right that you're doing all the work." Rebecca tried to sit but was still not used to her taller size.

Lilith took a deep breath. "I guess you can help with the sorting. I have an extra dress for you to wear tomorrow. There is going to be a funeral. The half-dwarf and his half-elf wife are getting buried tomorrow on the mound. He died a rather painful death." She suddenly started to cry. "I could not heal him. I tried every type of healing I know but it had no effect. I have the powers of a god and yet...I was unable to stop his suffering. I do not understand what is going on but I think something very bad is going to happen soon."

They headed home and snuggled in the bed as they fell asleep.

Rebecca tossed and turned all night. "Four hells, out of all the days to be injured. I was looking forward to helping her explore. I guess it would be a bad time anyways." She watched Lilith sleep. "She is getting better at expressing her emotions. I guess this place would get to anyone."

"So much death…Mother, Father, all my siblings." Rebecca cried herself to sleep.

* * *

"You sure you want us to wear this?" Rebecca asked as Lilith smiled while holding up a black silk dress with a bright red cross in the middle.

"They are matching, and I like the feel of the silk." She rubbed it across her face.

"I think these belong to a cult. And I think I know what cult. Where did you find these?" Rebecca sounded slightly off.

"One of the people who were digging up useable stones fell into a deep basement. There were hundreds of these there. Do you not like them?" She held one up to Rebecca to measure.

"Was there a dark red table in the middle?"

"Yes, why?"

"They belong to a cult that worshiped the dark elf goddess, Melania. They used that table to sacrifice people." Rebecca pushed the dress out of the way.

"Why would humans worship Mother? She hates humans. I do not understand. It is not the dresses' fault that bad people used them for that. Maybe if we get the tailor to cover up the red cross in the center, we can use them?" She kept looking at the two dresses.

Rebecca looked at Lilith. *Her eyes show her emotions.* Lilith looked at her puzzled. "Alright, fine. It will also need some other alterations. We do not want to offend the elves."

In the center of the vast emptiness was a freshly made mound of dirt and marble steps that led all the way to the top. There were three fire pits with bright white flames. An old elf was singing a tune in the elven language. Lilith became a little sad as she listened to the song.

"Do you understand what she is saying?" Rebecca asked, trying to follow the words.

"It is about their goddess, Altaytay. Her real name is actually Alfife." She jumped as someone placed a hand on her shoulder.

"It is rare anyone knows her real name. The name Altaytay came about because our language cannot pronounce her name properly." It was a dignified male voice.

Rebecca looked at him and said a little rudely, "Sir, who are you to touch my mate?"

Lilith looked at the man. He had on a fine silk robe lined with gold. "This man is the high king." She smiled a little "It is because when she made your language, she wanted to see how her name would sound if some key letters were removed."

Rebecca just stood there. She tried to speak but ended up sounding like a gibbering idiot. "Sor…sorry. I did not know."

"If she truly is your mate, then I will have to speak up to you for I am beneath you, Lady Dragonblood. Lilith, how is your mother?" He smiled and patted her shoulders.

"She is fine. I am surprised you remember me." She turned and bowed her head.

"How could one forget someone who looks like you?" He nodded at them both and walked off to greet more guests.

"You know the high king? How do you know the high king?" Rebecca gripped Lilith's hand tightly.

"My mother showed me where I needed to go to gather information. His kingdom is one of the twenty places I was assigned to spy on. I told you. She is a goddess." She watched the elf king as he walked around.

"I think it's weird he is not crying. This is his daughter that died." Rebecca said in a soft tone.

"He also be paying respects to her husband. This be a dwarf custom. Ya remember the good things about them," Onyx wheeled himself next to them.

"It is also the drug. I can smell it on his breath. He is very sad inside. He is doing all he can to make sure he keeps his composure here. Mother told me this was his favorite child out of all his children. Even his other wives adored her." Lilith closed her eyes and a lone tear rolled down her cheeks.

A female elf with long pink hair that touched the ground cleared her throat. "Guests, sorry. Human not good, but I speak, so understand."

She looked deeply into the white flames. "My sister kind, loving, brave. My *heat zati, ousoo* divided. Spend last days with dwarf. When meet him before death, knew why sister *mwagee*. He *zati*, made me cry. *El oula* as my brother." She bowed low as tears fell from her eyes.

"She mixed in some elf words. What is *zati*?" Rebecca watched as they performed a dance.

"It means broken. *El oula* means she accepts. That she views him as family. The o is silent. The dwarfs and elves have a long history of hatred. This union started something and only the future can tell the outcome." Lilith stared into the flame.

Another elf walked up. He had silver hair. "*Geetul aulatay geetimwa. Iayati siegee.*" All the elves held up a hand and bowed their heads.

"He said he will always love her, and she died with honor. I think he is a younger brother from a distant elf clan. The female elves outnumber the men by a lot, so they tend to have more than one wife. The king has to have one bride from each clan for each clan to have ties to the royal bloodline." Lilith watched intensely as a group of young elves did a dance.

Chanting started to overtake the sound of the music. From the other side, a group of human enchanters casted a levitation spell on a large marble object. Every time one would be drained and pass out from the spell, another would quickly jump in.

The object was a large marble sarcophagus with a carving of Rose and Ugthar. The king fell over crying, and the elves rushed over to help him up.

"Aye, I guess the drug wore off. So much of that wee black stuff made their bodies too dangerous to burn, so they be in there. He be at peace now with his love." Onyx cried as he wheeled his chair into the crowd.

People slowly dispersed back towards the camp. Hundreds of gravestones were starting to be placed. Some only had a finger with a ring on it to be placed in a small box and buried; others only bits of clothing or random tidbits.

There was a man standing in front of their tents. "I have a letter for a Lilith. I was told she would be in this tent."

Lilith held her hand out. He handed it to her, saying, "Well, I have many more letters to deliver," He then left.

Lilith opened it. "It is from Father. He needs my help. The group of people he helped have been attacked by soldiers."

"Who would attack a bunch of helpless people that just survived this horror?" Rebecca took the letter and slowly looked over it.

A man ran to the middle of their tent district and shouted, "All hail the new king, King Loux. He will send aid to help us as his first act." The people rejoiced after hearing the news.

"Your father was helping people who had relatives from other countries, right?" Rebecca slowly walked backwards towards their tent entrance.

"Yes, a lot of the surviving dwarfs had relatives back home." Lilith looked at her, a little puzzled. "Is there a problem?"

"I remember Loux had a problem with other races, mainly dwarfs. I have a bad feeling about what the second act is going to be. The man said they are sending in troops along with the aid. Half of the people here are part of the Holy Army so there is no real need to send more troops. I just hope the feeling I have is just me being silly." They both went inside and packed their bags.

CHAPTER 15

ACTS OF THE KING

"**M**y lord, there are reports that men dressed in armor and wearing your marks are attacking the dwarfs who are trying to get back to their kingdom after their home was destroyed." A plump man dressed in fine robes was looking over some papers. He adjusted his glasses before reading more. "People are also complaining about the large number of troops you sent to aid with the building of the massive grave site. They thought you would send more skilled workers to help carve the stone. The soldiers are being rather rude, and some have already been arrested for raping a few non-humans."

The king pounded his fists on the table. "What about the investigation of what really happened?"

The man cleared his throat as he said, "Well sir, it looks like it was caused by non-human magic, like you suspected. I still think we should deal with the bandits. The dwarf king is displeased about thi—"

"What if it was caused by the dwarfs? We know they have been displeased with us since my grandfather's days." Loux calmed down a little as he sat down.

"Sir, I think it is too early to point fingers at any—"

"You are a dragonblood. Your kind is above these silly things. Humans are at the bottom of the chain when it comes to the civilized races. The last war we had with the dwarfs was in my great grandfather's time. Some of those dwarves remember it because they were in the war."

"Also sir, before I forget, the elf king is on his way here to meet you. He has been staying at the campsites. His daughter was killed there." The old man sat down.

"How are the finances going?" The king pointed to a younger man dressed in similar robes.

"Well sir, our treasury is empty. All that is left are the payments to the troops for the month. Our allied kingdom to the east has one more payment to make. That will arrive by the end of the week. The only way to get more money is to raise the taxes or go to war. But we do not have the funds for a war." The younger man bowed and sat back down.

A guard opened the door. "Sir, the elf king has arrived."

The elf king shoved the guard off to the side and barged in shouting, "My good king sir, I welcome you as a fellow king. I have come to have a few words with you since that is part of the king's job."

Loux grunted a little and cleared his throat. He tried to sound kind. "Sir, it is with great privilege to welcome an important and highly regarded figure such as yourself. What is it you wish to speak of?"

The elf king waved his hand. "No need to stand up or bow to me. I did barge in on an important meeting. The soldiers you sent to the camps have been targeting non-human races—mostly the dwarves— with their thug-like manners. I do know that when you have a lot of troops in an area, they can get rowdy, but one told me that they were following orders."

"My high king, our investigations are leading towards dwarvish magic. Since we do not know for sure which race destroyed the city, we shall keep all under investigation." King Loux drank from his cup.

The elf held up a flyer. "I saw this on a wall as I came into the city. This is a very anti-elf statement. It also makes it very clear that you are accusing my people of the attack."

"Investigations," the elf said under his breath, but made sure he was heard. He looked across the room and raised his voice. "My daughter died in this attack. I too have done investigations. Our reports say it was not a dwarf but a monster of a divine nature." The high king's fury could be felt as he stared at the human king.

Loux was unable to hide his annoyance as he said, "Our scouts also think an elf used it to frame the dwarfs. We know how much your kind hates them. This would not be the first time that the elves have framed the dwarfs. I have known many elf lords to sacrifice their own blood to further their gains." He sat there with a smug smile.

"If you are unable to tell a dark elf and us apart, then you have much to learn oh great king. Your brother would have—"

"My brother was killed because he was foolish enough to not watch his back when he allied with races who have looked down on humans. A deer may make an alliance with a wolf, but when the wolf becomes hungry, being allies vanishes from his mind." Loux leaned back in his chair.

"This was your plan from the start, to divide us. After the grave site has been completed, I shall take my leave." The elf king turned and bowed to the dragonbloods.

"My soldiers tell me it shall be done in five days' time. I promise you safety until that time. I shall tell my officers to treat everyone as if they are innocent." Loux spit on the ground and smiled, lightly waving at the elf king as he left.

"Excuse me, I need to take leave. I have duties other than just sitting here." The king stood up and walked out.

He went straight into his room. The doll was sitting in a little chair of her size in front of the fire. "I can tell something is bothering you. What is it you need me to do, king?" The doll turned her head and looked at him.

"I need you to do me a favor. Can you hit people with your vines and not consume them?" His voice was dry as he asked.

She smiled and said, "I do love what you are about to ask me next. It brings me great joy, king. I can read it in your face. Yes, I am able to do so. However, I wonder how this will help me."

"With a wound that looks like it could kill me, I could make a decree that would give us the slave labor to dig. It has to look like an arro—"

In an instant, the doll punctured his chest and smiled. "My sweet king, I shall make it look like what I think it needs to look like. This will indeed make it seem that your life is on the line, because it is. Do not worry, however. Even if your doctor was a moron, you would recover from this."

* * *

"Sir, sir, how are you feeling?" A male voice barely made it past the ringing in his ear. A light flickered from the darkness as he slowly opened his eyes.

A man in a doctor's uniform stood above him. "Do you remember your name?"

Loux pushed him away. "I am your king. Get out of my face. My head feels like a rock hit it."

The doctor cleared his throat. "Well, that is to be expected. You have been out for over a week. That wound almost killed you. Do you have any clue as to who attacked you?"

"Yes, it was a survivor living at one of the camps. Fetch my captain right away." He reached around and grabbed a cup of water. "I have a new order that I must enact."

A day later, a messenger surrounded by soldiers arrived into one of the campsites, "People, listen please. By order of the king, any survivors from the devastation must be placed under arrest and questioned about the attack on his royal highness. If there are any survivors that have fled this area, let us know. And if any of you seeks shelter from someone outside of this area, and if that person does not confess that they provided you shelter—you both shall be arrested. You are all fugitives until determined otherwise." The man handed out some papers to the soldiers. "Nail these in the center of every town, village, or camp's message board that you know of or come across."

He took a deep breath and eyed the remaining troops. "Well, what are you waiting for? Arrest these people."

CHAPTER 16

HE IS MY SON

"Are you doing well at your new school, boy?" Taranis sat in his study and spoke without even glancing at Albert.

"I don't understand why I have to attend a school like that. I am of low birth and it shows in how I speak and act." Albert rubbed his nose on his sleeve.

"I guess I should have taught you myself but it is a bit late for that. I told the teacher that your mother took you from me when you were born, and then she fell into some hard times and died in the streets. I'm sure it's fine as long as you show improvements. You have to pass as my son or I may have to kill you. If my master finds you, I'm not sure I can keep my promise to keep you alive." Taranis looked at him and smiled.

A loud thud echoed as the door opened. "Taranis, Master has a task for you."

"Aeron, I see you are still her dog. I can only assume she has started to stir again." He stood up in a strong stance.

"I see you have a snack. I didn't know you ate humans." Aeron smiled at Albert as he curled up in fear.

"He is my son," Taranis said quickly.

"He smells of fish, not of you." Aeron lowered his head and sniffed harder.

"My step-son. I was married for a while out of boredom. I offered her to my lord, and I have taken a liking to the lad." He pulled Albert behind him.

"You have lived as a lord in the mortal realm. It somehow suits you. I bring you a communication stone from Master. She has started to make her move. I suggest you off the boy now. It would be kinder." Aeron smiled and handed him the stone. "I have to go. I am needed to cause a problem." He slowly walked off.

"See that, boy—his lack of manners. He did not close the door." Taranis took a deep breath.

"Lord, are you alright?" Albert fetched him a glass of water.

"From now on, you need to call me Father. It is the only way I can keep you alive. I have never actually hated mortals. It is why I can blend in with them. But my lord and Master both wish to destroy this realm. They started two major wars. I have learned that their plans will never come to be, but I am duty-bound to follow their orders." He took a sip and held up the stone.

"Master, it is I, Taranis." His voice cracked near the end.

As the voice replied, both Albert and Taranis trembled a little. "I am in need of your brilliant mind. Something only a general could do."

"How may I serve you, Master?"

"I need you to take control of the dig site. Humans seem to have morals. After a while of working others to death, they grow emotions and try to put an end to it. The king is a useless man in these matters." There was a small pause. "How is your mission to revive your lord going?"

He cleared his throat and said, "Your betrothed is almost free. He only needs your sword to free him. Or your sisters."

"If you find my body, I shall give you my sword to free him." The stone became dark and the voice stopped.

"Boy, remember that voice. It is the voice of true evil. It looks like you will get your wish and I will have to school you myself. Just be warned, you will see things that will disturb you to your core. Learn from them. May that be a reminder of how the world really is." Taranis patted the boy's head.

Albert cleared his throat and tried to respond calmly, "Yes si—, yes, Father."

* * *

"So boy, we have been here for over two weeks. Tell me what you think." They stood on a tower looking over a campsite full of dwarves and elves.

"The beasts are basically useless for both digging and keeping the workers working. They eat the workers before they die, which causes these delays." Albert pointed to some fog that was about to come in from the north. "Also, I think we are about to get attacked." Albert started to sound more like a noble.

"That is right. It seems some dwarf refugees are trying to save their kin. This is the problem with Master's mine. Our only safeguard is that no one knows our true goal or the main army would invade to stop us." He scoffed as he watched the slaves pause while digging to cheer.

"You there! Dark elf. Ready the trap. I think it is time they learn to lose all hope." The dark elf bowed and ran into a building.

Loud thudding sounds rang under the ground and the earth fell from beneath the charging army into a large pit full of tar from where they were looking. Taranis tossed in a torch and the screams of the dwarves that fell in demoralized the ones waiting to be saved.

"Father, if you do not really agree with the mission, why bother doing all of this?" Albert watched as the fire burned. He stood unflinching despite their screams.

"I am bound by duty. I hope you learn from me and not fall under the same monster I did. However, no matter whom you serve and for what reason, always make a lasting impression on all those who get in the way of your mission." Taranis smiled as he walked back into his office.

"Why are you smiling, father?" Albert slowly followed him.

"In a week or two, we will start to get elves, and humans." He sat at his desk and looked at some paperwork.

His communication stone started to glow.

"Yes Master, what is it that you need?"

"How is the digging going? Have you found my body yet?"

"As we had planned, the king thinks that I am working for him. He only knows what I report to him, so that front is going well. As for the other part, it is not easy with what I have. We are spending more time setting up fortifications to fight off the constant attacks. Also, the nal and nox are eating the healthy workers. Remember that my lord created them. Therefore, only he can control them. I can just give them directions." He stood up and looked out his window.

"I will soon have a new man in charge. The puppet king is about to outlive his usefulness. He will leave me alone with his son who will be perfect for my vision. We will visit as soon as we are left alone." The stone went dark again.

"A human for her plan? I guess thousands of years of resting can really change someone. I do not like the way she mentioned this new man—she is promised to my lord." Taranis sat back down and stared at Albert.

"I know, Father. I will fetch my school books." He slowly walked towards the bookshelf.

"I shall teach you something more important than your mortal studies. I will teach you the history of my people. If the master is starting to add humans to her plans, then she may allow you to live. In case she may ask you questions, knowing the real history could save your life." He continued, "The first thing you must know is that we gods are not immortal. We only live longer than you do." He spoke slowly to make sure Albert understood everything.

"Then why are you called gods?" Albert looked at him, confused.

"Because we created everything you see." Taranis smiled as he looked at a painting of a starfish. "For example, I created that magical creature."

CHAPTER 17

CROSSING BORDERS

Rebecca tugged on Lilith's arm and sighed. "Well it seems we have lost them—again. You need to stop spacing out like that. What's on your mind? Must be something good to make you wander off so much."

"Sorry, but I never really looked around before. By traveling on foot, I get to see things I have never seen before. I also am thinking about Mother. I feel she may send Sister after me soon." They started to walk towards a worn-down trail.

"I told you, you can go and come back. You have been with me for two mating cycles now. and we didn't waste the last one. We are now officially mates. I will wait for you." Rebecca smiled at her gently. "Now let's hurry up and find your father with the group." Lilith blushed as Rebecca pulled her along.

"If I go, Mother will not allow me to come back. I sent her a letter. It should have arrived by now. I told her about you, and that we are a family now." Lilith picked up a white berry with yellow spots. "I never seen this before. It must only grow around here."

"This means we are close to the dwarf kingdom. Don't eat it—it's poisonous. I don't want a repeat from last month." Rebecca swatted the berry out of her hand.

"It looked like a blueberry. They both had the same color. I just thought the sweet smell was because it was extra good." Lilith looked around.

"Looks like we are about an hour behind them." Rebecca's face became more thoughtful. "Well, now that we are alone, we should talk about something." Her arms started to shake a little.

"Is it about what the white dragon said? That when only one member is left in the family, the instinct to lay eggs takes control? I really do not mind. We said we wanted a family, and since I am a female, it is the only way. You finding the suitable man to mate with will be perfect." Lilith smiled at her.

"You're getting better with the smiling. I'm not so sure about this. I'll feel like I am cheating on you, but it's getting harder to ignore. Are you sure it's what we want?" She held her hand more tightly.

"Look, just find some guy who wants no attachments. Sleep with him and leave. We will then have a real family." Lilith looked at her with a grin.

"Um, everything you just said does not seem like you. And that look on your face sort of makes me uneasy. Are you feeling well?" Rebecca slowed down her pace. "Did you eat the berry?"

"If we have a family, I am sure Mother would let me stay with you. We are both females, and so we cannot make each other pregnant. I am not even sure if I have the ability to have kids. But you have that instincts to save your clan. This is what I want—little versions of you to raise." Lilith wrapped her arm around Rebecca's.

* * *

"I see, you got lost again. Do I need to tie a rope around you?" A man chuckled behind the fog.

"Father, I am sorry. I got carried away with all the new things I was seeing. Rebecca stayed with me." Lilith's voice was full of emotion as she ran up and hugged him.

"If it were anyone else, I would have assumed them to be dead by now. The two of you are the most perfect pair," he said with a smile.

123

"We are going to have kids. Rebecca is going to get pregnant so we can have a family." Lilith had a childlike smile while Rebecca choked on her own spit as Verus laughed.

"Well, I hope I am alive long enough to be a grandfather." He patted her head and they walked off.

Rebecca slowly walked behind them as she watched. *I wish she talked to me like that all the time, instead of just at random moments. Why did she have to tell him that anyways?*

They approached the camp where the refugees were resting. Lilith walked to each one of them to ask if they needed anything.

Rebecca took a deep breath. "So, looks like we lost half of our numbers. Why would the king make an order like that anyways?"

Verus eyed the camp. "We are down to twenty. We have lost more than half. If what I hear is true, they are looking for something. Loux has always been a little shit. He hated other races. He barely put up with the elves. I think after we drop these people off, we should head to the elf territory." He looked at Rebecca. "Is something bothering you?"

"A few things."

"How is she now with showing her emotions to you?"

"Slightly better, but still not on the same level as it is with you." Rebecca sighed.

"I gave it some thought, and I think I understand why. Even though she calls me Father, she was not created by simple means. A normal child will have the traits of both parents by natural selection. She was created as a copy of both, with traits picked out by the creator. When she looks at me, part of her feels at home. It is more like we are part of the same being. With you, she does not have that connection. But don't worry, she is getting the hang of it." He placed his hand on his sword and looked around.

"So, how far do we gotta go before we cross the border?" Rebecca let out a whimper and sat on a log.

"It will take maybe two more days. We would have been there already if it wasn't for the bounty hunters after us." He stared off into the fog. "There is also what Lilith said yesterday."

"You mean about the odd human-looking monster with fangs? I heard vampires were killed off almost twenty years ago." She slowly stood up and looked around.

"Hosberg once told me he might have missed a few. The vampire king cried out to his father before he died. If we account for all the refugees that we know who died in battle or left the convoy, we still have fifteen unaccounted for. We are also not too far from the vampire king's domain." He pulled out his sword.

Rebecca slowly walked towards the group and signaled them to pull out their weapons. They formed a circle to cover each side. The fog became thicker and the air became heavier. There was a dead silence; not even the insects made a sound.

Screams echoed in the distance. Red mist painted the fog, and growls followed shortly.

Verus slowly backed up towards the group and whispered, "It must be the group of bounty hunters that followed us—I guess they made camp not that far from here."

A man in full chain mail ran out, begging, "Sir, help me, forgive me. I swear I will not huntcha' no more. Save me, sir I... I...Beasts, ripped us apart."

A man with purple skin jumped out and grabbed him. His fingers pierced the armor and ripped off the hunter's arm. The purple man smiled and drank the blood that rushed out of him.

Lilith began to shiver. "Rebecca, what is wrong with that demon? He seems a little different from the ones that would visit mother."

The purple man stood up and smiled at her. "I see, you're her daughter. You can see past my illusion. I have been blessed by my lord and master, Turiacus. You willingly walked into one of his domains. This means you belong to him."

"Rebecca, we must run away. Mother told me of Turiacus. She said he is very dangerous and powerful."

The purple man's body started to change. He resembled more beast than man. His teeth developed points, the thickness of his arms tripled, his eye had a blue glow, and his face resembled a frog.

"I am Lucard, fourth general to my lord. I will grant you a small favor since your mother used to be my queen. I shall spare you and the two you seem closest to. Everyone else will have an hour. I love a good hunt. I think an hour should make the game more fun." He grinned as blood trickled down his face. "If you make it off his territory, I will allow you to live."

The people started to panic as Verus tried to lead them north.

Lilith grabbed his arm and pointed. "Father, we have to go this way. Why do you seem so lost?"

He looked at her and took a deep breath. "Shit, the fog is magical. Everyone, follow her." He tried to wave down as many people as he could.

They kept running until they couldn't any longer. Rebecca tried to help the smaller ones keep up until everyone was out of site.

"Oh shit, Lilith!" She shouted as she held on to one of the shorter dwarfs.

"Aye, lass. If ya grab any tighter, me arm will break." She let go and counted them.

"There's five of us. We have to remain as a group. Where is she?" They stumbled around in the fog.

One of the five screamed as he disappeared into the fog. He vanished like lighting as the red mist painted the fog. Soon, another one let out a scream.

One pulled up a large stone and tossed it blindly into the fog. An arm reached out and pulled him in. Rebecca huddled the other two close to her and covered them with her body.

"He said he won't kill me. Just stay close and wait for Lilith." They began to cry as fear filled their hearts.

"I did say I will allow you to live, but didn't say anything about not harming you. You can still live with a missing arm or a leg." They heard a chuckle.

Lucard slowly walked into view. His teeth had bits of flesh stuck to them and fresh blood dripped off of his body. Before he could strike, someone in leather armor jumped out and shot him in the arm with a bolt.

Irritated, he shouted, "Samantha! I am honored to see my lord's betrothed in my new territory. Have you decided to return to his side?"

Her face looked like that of an aged old man: faded brown hair, slight elf-like point in the ears, but her voice was youthful. "Lucard, I do not recall ever agreeing to be his anything. I do however remember you forcing me to drink from that cup." She shot him in the shoulder with another bolt.

"You know that will not work on me." He winced as he pulled out the bolt.

"I know, I just enjoy annoying you." She shot him again and smiled.

He became frustrated as he pulled out the new bolt. "Who is it you are seeking?"

She dropped her crossbow and clenched her fist till the skin on her knuckles turned white. "Your brother Ducard! I am going to kill him first."

"Ah yes, he killed the man you were having relations with. Cheating on my master. I care not what you mortals do, but you are my master's wife." He grinned as he licked his lips. "Allow me to kill these mortals and I shall tell you about Ducard."

"You know I can't allow that. I will fight you with everything I have to keep them alive." She pulled out a flask.

"I don't want to risk hurting you. Master would not be happy. He speaks of you. He screams for you. I will allow these three to live and tell you Ducard's location if you drink from the cup again. I know you crave for it—I have been watching you. you have been trying to keep it hidden, but I will give it to you now." He turned around, exposing his back. When he turned back, he was holding a cup. It was full of a red liquid.

Lucard snickered as he spoke. "Should I grab a mirror for you while you drink?"

Her body quivered as she looked at the cup. She pointed towards the right and hurriedly said, "Dragonblood, if you head that way, you will find your group. You are not far from the border."

Rebecca's voice trembled as she said, "Tha... thank you, mi—

"Go! Now! Before he changes his mind." They ran off. Before the fog fully blocked the view, she looked back and saw the woman drink from the cup.

They ran in that direction for over twenty minutes. Even though their legs begged them to stop, they kept going. The fog became thinner and thinner the more they ran. Then, as if they had just walked through a door, it vanished completely.

Rebecca panted hard as she collapsed. Before she hit the ground, Lilith appeared and grabbed her, embracing her in a hug.

She cried as she said, "I am so sorry. Forgive me. I lost track of you when everyone got separated. I was worried I lost you." They kissed deeply and held on for what seemed like forever.

"It's alright, Lilith. I'm fine. We ran into some minor issues but a vampire hunter saved us." Rebecca gently combed her fingers through Lilith's hair.

"I will never leave you again. I love you. I really lov—" Rebecca stopped her from talking with a kiss.

Rebecca collapsed onto the ground, gasping for air. "I told you— you talk too much. I just need to rest a little." She looked around. "What is that smell?"

A dwarf smiled as he walked around in a trance. "That be the smell of the mines. I not been here for almost hundred years. Glad the smell still be the same."

Another dwarf walked up to Verus and held his hands. "We be grateful to ya. From here, we be fine. Me brother's village not too far from here. I can see it in ya face, something be bothering ya."

Verus looked at everyone who was left and took a deep breath. "Eleven, we lost half in the fog. I am deeply sorry that I could not do more."

"I know ya did ye best. The other soldiers left as soon as they heard they be wanted and hunted. Ya stuck around, that be saying much. Just me and me wife made it from my family. I'll tell the king of what transpired. I be sure ya be a hero, I may even have a song aboutcha'." The dwarf bowed and signaled the others to follow him.

"Father, what do we do now?" Lilith sat next to Rebecca and held her close.

"After we get some rest, we will head towards an outpost. The only one I know that would accept me is a few months away. It would be quicker if all of the vampires were truly gone. Also, winter will hit next month and we may get stuck. It snows in this region." He pulled out some stale bread that he had in a small sack.

"I have never seen it snow. Rebecca, if we get stuck in a town, it will be the perfect time for you to get pregnant." She smiled at her with sparkling eyes.

"Are you crazy? Even if I agreed to have a brood, doing so on a trip like this would be the dumbest thing I could do. I would be almost useless and a burden for months." She tried to sound angry but had a hard time with the look Lilith was giving her.

"Lilith, it is not as simple as just sleeping with a man. He has to have something about him—a scent, something that my instincts would want in a brood. To make sure it survives, and carries the—" Lilith stopped her with a deep kiss.

"You talk a lot. Your lips are much better on mine." Lilith started to hum the Ballad of the Unnamed Goddess.

Verus tried to hold in his laughter as he said, "It must be rough having a goddess as a lover. I would worry she might smite me for any disagreement."

"You should have seen her when we first met. She was trying to help me hook up with someone. I think it all worked out for the better. It's handy because I can say our relationship is divine and blessed: a gift from the heavens."

Lilith looked at her. "I will have to introduce you to Mother soon. After we have our own family, I will no longer be an experiment. I will be a person."

Rebecca looked at her with a confused gaze. "I don't understand what that is about, but I'm sure you'll tell me when you're ready." She slowly rested her head on Lilith's lap and nodded off.

CHAPTER 18

FOLLOWING THE HEART

"Rebecca, I need to make a stop at the next town." Lilith tried to catch up to her.

"Tell that to your father. He is the one leading us." Rebecca seemed annoyed. "It's alright, Lilith. You don't have to run everything by me —I told you that over a month ago. I have forgiven you."

Lilith grabbed onto her arm. "I know, but this is different. We will need to stay for a few days. I think Mother is going to communicate with me."

"Have you started to have visions again? I thought they were only for bad things." Rebecca tried to get her to walk faster.

"No, I do not know why but they stopped after the city blew up. I just know Mother would have responded to my letter by now. The only town whose name I remember is the one we are about to enter— Belvest." She tried to pick up her pace as she talked.

"I know every time I ask about your mother, you always say that it's hard to talk about. Can you at least tell me why dark elves worship her when she hates them?" Rebecca was slightly out of breath.

Lilith looked up into the sky and then looked around. "They are not watching, so I guess I can tell you more." She paused. "She created gnomes. The dark ones started to worship her mostly out of confusion about whom their god really was."

Rebecca noticed her looking at the sky. "Who is not looking?"

"The Watcher and the Seer. They make sure no one says or does anything forbidden in this realm. I heard they used to be lovers but were forced to separate. Mother told me they have a son." She smiled and walked a little faster to catch up to Verus.

Rebecca noticed a sign that was posted on a tree and shouted, "Hey! I think Lilith and I might have a problem in the next town."

Verus walked up and read it carefully. *"All non-humans are forbidden in the city by order of the king.* Well, it matches what we heard when we took the dwarves back to their lands."

He looked at Lilith, who was fidgeting with her hair. "I will go into town and collect some stuff. I will also see if you have any letters waiting. Let us hope they assume that Lilith is a human name."

As he walked off, Rebecca sat down on the trunk of a fallen tree. "What is it that you are hoping would be in that letter? Is it really that important that you hear from her?"

Lilith started to set up camp. "Well, it has been almost been a year, and she has not seen me. I do not want her to hurt you, and I am worried if I disobey her—"

"I will be fine. You are now fully grown—make your own choices. From what I understand of her, she will barely notice anyways." Rebecca stood up and started helping.

As night began to take hold, Verus showed up. "I have some basic things here and a letter for you." Lilith quickly grabbed it to read.

"So what does it say, love?" Rebecca snuggled next to her.

"She is mad about using such a pointless method of communication. I told her I wanted to experience new things by trying this out." She teared up as she read more.

Rebecca tried to look at the letter. "What language is this?"

Lilith threw the letter into the fire and cried. "She is very angry with me and told me to leave you. She demands I check on my uncle and report back to her at once. She said I must obey her and do as I am told. I do not know what to do."

Rebecca kissed her cheek and took a deep breath. "Is she going to smite me if you don't listen?"

"No, she said she will banish me if I stay with you. I love Mother. Why does it have to be one choice or the other? It hurts so much." She pointed to her chest.

"Well, my little lost duck, you have to make a choice. The only real advice I can give you as a father is to make your own choice. You have grown a lot since the time we have met. Maybe it is time you left the nest." Verus stood up and walked off into the woods.

"Lilith, look love. I will support your choice regardless of what you pick." Rebecca lightly kissed her cheek.

"We will have a family and Mother will forgive me. I love you, and I promised I would never leave you again." She looked up at the sky. "They are not watching so it should be fine." Suddenly, wings sprouted from Lilith's back. One was covered in red feathers and looked angelic while the other was covered in brown feathers and looked more like a bird's wing.

Rebecca gasped. "What are you doing? I thought it was unsafe to show them?"

"They are not as big as Mother's or Sister's. I only have a ten-foot span. Do you like them? I told you I would show them to you some-day." She stood there and smiled.

"The brown one looks like a bird's wing." Rebecca gently rubbed it.

"I wanted to show you because I need you to know that I am committed to us. I have picked you over Mother. Rebecca, I love you with all my heart." Their eyes locked, and the only sound was the crackling of the fire.

CHAPTER 19

CHANGE OF HEART

"I see that you have not reclaimed your scale yet. With this rate of decay, I would say you have maybe a year left. These methods that I have told you about will not last very long." Taranis slapped some lotion onto Aeron's back.

"I see you have failed to find Master's body. I think your failure is worse than mine." Aeron growled in pain as the oil was absorbed into his skin.

"This failure occurred because she relied on humans to make the plans. I think we have been spotted by some elf scouts. It is only a matter of time before they send a proper army. Can we just kill the puppet king and prince?" Taranis scoffed as he looked out the window, watching over the site.

"She will not like it if we killed the prince. I fear Master has been on this realm far for too long. She has taken an interest in the young man. I think she plans to mate with him when she gets her body." Aeron stood up and checked his body for signs of rot.

Taranis snapped back and his eyes flared. "She is to wed my lord! It is the agreement they made when he took that vile filth into his body!"

"From what I recall, she said nothing of the matter. He did all the talking. Regardless, I can see what she is thinking. I shall carry out with her orders." Aeron smiled as he walked towards the door.

He stopped before flying off. "I thought I would give you the news before I left—he is active." Aeron said as he twitched a little.

"How is his state of mind? Do we know what his goal is?" Taranis tried to sound unaffected but his tone gave away his worry.

"It was like the last time we saw him. His mind is as chaotic as ever. Vampire sightings have started to catch my ear, which means he is no longer hiding." Aeron took a deep breath and flew off.

"That is the only being that can ruin everything." Taranis went into his office and sat at his desk. He banged his fist with one hand while the other shuffled some papers.

"Father, that man was back. Every time he is here, you get angry about something." Albert said as he walked in slowly.

"Everything is not as it seems. Boy, what do you know about vampires?" He reached towards his desk and grabbed a notebook.

"Nothing much. They drink blood and people turn into them. They were all wiped out."

"No, they were not. The vampire king had a father, and he was a god. He has defeated us twice in the past. If he is active, then I fear we must act quickly, my boy." He tossed the book to Albert.

"Inside that is everything you need to know. I no longer wish to pursue this folly." He placed his hand under his chin. "In all the years I have spent in this realm, I have learned that things balance out. She will fail. I will fail. I fear he will intervene in our plan as he always has."

"Is he really that powerful?" Albert softly said as he looked over the notes.

"Only a few gods in history had power like him, but he became cursed, which ate away at his mind. That alone makes him unpredictable. There are moments when he is his glorious self, and then at times, he is as dark as our master." Taranis looked towards the window. "I must try to convince my lord to not follow her anymore. I feel Turiacus will kill us this time."

"But Father, what if he won't listen?" Albert slowly flipped through the pages.

Taranis stood up and tried to look dignified. "We were friends while growing up. I am sure he will listen to me this time. He is going to owe me a favor after I free him. But if he refuses to listen," a long deep breath exited his lungs as he thought his next words, "then I must kill my lord," he finished in a dismissing tone.

<h1 style="text-align:center">CHAPTER 20
THE ELF QUEEN</h1>

"We made it to the forest. We must be on our guard now. The townspeople said this outpost has been on edge and killing everyone who enters." Verus cleared his throat. "Also, a warning. Once you enter, your body will glow for a little bit."

As they took a step into the forest, Verus's body starting having a white glow around it. Rebecca had a pink glow and Lilith had a red glow with gold specs.

"It's like I'm on fire, but I feel more refreshed." Rebecca moved her hands around and watched the aura dance.

"When you use magic, it drains your life force. This forest can restore some of it. Humans are immune to these effects." He pushed some bushes out of the way and took lead.

"Then why are you glowing, Father?" Lilith said as she danced around.

"I am an anomaly. Every few thousand births, there is an anomaly. Your mother said it is how nature balances itself. It is proof the world is still trying to perfect its own creation. It enhances one of our abilities and—"

"Your combat skills. You have an enhanced perception of your opponent's reactions. So that is why we have never seen you lose a fight." Lilith jumped up and hugged him.

"Something like that. It burns up some of my life force. You seem to be a little excited." Verus tried to gently push her away.

"I feel more awake and full of energy in here. I never knew I could feel so alive." Lilith jumped towards Rebecca and kissed her. "I forgot how this felt. It has been a while."

"I like this energy you seem to have, but I think restraint will be best." Rebecca looked around. "We are being watched."

Verus raised his hands and shouted, *"Tiol sieual samoa. Yultay siegee tiol."*

A female voice shouted back, "Verus, you are still lousy at speaking elvish." Someone in a green robe descended from a tree and stood in front of him.

He bowed and kissed her hand. "You are still the more lovelier of the queens."

She removed her hood, exposing her long pink hair and emerald green eyes. "You have always been such a sweet talker. It has been good to see you. I am sorry I didn't visit you after your wife died."

Rebecca looked around at the trees and Lilith jumped in front of her with a grin. "Fifteen, there are fifteen others hiding in the trees. Half of them have their bows ready." She held up her hands. "I can kill them in an instant if they bother you, my love. Just a single spell."

"No, it's fine. Why are you so excited? Even your voice is off." Rebecca tried to push her away.

Verus chuckled. "She normally sleeps to regain her energy but this forest is restoring it. Her body is overwhelmed with emotions and power."

"I thought your daughter was in charge of this forest. I was told she liked to kill on sight." Verus slowly walked with the queen.

"Yes, I have sent her off on a task to find one of our kin. I have made some changes. We wish to bring back peace. Who is that funny-looking girl? She is not *hummao*"

"In short, my daughter." They continued to walk until they reached a small fort made out of ironwood. Inside it was a small but long court-yard with some stairs at the end that led up to a tiny throne.

"Father, if you know her, why do you not call her by her name if you know her?" Lilith whispered into his ear.

"It is forbidden for anyone who is not an elf to say their real name. Most elves adopt a human name for when they interact with other races. She adopted Queen as her name, which is also her title." Verus looked around and saw a portrait of Rose.

Queen clapped her hands, "*Olaitay! Ousoo geetul osuoo.*"

Verus bowed. "I thank you." He paused for a moment. "I want to ask something of you in private." They continued to talk as they walked off.

"Lilith, are you alright? You are acting like a kid who ate a lot of candy." Rebecca tried to hold her hand to calm her down.

"I feel so alive. This energy—every time I visit the elf forests, I get filled with such emotions. Now that I am here with you, it is non-stop joy. Let's have sex. I want to mate with you right now!" Rebecca looked around in a panic, trying not to choke on her own saliva.

"Keep it down. We can talk about that when we're alone." Rebecca tried to hide her embarrassment with a smile.

"Well, as long as we can do it tonight. I feel like we can go longer. I know I normally get tired and fall asleep when you want to keep goin—"

"That's only during mating season, you moron. My drive is much smaller during the off seasons. I told you this before. Are you sure you're alright?" Rebecca put her hand over Lilith's forehead. "I think you might have a fever."

"Girls, over here!" Verus shouted as he waved at them.

"Queen has just told me that Aluxes was here a few days ago." Rebecca smiled as she hugged him.

"I'm so happy to know that she survived. I need to write her a letter." Rebecca tried to walk off when he cleared his throat.

"I also wanted to let you guys know that today is a holiday in the elf kingdom—a day just for couples. So, you two will be getting married today. I arranged it with Queen." He smiled as Lilith jumped in joy.

"Sister told me of this, and I have seen it many times during my missions. I get to be a wife. Thank you, Father. I promise I will make today the best day." She ran off while singing.

Rebecca looked at him. "But why do you want us to be married?"

"The clay doll can only keep me alive for so long. I was told that if I am careful, I can live for maybe five years. I want to see the two of you have a family before it's over." He smiled and held out his arms. "You are now my daughter. Promise me you will take good care of her."

She hugged him with tears in her eyes. "Thank you. And I promise you, I will take care of her."

CHAPTER 21
BATTLE OF THE GRAVES

"Rebecca, get up!" Lilith pushed her out of the bed. A loud ringing echoed as the sun rays started assaulted her eyes.

"Why is there a bell ringing?" Rebecca grabbed a pillow and covered her ears.

"He has been spotted—that dragon guy. He is heading towards your friend. We are going to try to meet them at the massive gravesite." Lilith grabbed their clothing and she quickly got dressed.

"You mean that guy that almost killed me? Maybe I should sit this one out. I will only be in the way." Rebecca curled up on the floor.

"I understand you are scared but I will protect you. I am your wife and you are mine. You can help with the support." Lilith took a deep breath. "Besides, didn't you wish to see her and hand her that letter?"

"That monotonous voice of yours can get on my nerves sometimes. Alright, I'll go." She stood up and slowly got dressed.

Outside, the elves stood in formation while Queen stood in the front counting the numbers.

"There are a lot more than I remember." Rebecca looked at them as she was handed gear by the quartermaster.

"Well, they arrived last night. Father told me they had been tracking him for a while now. He is waiting for us at the gate." Lilith helped her put on the padded armor.

"What kind of armor is this?" She moved around, trying to adjust it.

"I told them you wanted support. This armor will keep you protected from random things flying at you. It will keep you safe." Lilith kissed her and dragged her towards the gate.

"Girls, I hope you enjoyed your wedding. I am opposed to you going with us, but I cannot stop you from wanting to help, Lilith." Verus tugged on a leash and a six-legged horse walked out. "I hope you know how to ride a landstrider. They're not very good for battle because they run off when scared, but they are very fast at moving. The two of you will share one."

He pulled Rebecca off to the side. "Promise me—if it gets danger-ous, you'll run away with her. Reports say that he is getting desperate. When someone that powerful is desperate, they can lash out in unpre-dictable ways."

"Yes Father. I promise I will take Lilith away. But I think you will have to knock her out first." They both chuckled.

"*Lu-yatay zaho mwayeo, yasoo aisa. Ousoo ol siegee ol iayati zi mozsa!*" Everyone cheered as Queen ended her rally speech.

She walked over to the girls. "Honored friends, we are now family. After today, you will be our kin like Verus." She helped them mount and kissed their feet. "We do this for luck in my tribe. May it bring you blessings."

Lilith mumbled something and then spouted out a question. "That string instrument that played during the wedding, what was that?"

"That was a harp. The smaller one was a lyre."

"After the battle, can you teach me how to play them, Queen? I want to play them for our children after we find someone to get Rebecca pregnant." Queen laughed as Rebecca blushed.

"Yes, young one, I shall teach you after the battle. You are such a carefree soul. It has been refreshing having you around. You remind me of when my daughter was so young. I hope for a long, happy relationship for you two." She patted the strider on the back and it began to gallop.

"Lilith, I always wanted to ask you more about your mother but you always changed the subject. Why do dark elves worship her when you claim she hates them?"

"I was only able to talk about her when I was not being watched. And for the past few days, they have been ignoring me. It is related to my ability to heal humans and gnomes. She created gnomes— the dark ones—as she calls them. Their god joined the Fallen. After she killed her, they assumed she was their goddess." Halfway through finishing talking, they exited the forest and Lilith's voice became more emotionless.

"The Watcher and the Seer—can you actually see them when you look into the sky?" Rebecca tried to look up but was scared of falling off the beast.

"No, I can feel their gaze. At times, I can hear them in my head when I look at them. They seem sad. I think they want to be together. As for their son—I think they want him to have a life." She squeezed Rebecca tightly.

"It's hard controlling this thing. Following the group is even harder. Is this how fast you can fly?" Rebecca gripped the reins tighter.

"No, I fly much faster. But it wears me out. Rebecca, do you regret meeting me?" Lilith asked out of the blue as she rubbed her face on Rebecca's back.

"Sorry, I didn't hear you. What did you ask?" She turned her head.

"I asked if you thought I looked cute in that dress I wore during the wedding. I have never worn such a fancy dress before, weaved out of gold." She kissed the back of Rebecca's neck.

Verus rode up next to them after a few hours. He spoke louder and slower to make it easier to hear him over the beast's gallop. "We are almost there. We will dismount and walk the rest of the way."

"We did a week's worth of travel in half a day. My father told me elves are always able to travel faster. I can see why now." With some difficulty, Rebecca stopped the strider.

There was a small camp up ahead where they all met up. The

scouts had everything already set up. As they tried to deliver some information, a large explosion echoed.

"I remember that sound when the city was attacked. Lilith, I'm not going over there! I cannot do it. He will kill me." Rebecca stood there as her face became pale.

"Love, it is alright for you to stay here. You will be fine. I will come back for you when it is safe." Lilith hugged her and started to walk off towards the battle.

"Young one, being scared is nothing to be ashamed of, but I will give you some advice—the only way to overcome fear is to face it. I know how strong dragonbloods are and we could use those muscles of yours." The queen stood next to her. "I will tell you a little secret. Promise me you will share it with no one. Eirfel—that is my name."

"That doesn't sound like an elven name." Rebecca shuffled her feet.

"We have an ancient language that died out thousands of years ago, which is different than the one we use now. We use the ancient language for our names. Now, we are true kin and I trust you with my life. Knowing you have my trust, you will eventually show yourself. I will deliver your letter to her. You may take your time to think about what I said." She slipped her hand into Rebecca's and took the letter.

"I...I don't want to die. I'm the only one left in my clan. I have to...I need to...I—" She looked around and noticed she was alone.

What do I do? If I go, he will kill me. He said so himself. He wishes to wipe out all dragonbloods.

Another loud explosion echoed and she quickly raised her head. "Lilith! She's my mate! I will kill him if she's hurt." Rebecca ran towards the noise and saw dead bodies scattered all around her.

She heard some screaming from where the blast had come from. "That's a female's voice. Please be okay, Lilith."

As she got closer, she realized that it had come from the queen who was lying on the ground, rolling in pain.

"Holy shit, your arm! Let me, I know some healing magi—"

The queen grabbed her shoulder with her other arm. "Burn it! Just burn the wound! The arm is gone. Use that burning wood over there. Hurry before I bleed out!"

Rebecca quickly grabbed the burning wood and held it close to Eirfel. "What do I do now? I've never done this."

The queen removed parts of her clothing to expose the wound. "Place the flame here, now!"

As Rebecca cauterized the wound, the queen screamed out, *"El oula ol siegee iayati!"*

"I don't speak elvish but I do know you said something about death. Don't die, please! I know some healing magic that Lilith taught me." Rebecca held up her hands and started enchanting, *"Gala luye ya arta."*

"The third queen of the high elves being saved by a dwarf healing spell. I guess it is better than dying." The queen chuckled despite the pain.

"Sorry, it's the only spell she taught me. I'm not a white dragon. I'm a lightning dragon. I'm not strong enough to do magic…I'm sorry. I can…Where is Lilith?" Tears fell from Rebecca's eyes as she panicked.

"You are doing fine, young one. The bleeding has stopped and that spell has done enough to keep me alive for now. I have not seen her. That last attack... I must rest now. Go find her, she may be in danger." The queen put her head back and passed out.

"She's still breathing, I guess that's fine. Lilith—I need to find her. Lilith!" She ran around frantically.

The sound of combat took over the eerie sound of burning wood. Grunts and screams followed by the sounds of clashing metal.

A group of elves surrounded Aeron and kept stabbing at him with pikes while others shot arrows at him. He swung around violently, killing a soldier or two with each attack.

"Filthy elves, I will kill you all!" He growled and cried with each jab.

Wings sprouted from his back, and the flapping caused a huge gust of wind to knock the soldiers down. He leaped into the air but was hit by a flying object. Lilith flew up and stabbed him in the chest, pushing him onto the ground.

"You hurt my Rebecca. I will kill you!" She stood on top of him and kept stabbing him with all of her rage in each thrust.

"Whelp, I applaud you for breaking many taboos. And doing it for the one you love is most respected by me. I did the same to save my creations." He grabbed her by the neck and stood up.

"But I can tolerate a lot of pain to gain an upper hand." His wounds were healing much slower and an odor came from his body.

"I hope this loved one you hold dear will have nightmares about me for as long as she lives." He grinned as he squeezed Lilith harder.

The archers hit him with arrows but he did not let her go. Her face started to turn blue and her eyes began to bulge.

Tears fell from her eyes as she could barely let her words escape, "Sorry...my love. I will have to break my promise."

Rebecca screamed as she leaped at him. Her body had a bright yellow glow to it as she punched him in the jaw. A bolt of lightning exited out the other side of his face and he flew into a tree, letting go of Lilith in the process.

Lilith gasped for air as she tried to talk. "Yo...you used...breath attack... I thought you—"

Rebecca coughed up some blood. "I did, and it can kill me. My training was for me to tolerate the pain more. I have not practiced it but I do think I can do it maybe one more time."

"Dragonblood! I guess you survived. I can see why I am the object of your nightmares." Aeron stood up slowly.

"What's wrong with him? He is barely being held together." Rebecca held her nose as she talked.

"His body is at its limit. His soul is not able to hold it together. That smell is him starting to rot." Lilith tried to get into a ready stance but fell over.

Aeron used the diversion to charge his way towards them and pushed Rebecca out of the way. Other soldiers tried to hinder him but he plowed into them as he took off into the air.

"Lilith, wake up!" Rebecca checked her vitals. "She's breathing.

Lilith, wake up. He flew off." She kept shaking her body but Lilith wouldn't gain consciousness.

A wagon came by filled with wounded soldiers. An elf jumped off and checked Lilith's body.

"She has several broken bones and her throat has been damaged. Do you know what race she is?" The elf stared at her.

"I... She is a goddess. How can she have broken bones? She always just healed on her own... How could a divine being get hurt so badly?" She sat there and cradled Lilith. "I... I don't know what to do."

CHAPTER 22
THE MINES

"Lilith, Rebecca, we are going to split off from here into separate groups. Queen says there's a camp nearby with slaves. They are mining for something. Keep yourselves safe while fighting that monster." Verus hugged them as he ran off with the other group.

"*Aulatay hoge.*" An elf put his hand on his chest.

Verus nodded. "Yes, they will be alright. I trust they will come out fine."

They approached a large field. Bodies littered the ground. Elves, dwarves, and humans were scattered all over.

Verus checked one of the bodies. "Worked to death, what are they trying to find? There is no point in making your workers work to death unless it's something they do not want anyone to know about."

A scout tapped his shoulder and pointed to the tree line. Next to a tree stood a well-dressed man in a black doublet with crimson eyes and hair.

"I am General Taranis. I knew this day would come. I do not wish for this but I have my orders. You fools would have fared better fighting that moron, Aeron." He waved his hand and the tress tumbled over, making a wall that blocked the way to the top of the hill.

In an instant, Verus raised his shield and arrows rained from the sky. "Take cover! The trees are preventing us from closing the distance."

In panic, the elves tried to find cover. Some screamed in pain and fear. After the arrows stopped, everyone came back out.

"Lord Verus, numbers low. We still good," an elf nodded.

More screams echoed and Verus looked around frantically.

"Who was that? Where did that come from?" He looked over and saw an elf hiding by one of the fallen trees. He quickly vanished, letting out a scream followed by a red mist.

A little black creature hopped onto the fallen tree and let out a loud scream.

Verus body began to shake. "It's the little shits that were eating everyone. Men, get out of the tall grass!" An elf repeated what he said in elvish and everyone tried to run back into the forest behind them.

One by one, the soldiers fell and screamed followed by a bloody mist. Verus managed to turn and block one of them with his shield. The beast sank its teeth into the metal and became stuck. Verus quickly slammed the shield down, crushing it to death. Out of instinct, he swung his blade, cutting another one in half as it leaped at him.

"I will not allow you bastards to get me now. I have a daughter to return to." He slowly moved backwards with his shield ready.

One of the nox mimicked what he said in a revolting voice, "I have a daughter!" It jumped into a small opening and grinned. "Is she delicious? I remember you. You died in the fall. You do not smell yummy, but I shall still eat you." Four more came into the clearing.

An arrow struck one in the back and it fell over dead. The others scattered as more arrows rained from the sky. *Good thing the enemy is not watching the field. I could kiss that archer,* Verus thought.

The sound of rushing air filled the valley as the air around him heated up. He looked off to the side and saw an elf mage rapidly aging as he cast a large fireball into the fallen trees. A large explosion followed and it created an opening. A female elf held the mage's hand as he turned into dust. She fell over crying.

Verus ran towards the group and started shouting commands. "Everyone with a shield in front! We will make a wedge formation!"

He held up his fingers, making a V. "I will be on point. It will not prevent all of us from getting hit, but it will help."

They came together and charged across the field towards the gap. Arrows rained from the sky as they reached the breach. As they entered the opening, dark elves armed with swords rushed in. The wedge formation became an automatic advantage as the shield wall blocked the gap in the wall of trees so they could not get surrounded.

After an hour of constant battle, the dark elves' losses became too great. They lost heart and retreated. The army advanced forward, cutting down whoever they managed to catch up too. As they reached the edge of the forest, General Taranis stood there with his sword drawn out.

They surrounded him as he bowed. "I have heard many tales of your feats, Verus. I wish to duel you."

Verus chuckled as he spoke. "I am not a fool. We have you surrounded."

"A fool, yes." He waved his hand and vines came out of the ground and started snaring everyone. "I am a god. With a flip of my wrist, I can kill all of you." He snapped his fingers and ten vines burst into flames, burning the soldiers.

"If we duel, I will allow them to go regardless of whoever wins." He hunched his body a little and held his sword close with the tip pointing at his target.

Verus slightly angled his shield to the side and rested the blade on the top with his tip pointing at Taranis. With blinding speed, Taranis thrust forward. Verus deflected him to the side and stabbed with his blade. Taranis used the momentum to sidestep, avoiding the blow with a quick spin and hitting the shield with his pummel.

The force knocked Verus back a little but he quickly flipped the bottom of the shield, hitting Taranis in the chin. Taranis thrust his sword, barely missing Verus as it bounced off his armor. Verus lowered the shield and rammed him with it. At the same time, he jabbed Taranis' arm with his blade. He then stood in a ready stance with his body hiding behind the shield.

"I see, the reports were all true. You have a heightened sense of battle. When you are focused on a target, you can actually see a glimpse into the future of their next attack. With sword skill alone, I would lose this match. However…" Taranis jumped forward, kicking the shield with both of his feet and causing Verus to fly backwards. Verus rotated slightly so he would roll as he hit the ground, and used the momentum to stand back up, swinging his blade and hitting Taranis in the leg as he tried to pounce on him.

"You can also predict what will happen to you. It is amazing—a human of your talent. But I do know a way around it. I have a slight trick." Taranis thrust his sword into a hole that the nox had made in Verus' shield when it bit into it. Verus spun slightly, snapping the blade and stabbing Taranis in the shoulder.

"I have won the duel, unless you wish to use your godly powers. But that would be cheating." Verus stood in another ready stance with his shield held at an upward angle.

"I will show you a cheat, boy!" He drew out another sword and with a single slash, cut the shield in half. Taranis swung the sword around like a maniac. Verus was barely able to avoid him. Each slash cut some of the armor as if it was made of butter. Taranis then kicked him to the ground and pointed the blade at his throat.

He smiled and slowly backed off while talking in a calm voice, "You are unable to predict a divine blade. I shall take my leave, boy, and declare you the winner."

"That sword—that is the king's sword! Where did you get that?" Verus tried to go after Taranis but a thick fog engulfed the area, and he disappeared.

Verus helped free the soldiers and quickly ran towards the mine. However, they stopped dead in their tracks as they approached it. There were thousands of prisoners at the bottom of the pit—alive.

Their bodies were mostly skeletal. Some that had the strength tried to cheer; others just sat there or laid on the ground. Some tried to cry, but their bodies had been denied water for so long that their tears could not be produced.

"They have been worked to death! Why would you work your

workforce in such a wasteful manner?" Verus and a handful of elves ran down to free the prisoners.

A dwarf who could still walk and speak came up to him and said in a raspy voice, "I thank ya, lad. It has been a long month for the most of us. Others more." He had a dry cough.

"That monster—I will hunt him down, master dwarf! I promise." Verus patted his back.

But the dwarf nodded his head from side to side. "Lad, he was no monster. The boy with the doll be the monster. Taranis kept us fed, even after the boy meddled in his affairs. He snuck us food and such. Just not enough to keep us alive." He pointed to what looked like a burnt garden, "Taranis had us grow crops and livestock. Kept us fed. We be slaves, but we be a workforce. Lad with the doll, the wee bastard ordered it all to be burnt. Said something about pure human empire. He talked like a lord. I swear I also heard the doll speak. Said somethin' about obeying the prince. King be gone on adventure." The dwarf fell over as he finished.

"Here, take some water. You did good, master dwarf." Verus looked over and noticed a female elf with an urn. She held it up to him as she cried.

She softly said, *"Saiegee iayati, saiegee iayati, saiegee iayati."*

Another elf walked over to him, " You—commander, you bless urn. We not live without him."

"The elf that sacrificed himself with that large fireball—you want me to honor his death?" He gently took the urn.

"It be husband. You taste ash, put earth from battle, pour mix to earth, leave her some."

The girl nodded. *"Tulooss."*

"He be younger elf. Name new alphabet. Honor to know elf name. You be her kin," the other elf said.

"Why do I have to put some of the ash in my mouth?" Verus stood there confused as he held the urn.

"It says you be dead not for him. Part of you he be. *Iayatai.*" Both of the elves kneeled as Verus took a pinch of ash and placed it in his mouth.

The widow elf handed him some dirt which he mixed with the ash and poured most of it out. He handed her the urn as she kissed his hands and slowly walked off while weeping.

"You first human to do elf honor death. You today are also my kin. We drink after, today sorrow."

Verus walked around and looked at all the prisoners. Some were more ghostly than others. The elves and other half-human variants had suffered the worse. The smell of rot and decay was almost unbearable.

He walked up to an elf officer. He tried to keep an even tone but his voice broke out, "What's the count?"

He raised his fingers and tried to find the words. "Three hundred thousand."

"We cannot feed that man—"

"No, sorry. Dead. Only ten thousand live. We are going to be busy burying tonight." The elf sat on a rock and pointed to a small cave.

When Verus looked inside, He saw that it was full of bodies. He recalled not seeing a single child with the survivors. The cave was full of them, and the other smaller races.

CHAPTER 23
BOY AND HIS DOLL

"Albert, we must be ready. Master will be here with her puppet." Taranis rummaged through a chest full of clothing. "Here, this should fit. We must look our best, boy."

"This smells like death." Albert tried not to sound like he was whining.

"It was once a dragonblood's uniform. They are nobles. He...did not survive his capture." Taranis sat in his chair and inspected Albert from afar.

"You must look the part. Remember everything that I have taught you. How you speak, how you walk—even the smallest of gestures has to have meaning." He stood up and walked towards him, holding a ring.

"I had this made for you. It is the crest of my house. We managed to find some gems and rare metals in the mine. A good leader will always make everything better when he leaves." He smiled as they walked out the door. They watched as the workers worked the farms, fed the livestock, and brought up wagons full of earth.

A horn echoed as a pure white carriage with gold trim pulled up. A young man stepped out.

"I am Prince Tourmaline. My father, King Loux is off on a fool's mission. I am in charge of this mine." Taranis and Albert bowed as he walked towards them.

"I was not aware that this was a place for children. Is he human?" The prince waved his hand at them as they stood back up.

"He is my son. He is learning the family business." Taranis tried to take a step forward when he heard a dark, foreboding voice emanating from behind the prince.

"I did not know you had any children. He looks and smells like a mix of half-dwarf and half-gnome. It is by luck that he looks like a pure-blooded human. When has a devil ever taken in strays?" The doll looked over the prince's shoulder.

"Master, I am his step-father. My life has taken many turns during my time here in the realm." He bowed again.

"It may be as it has to be, general. I have also changed my plans, and your son may be key. I found this prince to my liking. He has no soul." The doll smiled as she sat on the prince's shoulder.

"I heard you have taken a liking to a boy. I hope he proves to be of valued—"

The prince interrupted him, "How are things with finding her body? Our plans cannot wait long."

"Sir, you may be a prince, and I may be courteous to you, but I do not take orders from you." Taranis stared into his eyes.

"Forgive the prince. The offer I made him has gone to his head again. I keep telling him—after the ceremony." The doll covered her cheeks with her hands as if to imitate feeling shy, "Oh, what is a blushing bride-to-be to do."

"You are already promised to my lord." Taranis grunted out.

"I promised nothing to him. His personal lust for me is what drove him to his failure. If we did not need him to control his beasts, I would have just devoured him after his loss." The doll ripped a button off of the prince's shirt and threw it.

"My love, should I be worried about something?" The prince hugged her and smiled.

"Just an old jealous boyfriend I broke up with. He is only a mere god. I will protect you." She kissed his cheek.

"He is the son of the god king. His very voice could kill lower gods." Taranis grinned at the prince.

"If she tells me I am protected, then I trust her. I am part of her plan. My foolish father did teach us a lot about plotting. We just decided to make it grander." The prince looked down at the camp.

"My general, I have changed my plans. I no longer wish to devour the world. The plan was for me to devour everything to only be devoured myself in the end." The doll looked over at Albert.

"I infected one of the maids at the castle to test a theory that I had. I found out that when she was near someone she loved, her energy grew, and I was able to feed off of it. But the foolish king killed her when he got her pregnant." The doll stared into the mine pit. "I also hid inside a temple of one of the gods. I was able to feel the energy of the people as they worshiped. I was able to consume it as I do with the fire. It got me thinking; if I created a church for Father, he would be able to absorb their energy. Therefore, I must make an empire that worships nothing."

"I want you to stop feeding the slaves," the prince said calmly.

"That is a foolish order. Only a moron would starve his workforce," Taranis growled.

"Follow the prince's orders. Have them worked to death." The doll eyed Albert again.

"This is the king's orders. He wishes for a human-only empire. After his death, I will save them, and they will follow me into hell. Agrona will be my queen, and they will accept her." The prince bowed to them and walked off with the doll.

As he passed Albert, he handed him a ring. "Visit the castle once you become of age. You will make a great advisor to o—" He stopped himself from talking. "I cannot let all of our plans leak out." The prince waved to the carriage with the doll in his arms. His personal guards went towards the gardens and pens and started setting them on fire.

As they left, a dark elf whispered into Taranis ear. "A spy, you say. Let them witness this place. Allow them to report back to the elf kingdom."

He took the ring from Albert. "Follow me to the mines. They found something."

"Father, the ring—why take it?" Albert slightly shuffled his feet.

"I do not trust them. I do not like their plan. I have a plan of my own and you are a part of it." They quickly walked into the mine shaft.

The smell of wet earth and mildew filled the air. It was hard to breathe; the pungent smell of rotting flesh filled their nostrils as they went deeper. Soon, they found themselves on a walkway paved with bricks.

"This is the sewer of the city. Watch out for ghouls, boy." Low growls echoed down other pathways. A dark elf guard was posted at every turn to fight off ghoul attacks.

They ended up in a small room that had some rusted weapons, rotted wooden chairs, and a table with a broken lamp.

A dwarf came up to him holding a sword. "We found this. It be the likes I never seen."

"You found a sword and decided to turn it in instead of using it to fight your way out to freedom?" Taranis eyed the dwarf.

"Aye, you'd have us all be killed. One sword will not change the outcome." He kneeled and held up the sword.

"I know this blade. I remember it well—it was given to the humans." He took the sword. "Boy, I will tell you another secret." He continued, "Gods have two types of divine blades. There is one that they can summon, which is made of pure magic. It has the advantage of becoming stronger the more you put into it. However, that is also its drawback. I've seen many comrades die from this flaw. The other type of blade is made by a metal only found in our realm, though some of it has made its way to the mortal realm. It is called god's metal. This here is the blade held by the Unnamed goddess."

He grinned as he looked at his own reflection. "This can free my lord, and then everything will return to normal."

He quickly rushed out of the mine along with Albert and headed towards an elf officer. "We need to prepare for war. I have a plan."

CHAPTER 24
AERON

Badly injured, Aeron stumbled in the woods. He shouted at the shadows as he trudged along. "Taranis, where are you? You lost the mine!"

"I need you! My body is falling apart again. My soul can no longer repair it and I can barely see. I cannot mix the potion when I'm like this!" He fell over, blood slowly oozing onto the ground. "Taranis, my blood has become that of a human. I do not have much time. If I die, Master will hunt you down." A twig snapped and he tried to stand back up.

He swatted around, hitting the trees. "I can smell you, human! Come to finish me off, have you? I am still stronger than you by far."

"Sir, Father ask me to find you. He said this may happen." The voice was of a young boy.

"I remember that voice—Albert! I will rip you in half for his failure." He tried to head-butt the boy but missed and hit a tree, knocking himself down.

"I know how to make the potion. It is why I was sent. He also gave me this to make sure you aren't a threat to me." His vision was blurry but he saw the boy hold out something.

"That smell is of Master. I see that you have met her, and she has granted you a gift free of her curse. What is it that you wish for, boy? If the mas..." Aeron cried as the pain flared.

"Yes, they said they had something for me in their plans. Father has told me a lot. It is why I hardly fear you. If you kill me, you will interrupt her plans. And also, you will die as a powerless human." More twigs snapped and the blurry vision moved around more.

"You have become more fearless. I am guessing he had you kill a few ghouls, maybe even fuck a slave. But make no mistake, boy. I am a real monster." He tried to laugh but could only manage to cough up blood.

"Father has done no such thing. He filled me with knowledge, taught me a few spells, and even gave me his family crest." The sound of two solid objects striking followed.

"Making a fire—you are a foolish boy! The soldiers have scouts. They will see it." He tried to stand back up but stumbled over.

The sound of liquid being poured into a pot followed the crackling noise of the fire. "I do not think you are aware of it but you have flown a few miles. If I were to walk, it would take a day to get back to the mines."

Aeron struggled to stay awake. "Why did he abandon the mine? It was full of elves."

"He has his own plans. And if I am being honest, I'm sick of them. Even you have your own hidden agenda. I'm surrounded by gods but I see you guys acting no better than the people who are supposed to be lesser than you." The sound of stirring followed after he finished.

"Yes, you are correct. We are no different than you mortals. Even us gods are not immortal. We just live longer. What is your plan?" He tried to stare at Albert but was unable to tell between a stump and the boy.

"I honestly see nothing wrong with the doll's plan, and I see nothing wrong with Taranis' plan either. They both seem to be the same except that one has more thought behind it. I will just follow what I think is the right path for me." He placed the pot on the fire.

Aeron grunted in pain as he tried to move. "Taranis has no plan. He just wants to free his lord and is hoping that he will save the day. He is a foolish person tied by his blind loyalty."

"No, if he cannot get his friend to change his mind, he said he would kill him. He sees folly in following a path of destruction. He says it is meant to fail." Albert hunched down next to him. "You are not strong enough to take the potion into your blood so you must eat it. However, it will not heal you fully. There is a lot, and you have to eat all of it."

"I must say that I agree with him. I have lost the same wars that he has. It is why I was happy when Master told me she had a new plan. What do you think is my hidden agenda?" He ate the food that was mixed with the potion.

"You are easy. You love your dragons. The books that I was given to read stated that the dragons were hunted for sport. They were almost wiped out. Father said you put your soul and blood into your creations. I think you did it to save them because I have noticed that the gods do not care. I also think your master made an agreement with you about your dragons, and you do not fully trust her since her hunger has no bounds." He refilled the bowl.

"Yes, you are indeed a very smart boy. Taranis has trained you well. I think you are the first human I have enjoyed coming across. You will be a fine man. I think the master saw a talent in you. You are also good at potion-mixing. I am almost able to see now." The blurriness had become a haze as everything slowly came back into focus.

"My real father was a simple man who worked hard. I barely knew him but he was a good man. Mother was not happy and was seeing another behind his back. I miss them both, but this journey has opened doors to a world that someone of a lower birth like me could've never achieved. I am grateful to Taranis but I have little feeling for him. It was his doing that ended them both. I will use what he will teach me and make my own choices." Albert put out the fire.

"Boy, you know the full truth of this world. Your choices are few. I think the plan that the master has for you is worth thinking about. Her new plan is my only hope for my dragons." Albert nodded at him and walked away.

CHAPTER 25
AFTERMATH

Rebecca hugged Lilith tightly. "Lilith, you're awake! I don't know what I would do if I lost you."

"How long was I out?" Lilith slowly sat up and looked around, trying to see out of the tent flaps.

Rebecca cried as she hugged her tighter. "We are still here at the field. You were out for almost a week. In the first two days, you almost died. There was a moment when you stopped breathing. Father left to get some herbs. The magical spells would not work on you."

"I guess the fight was harder than I thought. I hate to think how much stronger he would have been if he was still in his godly form." Lilith patted Rebecca's back and gently pushed her off.

"I thought you could heal magically? I have seen you recover from much deeper wounds. That one time, you even broke your arm." Rebecca sat next to Lilith, combing her fingers through her hair.

"Yes, but I am also part human. My regeneration has a limit. When a god reaches their limit, they turn to dust and die. When I run out, I become human, and so I recover slowly. It returns in time, but their limit is much higher than mine." She looked at the splint on her leg. "Gods are immune to most mortal spells. Only when casted by a higher being do they have any effect. If I was created in the natural way, healing spells might have worked on me." She noticed the wrap around her neck.

"You had a crushed neck. An elf doctor had to perform surgery on you. You may not have noticed because of the herbs they forced you to drink but you sound like a frog right now." Rebecca lightly giggled.

Lilith moaned slightly as she tried to move. "My body is aching. What happened to him?"

"He got away. He was also seen over the mine that was liberated by the other half of the army. He got into a short fight with them and then flew away." Rebecca shivered a little as she rubbed her arms. "He is a real monster. Even when he was near death, he was stronger than anyone else."

"He is an ancient god. The power of dragons is the testament of his true strength. Mother told me that Aeron is proof of the god king not understanding his own subjects. He joined the Fallen out of desperation when the dragons were being wiped out for sport. He is the only god who joined them without any influence of the dark substance." Lilith tried to reach for some water but her arm fell back from lack of strength.

Rebecca held the cup of water to her mouth and gently gave her some. "You are always so strong and brave. Allow me to be the strong one this time."

Queen walked in. Her sleeve was stuffed to make it look like she still had her arm. "I am glad to see you are awake. We will have a ceremony once you are able to walk."

As the numbness in Lilith's body started to slowly dissipate, her tears became more abundant. She tried to speak normally but her throat was hurting, "How many are alive?"

"Mostly only the support survived. Only a hundred and fifty soldiers lived out of fifteen hundred. Most died from their wounds. By the Unknown Goddess we managed to win—mainly by luck." Queen found a seat and sat next to them.

"I keep hearing this Unknown and Unnamed Goddess. Mother never told me of such a person with no name." Lilith tried to sit up again but was unable to.

"Well, you probably know her by her real name. They are the same person. Originally, she was only worshiped by humans, but the legend says that her name was erased from mortal minds. Therefore, to the humans, she was unnamed. To other races, she was unknown. After the cultures mixed, the words became interchangeable. Some call her one thing. Others call her by something else. Maybe you can tell us her name, the one you know, little one?" Queen smiled at them.

"If she is who I think, her name is forbidden to mention. I am sorry. I truly am. I have already broken many laws by showing my wings to mortals. Please tell them to not let anyone else know about them. They will take me away from Rebecca and erase me from her memory." She coughed and spit out some blood.

"It is alright, little one. We will keep your secret. You are one of our kin, my sister. Your father should be here any minute now with more herbs. I am sorry. We ran out trying to care for the wounded." She gently placed her hand on Lilith's head and hummed.

Verus walked in while holding some herbs. "Sorry it took so long. I had to fight others off. These things do not grow in abundance." He looked over at Lilith. "Oh, you're awake. Here, Rebecca. I hope this is enough to last her a while."

Rebecca grabbed them and quickly started to grind them. Lilith cried more as the pain became worse. Verus reached for a pouch that was lying on the table. He pulled out a small flask and tried to give her some.

She swatted it away. "I cannot drink that. It is toxic for me."

"It's just god's grass." He picked the flask back up.

"I know. It really is toxic for me. Give it to someone else who is in worse pain than me." She looked over and watched Rebecca as she mixed the herbs with boiling water. "The bonds that created me can be thrown off and I can become unstable. Mother never told me what would happen."

"I guess I still have a lot to learn about being a father to a half-god. Well, let me make you some soup. Do you like rabbit broth?" Lilith nodded at him, and he began to prepare the food.

Trying to hold back her tears at seeing how much pain her mate was in, Rebecca suddenly cried out. "How long will you be like this?"

"It can take as long as a year. Depends on how depleted I am… I think I shall nap. My body is feeling a little heavy." Rebecca handed her a small jar full of a greenish yellow liquid. She drank it and quickly fell asleep.

"How is she? Will she live?" Rebecca cried into Verus's arms.

The elf queen looked at Lilith closely. "She will be fine. Her bones have mostly healed, and the bleeding from her organs has almost stopped. The herbs are doing their trick. I'm just worried about how slow her healing is. It must be because of what she is. Creatures like her are created to die. The fact that she has been alive all these years must be putting a strain on her magical bonds."

"When she heals, we will go on a vacation. I want to surprise her with some time off. I hope she is well during my next mating cycle. I want to make her wish come true." Rebecca sat next to Lilith as the others left. She rested her head back and fell asleep.

CHAPTER 26
EMBERS OF DARKNESS

"With the girls on vacation, I can now get to business—the mine. I don't think they were after rare minerals. Back when I used to be a guard in the sewers, I always had a feeling that there was something darker down there, and I think they were looking for it." Verus looked at the council of elves.

A male elf wearing silk robes stood up. He said, "Lord Verus, you *hummao*. You sure we know something down there? No text claims to be so." He turned and walked away.

"There was an area ghouls refuse—"

"They dumb beast. Only worry when alone and they many. If dog scared, we scare also?" A female elf in armor stood up and also walked away.

The other six stood up and bowed before leaving. One stood at the entrance and turned around. He looked old; his life seemed to be near its end. He had a strained voice, but he carried it with respect.

"I have been around for seventeen hundred years. I remember my father telling me that ghouls remember the things that we forget. They still worship ancient relics that used to be important to every-one. I will grant you my troops and I will assist you. I am sorry but I could not let the others hear me agreeing with you. They only agreed to let you speak out of respect." His human speech was almost perfect.

"Sorry sir, but we have not met before. Who are—"

The old elf raised his hand. "That young man you honored was my great-grandson. We are kin, so it is the least I can do. I was raised by humans, so I do not have an elf name to honor you with. As for my name, I was named after a plant by tradition—Garlic."

"How many men are you bringing?" Verus asked as they shook hands.

"I cannot offer a lot. My troops bore the brunt of the damage during your raid on the mines. I can bring around fifty. Most of them will be from the reinforcements. If I allowed more, it would make me look weak in the eyes of the others." Garlic smiled and wandered off.

The elf queen walked in and laughed as she sat down. "I am glad you managed to get at least one to join you. He is one of the few that still remembers the lore and legends of our kind. I wish I could help you but after losing my arm, my husband insists that I need to stay at the fort and run it till my daughter returns." She let out a sigh and mumbled in elvish.

"I have never heard words like that but I assume they are foul." He laughed a little as he sat down next to her.

"Yes, we rarely curse around humans. I just thought I should see this till the end." Her face lost some of its color and her eyes locked onto a corner. "When that beast blew my arm off, I felt something. There is an evil that sleeps under this ground. If what you said was true —ghouls refusing to go to some areas—then I fear it is something that the entire world should fear."

She stood up and bowed before she left. As she turned around, she tilted her head slightly and looked at him. "I cannot give an order but they can volunteer to aid you. Twenty of them decided to help you. They are not soldiers, but I think they will suit you the best." She walked away as Verus bowed. He quickly ran into his tent and checked his supplies: a short sword for a narrow passage, a long sword, a buckler, and extra bits of armor to attach to his ankles. He looked at the playing card he picked up from the sewer. His wife's writing, now nothing more than smudges, was still as clear to him as when he first read it.

He stepped out and was greeted by the elf officer that was with him during the raid. "I be your translator. Your elf language not so good."

Verus chuckled. "Well, I guess I should work on my elvish." The elf patted his back and nodded.

They headed outside and he was greeted by a dwarf. "I be ya help, lad. The ones able to move agreed to stay and help ya."

"Master dwarf, I cannot ask you to help. You have been through so much." He tried to touch the dwarf's shoulder but his hand was swatted away like it was an insect.

"Aye, I know whatcha' mean. But we gotta know what that wee bastard was starving us for. I be the only survivor of me family. I gotta know why they died." He put his fist over his heart. "I be Granite."

"Well, with a strong name like that, I can see why you survived." They both nodded and shook hands.

"Alright, we will be heading into the sewers. Ghouls have made a den out of them so they will probably attack. Let us hope they not have grown any lords." Verus drew a map in the dirt. "We will be looking for a blockage. It should be around here. Ghouls only block passage-ways if they want to make a trap or if they fear what is on the other side."

Granite spit off to his right and shouted, "We to believe that ghouls have brains? Those dumb beasts do not even speak, barely understand tools, and here ya saying they can make traps?"

Garlic cleared his throat. "My good master dwarf, legends say ghouls used to have an empire but it brought about civil war, and so they agreed to never have it again. They do have a language, and it is one of the only surviving ancient dialects still around. Have you ever come face to face with a ghoul lord? They do speak. They even try to barter."

"Aye, be fairy tales. I would rather find out if dragons fart fire than to talk with a ghoul lord. But I will follow ya orders. Ya did save me life." He played with his ash-colored hair.

"I hate to say this master dwarf, but since your kind can see in the dark, I would need one of you to take point, and in key spots along the formation. If we use torches, they would be drawn towards us." Verus held up a pouch of dust.

Garlic took a sniff and said with some excitement, "Gnome dust. Sir, it is an honor being your kin. It must have been a costly penny."

"No, I am related to royalty. Stuff like this was gifted to me. Ghouls are unable to see the light it creates. I only have enough for about three hours of light, and it's extremely dim at that. Once we run out, we will have to use torches or magic." He handed some to the dwarfs.

They formed a line in groups of three and walked into the mines. Once they entered the sewer, the dwarves took out some gnome dust and clapped their hands. Like little fireflies, the dust danced around them. The darkened area made the dust look like stars in the night sky. The elves had a hard time making out the shadows as they had bows and spears at the ready. The light barely lit ten feet in front of them.

A dwarf pointed down a hall. He tapped his foot three times and nudged his hand once. An elf took a shot and the ghoul let out a loud scream as it fell over dead.

"I see that you know of the elf code. I am sometimes amazed by what the dwarfs know. We are an ignorant race indeed, thinking we are better than everyone else." Garlic smiled as he nodded at the dwarf.

"Aye." The dwarf nodded. "Trick I learned from the war."

They walked down the pathway for over an hour. Verus was going off of memory to try to find the spot. Every now and then, a ghoul would pop up and an archer would take him down. Eventually, they hit a dead end.

"It has to be around here. Look for something that looks like melted rock." Verus said softly as a group moved their hands along the walls.

A dwarf shouted, "*Luon!*"

Granite pushed him over and pulled at a stone. "He said it be loose."

The wall tumbled as they pulled the stones out. The dwarf fell over as he looked at the wall that was behind it. It was a grey mesh that looked like melted rock. "All me years never seen a rock like that. What it be?"

Verus cleared his throat. "Ghouls would eat fat and dirt. The digestive acid in them melts and mixes the two together. After a while, they vomit it out. If they mix it right, it can be as hard as brick."

The sound of something being dragged echoed from behind. A dwarf let out a scream as the others scrambled into a defensive line. It came into the light slowly and was barely visible. A ghoul the height of a forest giant walked out.

"A ghoul, lord!" Garlic shouted in excitement.

It was hunched over to fit in the small area, dragging its knuckles along the ground. One of its hands held a stone that was cut in the shape of a sword. It was too crude to tell what kind of sword it was supposed to imitate.

It barked and let out a low growl. "Hum...hu...humans, de...dea...death is here."

"I be a dwarf, you dumb shit!" Granite shouted.

Verus pulled him back. "To ghouls, all things that are not ghoul are the same." Verus lit a torch and raised it. Two more ghoul lords stood behind him.

"Soldiers, form a spear wall. Everyone else, tear down that wall!" Verus shouted as the soldiers formed a line in front of him.

The ghoul lord made some barking sounds that almost sounded like speech. A bunch of ghouls came from behind and rushed at them.

The elves and dwarves battered at the wall with hammers, pics, and anything solid they could find on the ground. As they pounded away at the wall, the ghouls kept running into the spear wall, wearing down the weapons. Eventually, some of the tips broke and the formation buckled. Verus held his buckler over his head and tried to fill the gap.

One of the large ghouls reached its long arm and grabbed a soldier. Another tried to grab Verus but he cut off its finger.

One of the dwarves managed to knock out a hole in the wall and everyone rushed in. The ghouls stood there, not willing to go past the wall.

"Foo...fo...foolish humans. Evil li...lives there. We go." The ghoul lord nodded and they all left.

"Why they never attacked us like that when we diggin' up the mine?" Granite asked as he tried to catch his breath.

"Taranis, ghouls know when true danger is near. They avoid it as much as they can. The first time I faced a ghoul lord, he ran away before he could finish me off because a dragon flew by. Whatever is down here is far worse than fighting three ghoul lords." Verus said as he double-checked the opening to make sure the ghouls had left.

"We bloody lost half of our men. How the hell we get outta here after we find what we lookin' for?" another dwarf asked as he picked up a stone.

They followed the path until the dark red stone became a bright white color and a white light lit up the area. It was as bright as day but they couldn't see the source.

Garlic looked at the stone and rubbed it. "I remember my grandfather telling me of stones like this. This piece is over thousands of years old. Only gods can make this type of stone."

They found some stairs that went down. They kept going on for almost an hour. The second they were back in a hall, the dwarves complained about their feet hurting. Verus and Garlic kept moving as the others rested.

At the end of the hall was a large door that looked to be made of glass. Granite managed to catch up and rammed into the door.

He let out a cry as he bounced off of it. "Aye, shit. It be pure diamond. I never seen diamond this clear." They tried to find a way to open it but it was locked shut.

As the rest of the group caught up, they began trying to find a way in. They poked and prodded everything but found nothing. Right when they gave up, the door made a grinding sound and opened up. Garlic stood there with a grin.

"I managed to find a hidden button." He slowly walked his way in.

The path went around in circles until it led to a large open area. In the middle was a floating diamond casket filled with a dark liquid.

"What in the four hells is that?" Verus stood there staring at it.

"That be what the wee bastard wanted us to find? A bloody casket?" Granite jumped down and walked towards it.

Before anyone could speak, his body started to wither away and became dust. Everyone stood there in shock, not knowing what to do.

* * *

They set up a small camp and rested. Verus sat near the casket and stared at it. He tossed a coin at it and watch it turn to dust.

A dwarf sat down next to him. "Where the dust go?" he grunted out.

"It consumes the dust into nothing." Verus tossed another coin.

The dwarf tossed a small tool and it had the same effect. "Whatcha be doin?"

"Seeing if there is a limit but it seems there is none. I ran out of pebbles that were stuck in my boots." He pulled out a dagger and thrust it in the air. Half of the blade turned to dust.

"I might try something." The dwarf had one of the diamonds in his hand. "I found this lying on the ground. I don't think it be diamond." He tossed it. It made a ringing sound as it hit the ground and slid across.

Verus quickly looked for more and grabbed a handful. "Maybe if we make a suit out of..."

"We need a forge, ya daft bastard. If ya forgot, there be a wee ghoul problem. We not even sure if a forge can melt that." The dwarf spit into the affected area.

Garlic walked up and grabbed one of the stones. "I once read something in an ancient book about a stone and a casket. In the story, the stone would protect the holder from dangers." He walked towards the casket and was unaffected by the devouring air. He kept going until his fingers reached it. He turned and smiled at them as he bowed.

"This old elf has been blessed with a lovely sight. Inside it is a really beautiful naked woman. I have never seen such a perfect body." He slowly walked away as the others grabbed a stone and ran towards it.

Garlic walked up the hall a little and looked around to make sure no one was nearby. Then, he pulled out a communication orb.

"Sir, it is I. The disguise has worked perfectly. We found her body, Lord Taranis." He grinned.

"Good. After I awaken my lord, he can free her body. It will be favorable to him."

"But my lord, what of the mortals?" Garlic asked with excitement. "May my spiders have them? After having some of the king's men, I felt young again. I want more."

"No, I have other plans. Most importantly, that human needs to survive until I have returned."

"Yes, Master." The elf grinned and slowly put away the orb.

CHAPTER 27
MAKING A BROOD

Rebecca sat on a park bench, eating a pastry and trying to absorb the sun's heat. "Well, this place is rather nice. A small little fishing town. I wish we got here a few weeks earlier."

"Sorry, I know you really wanted to see her. I should have never gotten hurt so badly. If I had not, we would have been able to catch up to her." Lilith was next to her, rubbing where the cast used to be on her arm.

"I keep telling you that it's fine. He was a monster. It can't be helped. You are lucky that I love you so much and that it's mating season." She stood up to show off her mature form. "I keep forgetting how amazing it feels to be grown up."

She sat back down next to Lilith and imitated her sulking look. "So, how tall are you really? You adjust your height to match mine every mating cycle."

Lilith pointed at a lamp post. "About that height, maybe shorter by a little. I am sure I told you this after the city was destroyed."

"That's amazing! That is ten feet tall. But then why do you always stay so short?" She locked her arm around hers.

Lilith placed her hand over Rebecca's head. "This must be from the injury you sustained afterwards. I did not properly test you for memory loss." She continued. "My missions for Mother require stealth. It is easier to stay hidden when I'm shorter. After I met you, it just made things easier. Did you notice I was taller when I was fighting in the air?" Lilith looked around at the men that walked by.

"I was so worried about you that I didn't really notice. Why are you looking at all the men?" Rebecca pouted a little.

"You still have that desire to rebuild your clan. You need a man to impregnate you. I am looking for good matches." She got up and started running towards a drunk lying in the streets.

Rebecca stopped her. "Lilith, it's more than just needing a man. I need to have a scent of his genetics. There has to be a trait that I need for my broodlings. I do not have the luxury of picking any random person. I need to make my clan stronger to make sure this situation will not happen again." She took a deep breath and said under her breath, "That's what the white dragon told me I would be looking for."

"So how will you know you found the one?"

"She said that I will have this intense desire to breed with him and it would drive me crazy. I have never been attracted to a man before so it scares me." Rebecca held out her hand for Lilith to take.

They walked into a bar and ordered some drinks. Lilith had taken a liking to an elven wine which was common in most bars. Rebecca still drank her dwarvish ales.

A man stumbled in. He seemed to be drunk but his eyes were bloodshot with sorrow. His face was swollen, and the bartender gave him a drink on the house. Many sat with him and tried to console him.

Rebecca's head perked up and she stared at him. As a man walked by, she snagged his sleeve and asked, "Who is that man?"

"Oh, him, it's a sad story. His wife and newborn were killed few weeks ago. I heard she walked out on deck at night after being warned not to. Some monsters took the baby and ate it in front of her. Later, she jumped in and was eaten herself. He's a good lad. Sad to see that happen to him." The man said in a respectful tone.

"Rebecca, what is it?" Lilith's voice was still monotonous but had a hint of concern.

"There's something about him–I can smell it. I desire him. His scent pulls me in. It will make a strong brood." Rebecca stared at him and blushed a little.

"That is great. Get over there and have sex." Lilith smiled and waved Rebecca to go for it.

"You sure are dense. It doesn't work that way. I have to get him to notice me first but he is full of sadness. His family just died." She grabbed Lilith's hand and squeezed it. "Let's go have sex. I'm in full on lust mode and I am not ready for him yet. I can work on it tomorrow, but I need someone now!"

The following morning, they went back to the same bar. Rebecca sat at the bar table while Lilith stood nearby.

"The people we asked said he comes here in the morning for breakfast and later in the day, as we had seen him then. You know what to do?" Lilith stared at her with stars in her eyes.

"I have seen a few prostitutes attract men. I have an idea, I think. They are dumb survival instincts that I wish I could ignore. I am not attracted to him but I need to revive my clan. It's the only part of being a dragonblood that I hate." Rebecca sulked a little as she sat there thinking.

The man walked in and sat down at the bar stool next to her. His eyes were still bloodshot. She noticed dark bags under his eyes from lack of sleep. His skin was a pale color, and he had a smell emanating from his body. Lilith smiled and nudged Rebecca with her finger.

Rebecca cleared her throat and her voice broke a little as she said, "I am new in town. Do you know of something that can show a girl a good time?"

He looked at her and scoffed. "A dragonblood. I can smell that odor. You trying to attract me?" His voice was deep and empty.

"What? You're not into—"

He cut her off. "You are a very pretty woman, but I am cursed. I lost my family because of this curse. My great grandfather was right— I should have just taken over his work."

"Well, I did not come to find a husband. I just need someone to… well I mean." She lost her words.

"My blood gives me the ability to read people. I know what you want. I also know that girl who is looking at us with that strange childish look is your lover." He waved his hand. "Barkeep, I have lost my appetite. I'll be back later." He stood up and walked out. Rebecca and Lilith followed him.

Lilith ran next to him, trying not to shout. "She is a very attractive woman. She just needs your sperm. Most human men would just jump at the chance."

"Look, I'm not that kind of man. I know what it is that you want but I cannot help you. Find another man. You do not want my blood in your clan." He swatted at her as if she was a fly.

"You are a smelly man, and I have turned down much more attractive people than you. Just accept the fact that I am picking you and let me get my suffering over with!" Rebecca said, not caring about the attention she was attracting.

He went towards a door nearby and looked back at them. Doing his best to keep his temper down, he said, "Look, this is my home. If you walk in, I will summon the guard." He opened the door. He tried to step inside backwards but ended up tripping and falling over. He laid on the ground without moving.

Lilith checked to see if he was still alive. "He hit his head. I think he is knocked out. Take his pants off and just take what you need."

"I can't do that. I need his permission. I was a victim once. I don't wish to make others suffer like I did. Let's just take him inside and make sure he lives. I have about two weeks left." She kneeled down and helped Lilith carry him in.

"His house is a mess, and so filthy. I think I smell a dead rat." Lilith pinched her nose and dropped him.

"He's suffering. Poor thing, he really loved his wife. I know how he feels. If I had a house after my clan died, it might be the same." She dragged him to a bed and rolled him onto it.

Lilith started to clean up. "I think if we make him indebted to us, we can have him pay it off with sex."

Rebecca chuckled a little. "You are as fierce as a brothel owner."

Hours went by as they cleaned. Lilith stumbled into a small hidden room. "Come here quickly!"

"Lilith, you alright? What are these—books?" Rebecca stood by the entry, carefully looking at the pile of books. "They are all written by a man named Dumas."

"Mother told me about him. I think she was afraid of him. Looks like he has twelve volumes." Lilith picked one up and opened it.

"Put that down at once!" The man barged into the room.

Lilith instantly pinned him to the wall with her hand. "Why do you have all these books? How did you manage to collect so many?"

"They are a part of my family. My ancestor—I have his curse in my blood." He tried to fight her off but she was too powerful. He gave up and became as limp as a ragged doll.

"I only looked into a few of them. They have things that mortals are not allowed to know. I have been collecting them to make sure no one else finds them. However, I am not the only one who collects them. The king has one, and some vampire hunter has also been finding them." He started vomiting a little and she let him go.

"Mother told me these are forbidden. If any of the gods or devils knew you had these…" Lilith said as she wiped the vomit off her hand.

"Yes, I know. I read that in one of these, but it also said they fear him." He stood up and tried to wipe the vomit off of his shirt with his hands.

"But who is this Dumas?" Rebecca stood there still looking at the books.

"He is the only immortal human. He is an eternal. The original creations of the gods were eternal. It forced them to use up a lot of their own energy. When humans came about with self-reproduction, the gods copied them. Dumas is the oddity—he was created out of an accident. Mother never told me the details. Even the Fallen became fearful of him." Lilith pushed Rebecca out of the room before she could grab another book.

"Lilith turned to look at the man. "If his blood runs in your veins, then that must be why you are unaffected by her scent, and it is why she is attracted to you." She grabbed Rebecca's arm, "We must go. You cannot mix with him."

"Lilith, you are being rude to him. He cannot help his birth.

Anyways, if it's a trait my survival instincts say that I need, then I have to get it. According to Aeron, I am also an unwanted curse. Dragonbloods are a tainted race that he wants to wipe out." Rebecca pulled away from her and helped the man sit at the table.

He looked around and sounded a little off as he said, "You cleaned my house? Why?"

"It was filthy, and it was also our fault that you fell over. But you will have to wash yourself." Rebecca tossed him a towel. "I warmed up some water for you."

"I am not going to sleep with you," the man said in a stern tone.

"I am not doing this for that. You need help. I don't think your late wife and child would want you to waste away and die." She held out her hand but pulled it back when she remembered he had vomited. "I am Rebecca, Rebecca Crast. This is my wife, Lilith Crast."

He sniffed his hand and gave an odd look when he noticed how bad it smelled. "I am Holt. I have no family name."

CHAPTER 28
TEMPTATION

"I have been here for a week. Why are you not thanking me?" Rebecca had her hands on her hips as she tapped her foot on the floor.

"I did not ask for you to help. I was managing fine by myself." Holt slowly stumbled into the kitchen.

She pushed him towards the table and placed a plate of food in front of him. "You are clean, you smell nice, and you have started working again. You even have me and Lilith cooking you fresh meals to make you healthy."

"I didn't ask you to. You just forced it onto me." He glanced at the food and muttered under his breath, "Oh good, Lilith didn't cook it."

"That is my wife, sir! Do not insult her cooking. She is trying very hard and has gotten better." She looked over at a pot full of burnt stew from last night. "She was very sorry about burning it. I think she went out to get you a new pot."

"When do you plan on leaving? People are starting to think I have remarried." He finished his food quickly and stood up.

She handed him a lunch box and his coat. "And what's wrong with that? I am a very attractive woman. My cycle ends next week but mark my words, I will come back the next cycle. Lilith even talked about

178

knocking you out and bringing you with us. She really wants to become a mother."

"There are many other men out there with greater traits. All I have is my cursed blood!" He stormed out the door.

Lilith came in an hour later. She kissed Rebecca gently on the cheek and put the new pot in the kitchen. "Well, I shall try again today. I need to get better at cooking for a large family. We will have twenty eggs and all of them will hatch. Perfect babies."

"My brood was considered to be of a rare size. Four is the usual. I will be happy with just three." She sat down and had a solemn look on her face. "They think I'm his wife."

Lilith smiled and chuckled in an odd way. "You are acting like a wife. I have never seen you be so loving towards anyone but me. Has he agreed to have sex now?"

"I think this cycle is a lost cause. He is still sad from his loss. It was indeed very recent. Maybe I should just come back the next cycle." She folded her arms and planted her head on the table with a whimper.

Lilith remained quiet. Rebecca looked at her face and with a snap in her voice, said, "No! We are not going to drag him with us. We seem to always find trouble; it may kill him."

Lilith's face lit up. "I will talk to him. I have an idea."

"Do not hurt him, and do not make him feel worse. He is finally starting to become a decent person," Rebecca said in a concerned tone.

As the day came to an end, Holt finally returned home. Lilith sat at the table with her arms folded. She had an expression that he could not decipher.

"Did you and Rebecca have a fight?" He asked with some happiness in his voice.

"No, she is not allowing me to cook. She is starting to act more like a wife to you than to me. I was able to cook over the campfire just fine." She placed her head on her arms.

"She cannot help it. She has no real attraction towards me. It is the dragon side of her blood that is forcing her to protect her clan. She just needs to let this cycle end and find someone else during her next one." He sat down and started eating.

"I stayed up to talk to you. You were willing to have a wife and kids, so the cursed blood is not that much of an issue for you. So why is it a problem to sleep with her once?" She took a spoon and ate some of the food. "Is she not attractive enough for you?"

He blushed a little as he said, "She is one of the most attractive women I have ever met. Only a fool would pass on this chance. I just do not think it's right. If I have children, I want to be a part of their lives and they would also be a part of mine. I am not the type of guy to impregnate a woman and leave her. I want a family." He ate some more.

"Despite you being a slob, you are a decent person. Mother always acted like I was just a tool to help her with her goal...well, that is a story I cannot share." She ate some more.

Lilith stood up and got on her knees in front of Holt. She held his hands. "I am begging, please. We need this. I know why she needs to have your traits. It will make her clan stronger so that her ancient bloodline will not die out. This is the second time her clan has been down to its last member. I will do anything you want if you agree. Money, rare jewels, even...me." Tears fell from her eyes. Her voice had real sadness behind it.

"For a magical creation such as yourself to understand emotion is truly a gift. I do not need anything. I shall think on it." He helped her stand up. She walked off into her and Rebecca's room.

Holt pulled out one of the books and read it carefully. *Dumas, you had a plan. You told me yourself that you had a plan for me. Is it in one of these blasted books?* Just when he was about to give up, a sentence caught his eye: *His blood will carry on into the future. It shall be carried by the dragons, and they will carry on after I passed from this boring existence. She was lovely, hair of red. Gnomes are a gift.*

Holt banged his fist on the table. "Who writes like this? Each sentence is about a different topic."

He thought back to the times he had seen Dumas. Whenever he talked about something, it always ended up being about everything.

Things no mortal knew, and the pride of humans. He always spoke in a way that truly never answered anything. "Shit, he speaks in code!" Holt stood up and hit his knees on the table.

He noticed that the girls' door was slightly open. He peeked in and saw them naked and making out. Their fingers wandered each other's bodies and their lust for one another oozed out. Lilith opened her eyes and winked at him. He quickly ran off into his room.

She giggled a little as Rebecca sighed. "You are mean, you know. Do you think this will work?"

"I have asked around and looked into some books. How loud do you think we can be tonight? I want him to dream about us. I am sure he will oblige tomorrow." They went back to fulfilling their desires as the night went on.

CHAPTER 29

LUST

The girls sat at the table, eating breakfast and giggling. Holt walked out of his room and yawned. His clothing was disheveled and he was unable to fully open his eyes. Sitting down, he grumbled to himself. He groaned and yawned again as he laid his face on the table.

Lilith tried to pat him on the back but he pushed her hand away. "Rebecca, did you really have to be so loud last night? I know you guys have been doing it every night but usually I am able to ignore you." Lilith blushed a little and sat back down. Holt looked at her. "Wait, you were the loud one? You always seem so quiet and mostly emotionless."

Rebecca sounded happy as she said, "When I'm in my cycle, I can't control my lust. Normally, we do not do it as much. She has plenty of emotions when making love."

"I am starting to regret my choices in life. Thanks to you, I had a hard time resting last night. I know you two are trying to force me to give into my desires, but it's just too soon." He stood up and tried to walk off when Lilith stopped him.

"I have never been with a man before but I know how you are feeling right now." She pointed to his pants.

182

A little annoyed, he sighed and pushed her away as he left. Lilith noticed she was still holding on to his lunch. "I hope he will not starve to death."

"Lilith, are you sure it's working? I think it would be better if I was seducing him, not you." Lilith sat back down. Rebecca looked into her eyes and sighed. "You sure you understood him after you talked to him last night? I think watching women go at it is not really doing what you said it would."

Lilith looked disappointed as she softly said, "I was jealous from thinking about you with another person. I know it was what I said I wanted but…the reality hit me about how I really feel when we started living here. I want us to have children, and this is the only way. I will tell you what we talked about. Maybe you could persuade him to do it then."

Later that day, Holt slowly walked home. His face seemed drained of life. As he slowly opened the door, he closed his eyes and took a deep breath. He barged in and ran for his room but Rebecca grabbed him.

"Wait, I am sorry. I'm very sorry. Lilith did not tell me how you felt. I should have asked. I never knew it was because of such a simple thing. I should've expected it." She rested her head on his chest.

"I had a good father. I should've known I would pick a man who was also a good person. I will allow you to be a part of their lives. You would be their father. Just let Lilith and I raise them." He grabbed her by the shoulders and pulled her back a little. Then, he looked at her lips and kissed her deeply.

She jumped back out of his embrace and seemed startled. "Sorry, I have never kissed a man before. It's not something I think I enjoy. Your face is a little rough, but I can do it." She went back into his arms and they kissed again.

He lifted her up as they kissed and took her to his bed. She quickly stripped him down as he stripped her.

Rebecca looked at his naked body and seemed fixated on his privates. She shivered a little as she tried to touch it. "Sorry, it scares me a little. The last time I was this close to one was the worst day of my life."

"I'm really sorry. We can stop if you wish. You are only acting out on your dragon instincts to reproduce." He started to pull away but she grabbed his arm and pulled him closer.

"I'm just scared because it's my first time with a man. I have come this far so let's keep going." She laid back on the bed and he followed. He sucked on her breast and worked his way down. She moaned but kept looking at her discarded outfit that Lilith had gotten for her. Her mind was filled with thoughts for her lust of Lilith. Their sexual exploits were all she could think of when he entered her. When it was done, she opened her eyes and noticed that Lilith was standing there, staring at them and blushing.

Rebecca jumped up and ran towards her crying. Lilith grabbed her arm and hugged her tightly.

Lilith combed her fingers through her hair and whispered, "It is alright. I am glad it is done, and now we can have a family. I know what I said earlier but now I feel relieved. I love you, Rebecca. With every inch of my heart." Her voice was no longer without emotions.

Rebecca scoffed. "We have to do it more than once just in case it didn't take. I was just worried you would be mad. I promise all I could think about was you."

Holt walked out with his pants on and cleared his throat. "I am sorry. My body could no longer take it. I gave in to my lust."

Rebecca smiled at him and nodded. "It's fine. You know I wanted it so that I can have eggs. Tomorrow will be better." She took Lilith's hand and grinned. "She said she loved me with real emotion behind it. That's all that matters to me. Her monotonous voice is slowly going away. She is now able to express her emotions with her voice."

He cleared his throat. "Tomorrow?"

Lilith smiled at him. "We have to make sure she gets pregnant. So do it as many times as you have to."

CHAPTER 30
THE GOD PRINCE

"**B**oy, everything is falling into place. They have the body. They have a victory and now they will become lazy. I must free my lord now." Taranis looked at Albert and smiled.

"Will he kill me?" Albert said nervously.

"He has a habit of granting favors to the ones that do him a service. I will wish for you to stay by my side, untainted." He smiled at the boy and looked out towards at the sea.

"I am surprised you were able to find us a ship and a crew to take us to the cursed island." He looked around and sniffed the air. "I do like the smell of the sea."

Albert nodded. "I learned from my father whatever little I could. I also know what will happen to them once we land. You need them to feed him."

Taranis laughed as he talked. "Good boy, you have learned. I assume these are pirates."

"We be based near the cursed island. We never knew anyone willing to set foot on it that lived," one of the crew said as he walked by.

"Yes, good sir. I have been to that island many times." Taranis grinned as he looked at the man.

"So Father, what is that sword anyways?" Albert looked as the sword that Taranis carried on his hip.

"This is from a set of four holy weapons. There are four holy blades that became lost in the mortal realm: my lord's sword, Agrona's sword, Aeron's sword, and Etharia's sword." He placed his hand on the hilt.

Then, he pulled it out and handed it to Albert. The boy had a hard time holding it since it was heavier than a human sword. "I can hear a song," he said with strain.

"Yes, it is telling you the owner's name in our language. It also tells you the name of the blade. It is alive, boy. A living metal. It was how I was able to defeat that man. He can only read one living thing at a time." He gently took the blade back.

"Who is Etharia? The blade keeps singing her name," the boy asked as he rubbed his arm.

"She is the Unnamed Goddess. Her name was erased from mortal memory by the orders of the god king. His angels erased her name from all the books they could find." Taranis sheathed the sword on his hip.

Albert put his hand on his chin and pondered. "Why would the god king kill her? The history books claimed the Unnamed Goddess was the strongest of the gods, and the greatest weapon against evil."

"Even though she was my enemy, she was the greatest among us. The king grew jealous of her power and fame." He took a deep breath.

"Where is your sword?" Albert tried to look around to see if he had a hidden sword on his body.

"There are two other swords if you count mine and the cursed one. They are both being used to prevent my lord from being trapped forever. After he is free, I shall train you on how to use it. Just do not touch the cursed blade."

"Tell me about your lord. He must have been a great person for you to do all of this for." The boy sat down on a crate.

"He was my best friend. I was honored when I was appointed as his guard. It was even more moving when he named me his general. We used to love all the same things. I also have a duty to uphold, an honor

I have to fulfill." Taranis looked at him and closed his eyes, trying to remember. "When a man makes a promise from the heart, it must be fulfilled."

Albert looked out into the ocean. "Even if your feelings have changed?"

"He has been imprisoned for thousands of years. I can only hope that he has learned from his mistake. I only vowed to have him released. I still consider him a good friend, so I must give him a chance to see reason." Taranis pulled out a communication orb and walked into a cabin as Albert followed.

"I must now set my plan into motion—my plan to recapture the mine." His hand shook nervously as he rubbed the orb.

"Master, I have news to report. As I had predicted, the elves sent an army and captured the mine." Goosebumps formed on his skin as the orb blinked violently.

A voice, more terrifying than anything Albert had ever heard so far, came from the orb. "Do they know what we were doing there?"

"Yes, they have found the body and—" His armed bent backwards and a bone protruded from his skin.

"I would understand if they took the mine and you retreated for a moment in order to attack them in surprise, but they found my body. This is a failure I cannot allow." His body began to bend backwards. He tried to let out a scream but his throat was clogged with blood.

Albert shouted at the orb. "He has a spy there. They have no idea who the body belongs to, nor can they move it. He allowed them to take it to find out if your body is still consuming, and to figure out how to get to it."

The voice calmed down. "I remember that voice. My sweet boy Albert. Alright, I will hear him out." Taranis began to heal as his body stopped thrashing about. "What did you learn, Taranis?"

"You broke his vocal cords. He is unable to speak, so I shall speak for him." Albert cleared his throat, "Your consumption is active, uncontrollable. Our spy found a way to get to it."

"My boy, I can see I was right to pick you. Taranis, you better have a good plan on how to get my body back. Remember, part of me is inside you. Fail me again and I will kill you." The orb shattered into pieces.

"Father, are you alright?" Albert tried to help him but didn't know what to do.

"I will be fine. I just need some time to heal. I should be fully recovered by the time we get there." His voice was under a lot of strain.

After they arrived, they both walked off the boat and onto the shore. Some of the crew followed Taranis towards a small cottage.

"You actually have a cottage here, Father?" Albert was surprised.

"I sometimes hide things here. It is the safest place." He turned around and held up his hand to stop the crew.

"My son and I will bring out your payment. Just sit here. It will be a few moments." He snapped his fingers as they entered the cottage. Screams echoed as they stood inside and waited.

Taranis told the boy to stay there while he walked out. He looked up at the sky and saw the crack forming.

A deep but pleasant voice spoke through the crack, "My loyal subject, did you find it?"

"No, my lord, but I found something that would work. Etharia's sword is strong and will be able to break you free." He held it up and it hummed loudly.

He lowered the sword and stabbed the ground. He reached his arm towards the sky while his other hand still held onto the handle. A dark beam of light came from the crack and hit the hilt. The crack widened as a tearing sound ripped through the sky.

A dark liquid poured from the opening and a large naked body dropped to the ground. The man slowly stood up and grinned. He opened his eyes but there was nothing there except holes. The center of his forehead opened up to expose another eye. It was as red as blood, and it moved around slowly.

"There is a human nearby. Did you save someone for me?" the man said as he slowly walked towards the cottage.

"My lord, he is not for your consumption. He is my son. I wish for him to serve under you like I have." Taranis stood in front of the man and kneeled. "My lord Apophis."

He chuckled and touched Taranis' shoulders with his hands. "You always told good jokes." Taranis raised his head and looked into the empty holes that used to be his eyes.

Apophis stopped smiling. "You are not joking. What kind of fool are you? If you wish for him to be the last living thi—"

"Lord, Master has changed her plans. She no longer wishes to devour everything." Taranis lowered his head again.

"Oh!" Apophis squeezed Taranis shoulders tightly, causing him to wince in pain. "She is nothingness in body. How can she change her nature."

Taranis groaned a little and struggled with his words as the grip became tighter. "She found out that she can still gain energy if she is worshiped. I think she wants to become the ruler of the mortal realm."

Apophis let go and looked oddly delighted. "Ah, I see my love wishes to rule. I can agree to that. Why kill the cows when you can eat a few at a time to keep your food supply running?"

Apophis looked at Taranis' body and chuckled. "Forgive me, friend. It has been a while. Stuck in the void between worlds can drive one mad. I am in need of some clothing."

Taranis shouted, "Albert! There is a box marked as Lord Apophis. Bring it out at once and introduce yourself to our lord."

Albert came out dragging a large box with its handles. "He is a very bright boy, my lord. Master has taken a liking to him. She says she has plans for him."

Albert did not look at Apophis. He got down on his hands and knees and pushed the box towards him while staring at the ground. "Father has said much about you. I hope I can serve you well, my lord."

"He is a well-spoken lad. You have taught him well. I must be ready to meet my love at once. She will be pleased to see—"

Taranis cut him off and the prince growled. "She has been smitten with a human male—a prince. I think she plans on making him her king."

Like a toddler throwing a tantrum, the prince started to stomp on the ground and screamed out hellish sounds. He was about to hit Albert in anger when he paused, "My love wants you to live. I must refrain from destroying you." He looked over and saw a boulder. He smashed it into dust.

Albert cleared his throat. "My lord, Prince Apophis, if I may?"

"What is it, human filth?" He looked at the boy, trying to contain his rage.

"She is still trapped in the body of a doll. Her real body has been found. Father has allowed the enemy to take it so that you can rescue it for her." His voice was clear and he spoke like a proper noble.

Apophis' face lit up and his rage went away as fast as it had come. "If I save her body, she will see me as her hero. She will then allow me to kill this boy prince, and I can be her king."

He jumped up and down in joy like an excited child. He suddenly stopped and held his face in his hands, crying softly.

"There was something there. It took my eyes, my friend. I need to regrow them, or she will never be able to look at my handsome face." His cries became louder and he started rolling around on the ground.

"My lord, you are a god prince. Try to remember the dignity you once had." Taranis tried to help calm him down but his cries grew louder.

"Father, what has happened to him? He is nothing like you said he was." Albert stared at him and scoffed.

"The world between the realms is a place only a few have ventured into. It is a place I did not tell you much about. Everyone that came out lost something." He watched as the prince continued to move on the ground. "He was in there for thousands of years. His mind has been devoured by what lives there... along with his eyes."

Giant furry monsters slowly walked towards them, baring their claws. Taranis became nervous as he saw them. Twenty of them stood upright as the rest wandered back into the distance.

"Narshis. They are very strong." He gently pushed Albert behind him and held Etharia's sword.

One of the beasts slowly walked towards Apophis and tried to bite him. The beast howled in pain as his teeth broke on his skin.

Apophis stood up with a smile of pure bliss on his face. "It has been a while, my friend. May I kill these monsters on my own? I have some rage I need to let out." He punched the beast that bit him and its head burst into a red mist. The others growled at him and made their way towards him.

"I am glad to see he still has his strength. Not many gods can rival his raw muscle, and his skin is almost impossible to break." Taranis said. Albert and him stood there in amazement as the prince killed all the beasts with his bare hands.

"Father, I feel that he is dangerous. He has all that power but the mind of a child." Albert slowly walked forward to get a better view.

"He will regain his mind in time. I think we should continuing keeping the things we have not told him a secret for the time being. He may not hurt you as you are important to his love, but he may damage her plans all the same."

"I have a feeling something might happen. I think he aims to destroy her plans." Albert smiled as the prince finished the last one off.

Apophis turned to look at Albert. "Young lad, you are important to my love, and therefore you are important to me. But I am a lord, and you must learn to serve me properly. Fetch me some water so I may wash myself and remove this filthy blood. I also need a change of clothing." Albert bowed and walked away.

"Sir, you could just use magi—"

Apophis snapped his fingers, cutting Taranis off. "I need to talk to you. I do not trust him. I will not hurt him, but I need to tell you something. Once we rescue her body, we can only open her casket by using a divine being. This act will destroy both the blade and the user. What gods are left on the mortal realm?"

Taranis rested his hand on his chin and let out a deep breath. "Well, there is Aeron, but he is trapped in a human body. He also hates you and is Master's personal guard. Then there is your sister."

Apophis nodded. "She is too strong. We would end up killing her first. What about Turiacus?"

"His mind is gone. Remember that he is stronger than you, but his curse is almost complete." Taranis' face lit up. "Your sister has two daughters. One is the Amazon queen, and the other fought Aeron. I did not see her personally but I felt her energy during the battle."

The prince danced around singing and giggling. "I have blood relatives, nieces. I must see them and introduce myself—their long-lost uncle. I bet they have wondered about me."

Taranis cleared his throat and said, "Your father has forbidden even the mention of your name after your imprisonment. They have most likely never heard of you." Apophis' face melted as he cried.

"My father has erased my name? How could he? I am his only son! Only I can rule in his place after he is gone. He shall pay for this." He became quiet as he watched Albert slowly walk and pointed towards the cottage.

"Inside is a place to wash. I started the fire under the tub to heat up the water." Albert bowed and the prince patted his back and walked off.

"Father, I was able to hear everything. Do you wish for me to contact some of our spies to look for the girls?" Albert looked around as he heard more of the monsters growl.

"I think we may need to get off this island first. The prince may not wish to stain his hands again after taking a bath. I shall give him one of my spare uniforms. He cannot really see with that third eye. It can however see the life force inside others, since it was gifted to him by the master." They looked at the boat and checked the supplies to make sure it was ready to sail.

CHAPTER 31

NESTING

Rebecca placed her hand around her mid-section and rubbed it. "Well, the season is over, and I am still in my mature form. I guess that means I will be laying eggs soon."

"How long will it be until you start to lay them?" Lilith held her arm and squeezed it tightly.

"It can be in a week or a month depending on how many eggs I will lay. The more, the slower. I need to find a safe place for a nest." Rebecca looked at a map.

"Nest? You mean like a bird's nest?" She tried to help by looking at another map.

"Sort of. Normally, each clan is assigned a white dragon so we can go to her den for protection to have our eggs. With her gone, I am sure it has been taken up by another clans white dragon." She scoffed as she tossed the map.

"Why not just use—"

"I cannot use another clan's den. They would try to destroy the eggs. We may act more like humans but we still have our basic instincts as dragons. If I am killed, or unable to produce any whelps, then another clan can take over my family's ancient ties. It is what binds us to the original dragon of our clan. Other clans can become stronger when they grind up the bones up and eat them. But they can only do that when there is no one left who is feeding off of the bond." She ran out of breath as she finished and was now breathing heavily.

"I do not fully understand this but I think you are saying you need a safe place so they will not be killed off by other dragons?" Lilith slowly put the map down and seemed to be in deep thought.

"I guess that's the best way to explain it. It's more than that but yes, I need a safe place for our whelps." Rebecca sat down in defeat. "We need a new white dragon for our clan. We have to find a wild flight to acquire one. But I have been told it's rare a wild flight would allow a dragonblood to enter their den." She took another deep breath. "And the riders and their tamed flights are just stuck-up snobs."

Lilith handed her a small neckless with a purple stone in the middle of it. "Put this on. It will keep you safe."

"What's this for?" Rebecca slowly put it on.

"We are going to visit Mother. The air there is deadly to anyone without godly blood. And there is one safe spot—the village, but they do not like outsiders very much." She took Rebecca's hand, and they walked towards the forest outside of town.

"I should say something to Holt first. He needs to know. They are also his." Rebecca shifted her weight from side to side as she fidgeted her fingers.

"Look at me. Once we find a place, I will get him. Just hold on tightly. Flying on my own is not easy, mostly because one wing is larger than the other." Lilith's body grew and she towered over Rebecca. Her wings made a shushing sound as they popped out of her back. One was covered in red feathers and was a bit longer and more shapelier than the other. The other wing was covered in brown feathers and looked more like a robin's wing.

"Every time I see them up close, it amazes me." Rebecca jumped into Lilith's arms and held on to her shoulders tightly.

"If we took a boat, the journey could take over a month but I can fly us there in a few minutes. I would say less than an hour." With two flaps of her wings, they lifted below the cloud level.

Rebecca closed her eyes tightly at first. The feeling of the wind across her face caused her body to shiver. Her grip became tighter and Lilith slowed down a little.

"You need to not squeeze so hard. It is hurting my shoulder. Just open your eyes." Lilith's voice was a little deeper but had a hint of elation in it.

She slowly opened her eyes and gasped at the sight. "It's like an ocean of pillows—the clouds." The entire sky was blanketed in clouds.

"I use magic to move the clouds slightly to hide me. No one is allowed to see me fly. How is your breathing? The air up here can make you feel lightheaded." Rebecca looked at her and smiled. Lilith continued to fly at the slower pace.

After a while, the clouds parted and Rebecca could see the ocean. "This is amazing. I feel like a bird. I'm so glad I met you, Lilith. I hope we can do this more when the brood hatches." She looked up at Lilith, "Can you hear me? The wind is so loud. I can barely hear myself." Lilith did not take her eyes away from the direction she was going.

After a short while, Lilith stopped and nudged her chin, pointing for Rebecca to look somewhere. Off in the distance was a dark island. The black color made it stick out like an eerie sore on the green ocean.

"That is my home. My mother created me there. She will keep us safe." As they got closer, the jewel on Rebecca's necklace began to glow a bright pink.

They landed in what seemed to be a town in ruins. Houses were destroyed; some had scorch marks. In the center was a bright blue stone that pulsated a light.

"That looks like an elven memory stone but as big as a house." Rebecca was about to touch it when Lilith grabbed her hand.

"No! Sorry, Mother will be angry if you touch it. She is trying to share the real history of the world with everyone. To expose the lies of the gods. It is not finished yet." She let go and walked around for a bit.

"Mother is not here. She must be in her lab." Lilith walked over to the only house that was not destroyed. She pushed the door open and waved for Rebecca to follow.

Inside was a bright light and large glass tubes. They were full of half-developed bodies. Some copper wire connected them all and was jumbled across the floor.

"Mother mixed science with magic so it would be less of a strain. These are my unborn sisters—failures. She said I was only successful because of the soul of that one man. It was in the right setting." Lilith softly touched the side of one of the cylinders. Rebecca looked at the label: *Lilith thirty-four.*

"How many are there?" Rebecca slowly looked around. All of the bodies were in different stages of development.

"This is not all of them. Some of them died after development. The one before me exploded. I am the hundredth." She walked over to one that was a fully developed baby.

"My sister was created in the normal way but with the same interest—for science." She noticed a glowing red orb on the table. "Mother is not here but she left me a message."

"What's that thing?" Rebecca was trying her best to resist touching it.

"Your soul can actually record memories. If you know how to focus it, you can put that part of your soul inside this soul orb, and it will play the memory back like a message. The drawback is that you will have to give up a year of your lifespan each time." Lilith took it and placed it into a vase with copper wires connected to it.

"This allows you to activate it without using magic." She flipped a switch and sparks flew off as it began to glow brighter.

"Lilith, I see that you have disobeyed me. Your grandfather has taken your sister, so I must go and confront him. I will deal with you after I return. You know how important you are. Family is not something you need. I am ready for the second stage, so stay here." The orb turned dark.

Rebecca scoffed. "She sounded so...heartless. I can see why your emotions were stunted."

"Mother is Mother, and I love her very much. But I just want to have a life of my own." Lilith looked at a corner where there was a small bed. "That is where I grew up."

It was barely a bed, mostly falling apart with a tattered blanket.

Some toys were scattered on the ground but it was obvious they were never touched.

"Sister would give me toys but Mother would punish me if I played with them." She let out a hum and a tear rolled from her eyes.

As she turned around, the orb lit up again. The voice that came out was much kinder and Lilith's face lit up.

"Mother will try to cover my message so I hid it well. She told me about you finding love. I am so proud of you. I will deal with Mother—you live with your love. I hope I get to see you one more time before this is all over. I had a vision—it was about grandfather. You take care of her, and remember that you are your own person. May you have a happy life with her." The orb cracked and fell off the table.

Tears rolled down Lilith's cheeks and her nose ran a little. "My sister always told me to look for love so I could escape this hell. I was created to just be a shell for someone that Mother lost. I do not hate her, but I despise her." Her anger came out so strongly that it scared Rebecca. All the emotions she had been hiding started to come out all at once.

Rebecca, unable to find words just hugged her tightly as she cried into her shoulders. "Why did Mother never love me? I always did what she wanted. I always thought I would just follow her plans like she wanted and no one would ever know." Lilith just repeated the question over and over again.

After a few minutes she stopped and looked towards the door. "I know where to take you. There is a dragon's den nearby. The flight is rather large, but they are friendly towards humans. Sister took me to them once. I know they will shelter us."

They rushed out the door and quickly took off. Barely any time went by before they reached a mountain. Halfway up there, they came across a large cave. They landed in front of it and Lilith bowed down until her forehead touched the ground.

Rebecca was about to follow but Lilith stopped her. "I do not know if you remember me. I am Lilith, daughter of Melania. I come to beg you for help."

A deep, ancient voice echoed from within the cave. "Little one, I remember. You have no need to bow down to me. You are a goddess, and I am just a mere dragon."

"I have learned a lot about dragons in the past few hours. I have to beg because this is my wife. We are seeking an—"

He let out a loud roar that shook the mountain. Small rocks rolled, causing minor echoes as they bounced down the side. "She is a dragonblood with eggs growing inside of her. If you know of our ways, then you know we cannot allow her in. She is not of our flight, nor is she...how do they say it?…our kin. Our dragonblood kin is still large in numbers. We cannot bond ourselves to another clan."

"She is the last of her clan. Her white dragon was killed when the Holy City was destroyed." Lilith pressed her head down into the ground, causing it to bleed.

"I will not allow you to hurt yourself over this matter, little one. Stand up and come inside. I will allow her to come in while I discuss it with the elders of the flight." They slowly walked inside. The temperature was almost perfect.

The cave was large and seemed to be carved out by tools. The smooth edges with some designs here and there made it have a majestic feel. They followed what looked to be a hall that led into a cavern. It housed hundreds of dragons of all colors and sizes.

The whelps were about the size of a large dogs, while the older dragons could fill in a courtyard. Rebecca was unable to contain her excitement.

"Look, over there is a gem dragon! They spew molten glass. Father told me they are extremely rare." The dragon let out a low growl as she turned his head away from her.

There was a group of large dragons letting out low grunts. The one who seemed to be the eldest was a red fire dragon. His scales had lost their shine; some even had cracks.

He looked at them and lowered his head. His green eyes focused on Rebecca, and he let out more grunts.

"Holy crap, it's true! Dragons communicate by low grunts and body heat. Father said they are actually words that are spoken in a way that our ears cannot make them out." Rebecca couldn't contain herself.

"They are talking about what kind of dragon you are. He said that you are a lightning dragon. Then he pointed out that you are a runt, which is why you must be protected." Lilith kicked around a stone that looked like a large golden nugget.

"Of course you can understand them. I wish I was able to speak to dragons. I am a dragon myself." She stood there and tried to listen. She cupped her hands around her ears but eventually gave up and cursed under her breath.

The red dragon began to glow and his body shrank to a human form. "I have not used this magic in thousands of years. We have decided to give your clan a fighting chance. Your clan's ancient cave has been taken by another clan, thinking you were gone or were about to die off. They have yet to destroy your tie to your blood but I do not think they will wait long. We shall help you in reclaiming it, and we also have a youngling white dragon in need of a clan."

A dragon as white as clouds slowly walked up. It was barely the size of a house. The red dragon nodded. "She is not able to use magic to turn into the human form. Our blood kin are a large clan but we can spare her. We know of the ancient one you are related to. That is why we are being so generous."

The white dragon looked at Rebecca and lowered her head to sniff her. It let out a loud clicking sound. The red dragon grunted a little and made a sound like he was clearing his throat. He seemed to have forgotten he was in the human form.

"It appears that you are not going to be able to make the trip. You are a week in, and it looks like you are going to birth five eggs." He walked a little closer to her. "You will lay your first one by the end of this week."

He looked at the other elder dragons and started to make gestures with his hands. One of them let out a grunt and pushed him with its head.

"Just speak, you old fool." It was a low female voice. Not soft, but not rough. "Speaking in dragon tongue while in human form is as silly as watching a dwarf seduce an orc while drunk."

"She is about to lay her eggs. She is in a delicate state right now.

We are not really tied to any dragonblood clan. We only share one ancestor with them." He looked back at them and smiled. "She is also a runt. Even if she was at her best, that is not even half of what a pure-blood could do. I think we should prove to the world that wild dragons have changed."

"How come they keep bringing up me being a runt?" Rebecca said with some anger.

The young white dragon had a soft voice. Her human speech was still developing but they understood her. "In the wild, runts we kill. Even dragonbloods follow this at times. It means your clan was almost wiped out before and could not afford the loss of a single member. The elder has always admired the dragonbloods."

A blue dragon lowered his head and looked at Rebecca closely. His voice sounded like he was underwater. "Runt, you may be offended by us calling you by that title but that is how we are. We will allow you to nest here until the eggs are strong enough to be transferred to your nest, which we will clear for you. For now, you will be in the small den that was made for hatchlings."

A purple dragon lowered her head. Her voice also had a muffled sound to it. "All our whelps are now younglings, so you will not have to worry about them trying to destroy your eggs. We will work on training your white dragon to transform into the human form. You will need her for the birthing."

A loud crash came from outside the cave. The elder red dragon quickly transformed back into his dragon form and lowered his head with a slight growl.

A deep familiar voice echoed. It said, "Here, chick, chick, chick."

Aeron slowly walked in with a grin on his face. He pointed at the elders and howled at them. "You have an amulet I need!"

CHAPTER 32
THE TALISMAN

The elder dragon grunted like he was clearing his throat. "My lord Aeron, what do we owe to receive such an honor as your visit?" He lowered his head as if to bow to him.

"I see that you have allowed this filth into your den. Dragonbloods are a stain on my perfect creation. Allow me to kill her and I shall not harm any of you." He looked at the dragons and they backed away in fear.

Rebecca stood there and cried, "I have the blood of dragons in my veins. I did not choose this. Why do you hate us? My father worshiped you."

"My poor little lamb, I am doing this out of mercy. Dragons mixed with humans, and eventually, your kind was born. It is a weakness that I need to correct." He took a step closer but stumbled a little.

Lilith looked at him closely. "He has not fully recovered from our last battle. His body is still falling apart. I think I could beat him." Her wings popped out and she rushed at him.

Lilith slammed into him and crushed him into the cave wall. He tried to punch her off but his weakened body was unable to budge her. A tail came from his rear and knocked her to the ground. Before he could stomp on her, she bounced up and uppercut him.

In a desperate attempt, he grabbed a boulder and hit her in the face with it. He looked at the dragons and yelled out. "Help me kill them both! I command it!"

The elder red dragon came forward and said in a sheepish voice, "I understand why you did what you did, my lord. I was but a whelp when you started your war. But your war had dire consequences."

The others came to stand beside him. "You went to war with every race and lost. Every race hunted us and almost drove us to extinction. They would even hunt before your war but not to the extent that you forced them to. My brother was hunted by the blood pact child because he decided to carry on your war with the Amazons. His entire flight was killed because we became a threat. After we started to breed with humans, they left us alone. Many think of us as ancient legends, fairy tales."

Aeron's face turned red and he growled before he spoke. "If you help me, I will make you beyond legends." The skin on his arm began to split open.

"Lord, we will always think of you as our god but you have lost your way. That body is proof of that. We will be forced to fight you if you touch that young dragonblood. We have made a vow to protect her." The five elders surrounded him.

Aeron tried to make a dash for Rebecca but was slammed into the ground by Lilith as she dove into him from above. The impact made them fall into a lower cavern. Their grunting echoed as they fought. Rebecca slowly walked towards the hole to watch but Lilith flew through it and hovered above the hole.

A ball of fire followed her. She twisted her body, barely able to dodge. It caused an explosion as it hit the cavern wall, causing large boulders to fall to the ground. Many of the smaller dragons tried to dodge so they wouldn't be crushed.

Aeron climbed out of the hole and caught Lilith by the neck when she tried to dive at him again. He threw her to the ground and stomped on her chest. The smell of rotting flesh began to fill the air as the skin on his arm began to peel off.

He shot another fireball at the cavern wall and caused more boulders to fall. This time, not all of the little ones managed to dodge.

He looked at all of them and growled. "Give me the talisman. I know a human gave you an ancient artifact made by the elf goddess Ailtaytay. The necklace of Alfife. Give it to me now!"

The elder dragon made some grunting noises. "If we give it to you, will you leave us?"

"I swear to you as your god that I shall leave you be for now. I will even spare these two lambs. Just give it to me now!" He spit out blood as he spoke and readied another fireball.

The gem dragon walked forward. Her body began to glow a little and she turned into the human form. Unlike the elder who had managed to make the illusion of clothing, this one was naked. She headed towards a small cave and came out with the necklace.

She gently placed it around Aeron's neck and whispered in his ear. He smiled and kissed her cheek. A bright light flowed from her body into his and she began to age rapidly. Shortly after, her body turned to dust and he began to heal.

"She was of my flight, loyal till the end. I will honor her by killing you all when I get my scale back." He began to laugh as his body healed rapidly. He took his foot off of Lilith and kicked her into the wall. He then just stood there, wide open for her to attack.

She got up and dove into him but she bounced off. He punched her in the face a few times and each blow cracked bones. Rebecca tried to jump in but was stopped by her white dragon.

"If you do a breath attack, it will kill your eggs. She will survive this." Just as she said that, a large red tail brushed overhead and knocked Aeron to the ground.

He stood up and his body rapidly healed. "I shall return to finish you off. Dragons who do not obey their god shall be purged. Maybe I should start all over again and erase you all from this realm." Dragon wings sprouted from his back and he flew up, bursting though the top of the cavern.

Rebecca ran to Lilith as she cried. She checked her body and noticed that it was healing slowly. They embraced tightly.

The red dragon lowered his head and said, "Sorry, little one. If we attacked inside the cave, many of our young would have died. I fear we must prepare for war. Our god wants to now kill every last dragon."

CHAPTER 33
THE ETERNAL SPY

Verus looked around, trying to figure out how to open the casket. He slowly moved his hands across it, seeing if he could make out the women's shape.

A dwarf stood next to him and cleared his throat as he said, "Sir, we be at this for a month. I know ya want to touch her perfect tits but she be locked in there ya' know."

"Sorry, master dwarf, I know it seems a bit obsessive but I am going over every lore I know to figure out who she is. She looks to be in her early twenties." He walked off and sat at a makeshift stool.

"We been here for weeks. Ya scared off the ghouls, and we established an outpost. I feel it in me gut that we should prepare for an attack." The dwarf looked at the girl closely. "I think they be back for her."

Garlic came in singing the ballad of the Unknown Goddess. "My dear friend, I knew I would find you here. Do you fancy her? She is very perky despite her age."

Verus grunted a little and the dwarf walked off. "Have you found anything written about her? Something about her scares me. That black liquid looks like that tar I saw that devours people, and here she is simply swimming in it. I think she is the source of it."

"That stuff is pure evil. There are legends about it, but still, I have not found a thing on her." Garlic smiled and sat next to him.

"I think you should look for the books of Dumas. Legend says that they mention a history that we do not have in our books. An erased past." Garlic let out a deep breath and stared off into a corner.

Verus pulled out a small engraved dagger. "I used to be part of a guard force that would escort diggers. They would find artifacts that were never mentioned in any records. They once said that much of the evidence they found showed that the war that happened ten thousand years ago was not the war between the gods and demons; that was much older. The history books were amended to hide the real war." He grunted as he pondered over the matter.

"That was the Fallen War," Garlic said in a soft tone.

He then looked at Verus and smiled. "I have not seen your daughter for a while. Where has she gone?"

"She is with her wife in some town. They never had a proper honeymoon. I think the last time she contacted me, they had found a match to get Rebecca pregnant." He chuckled a little under his breath.

"She is Melania's daughter if I am correct?"

"I do not remember telling you her mother's name." Verus' vision started to blur a little as Garlic looked into his eyes.

"You told me about it last week, remember?"

"Oh, I remember now. She was created by magic, so I guess I am lucky she is as lovely as she is. I have seen many magical creations. They are by and large ugly." Verus rubbed his eyes as he talked.

"I hope her short vacation is going well." Garlic turned his head and mumbled under his breath.

"Well, I think we should head out towards the elf outpost. I have a feeling someone will be back to reclaim this body." Verus stood up and tried to walk away when Garlic grabbed his arm.

"I am just an old elf, but I do think you are a very interesting human. You have an amazing foresight. I just want you to know—you are valued." He let go and Verus stumbled around like a drunkard.

After he was out of sight, Garlic pulled out a communication stone.

"I am on top of it, my lord. I will send a shadow to find the younger one and will personally go to the Amazon forest myself."

A child's voice came out of the stone. "Father is a little busy. I am Albert. He has allowed me to take control of this mission. Only have the shadow gather information for the moment. We would rather have the Amazon queen—the other is just a second option. Take caution. This is a vital step."

The glow of the stone stopped, and Garlic took a deep breath. "That young lad has the sound of a future leader. I wonder what Master's plan is for him."

Garlic slowly walked out of the mine while taking in the sights. When he exited, he was greeted by armed soldiers. The ones in front aimed their spears at his throat as the others in the rear drew back their bows.

The elf queen stood on top of her horse so that he could see her. She had adjusted her armor to add extra padding to the empty spot where her arm used to be. "The spell you have cast wore off. Only a fool would use a name like Garlic."

He smiled and raised his arms. "Do you not remember me? I helped you learn how to ride a horse. I introduced you to the king."

Her vision became blurry, and she steadied her head with her hand. "Elves use names of flowers when given a human name. The spell will not work. We found the body."

"I see. I never really cared for the culture of the high elf kind. I am surprised how soon my spell has worn off." A dark shadow engulfed him and then it disappeared, exposing his true self. He had twelve fingers on each hand and a hunched back.

"What type of monster might you be, sir?" The elf queen had a slight smile as she asked.

"I am an eternal. I am usually just in my library, but I was bored and was offered something. I think this is a fine time to allow my children to feed. They are hungry, and I have been getting bored." He snapped his fingers and spiders the size of three horses came rushing out of the mines.

One of the archers managed to hit one with an arrow but it bounced off and made a sound like it hit metal. Spears had the same effect.

One spider leaped at the queen, but Verus intercepted by slamming into its flank with his shield. He went into his defensive stance, allowing the shield to cover most of his body. Each time the spider tried to strike him, he would deflect it with his shield. On the fifth attempt, he managed to counter by ramming with his shield, knocking it off balance. The spider tried to get back up but Verus jumped on its body shield first and crushed it.

Garlic winced in pain. "Ah, I see, my friend. I knew you would find a way to kill them. I have great respect for you, and I truly developed an attachment to you." He snapped his fingers and every spider took off into the woods. Each had one or two soldiers cocooned up in a web sac.

"Thirty will do. I will grant this to you as a thank you for being a good friend to me." A spider almost twice the size of the others came out and picked up the eternal and carried him off. His laughter echoed in Verus' mind.

"You have saved me again, my old friend. This has indeed become a bad habit of mine, needing to be saved by lower beings. With one less arm now, I think my fighting days are over." The elf queen was out of breath and each word was almost a struggle.

"My queen, I think me saving you is just part of the duty of being a knight." He looked around and tried to catch his breath. "I fear we are not ready for what is about to come next. I think that body is more important than we can imagine."

"As the high queen, I would say abandon it and save my people. But the gut feeling I have is telling me that we must defend it till the last." She made a movement as if she was trying to pull up a sword with her missing arm. She blushed slightly and used her other arm.

"Verus, use this sword. It will enhance your ability of foresight. I will provide every soldier I can muster. I will also send word to the high king requesting aid. I just hope they will get here in time." She handed him her sword but he hesitated to take it.

"Verus, what seems to be bothering your mind?"

He mumbled a little and then tried to find his words. "Everything that spy said. I feel he was trying to make a connection with me. I sort of feel like I just lost a good friend."

She smirked a little. "A good spy makes real friendships. It is why elves always made better spies. Humans just never have the time."

CHAPTER 34
BIRTH OF A CLAN

"Holy shit! I never knew it would hurt this much." Rebecca cried as she laid on a tiny nest that was made just for her. Lilith held her arms while the white dragon, who was in her human form, prepared a fire.

"Hold her tighter. We cannot allow her to budge even a little. She might crush the egg." The white dragon slowly walked towards them and motioned for Rebecca to spread her legs.

"How much longer will this hell last?" Rebecca tried to move her arms but Lilith was too strong.

The white dragon looked at her body and spoke in a tune that resembled singing. "I have never delivered dragonblood eggs before, but if it is like anything the elder has told me, I would say you'll have four, maybe five eggs. So two more days at the most."

"This was a dumb idea, getting pregnant. I think humans have it easier, and dragons." She cried out her words as she attempted to hide her pain unsuccessfully.

Lilith kissed her forehead and sang along with the white dragon as she spoke. "This is an amazing sacrifice you are making for our happiness."

"I can see why my mother was such a bitch at times. These

bastards owe me for this pain." She grunted as the white dragon told her to push.

After a long grunt and a slight sigh of relief, the dragon pulled out a yellow egg with blue stripes. It was the size of a small pumpkin but was slowly getting bigger. The egg was gently placed in a nest by the fire.

"I think you will have another hour before the next one is ready to be pushed out. Dragons just lay them all at once. This is more of a strain for me and the mother." The tone of the dragon's voice had lowered and she sighed as she sat down for a moment.

Lilith, unable to hide her excitement, ran towards the egg. She had the look of a child in a candy store. "This is so beautiful. I have never seen such a perfect thing in my life. How long will this take?"

The white dragon snapped at her, "Do not touch the eggs!" Then she took a deep breath and calmed down. "Sorry, the eggs are very fragile. Depending on how strong the father's blood is, it can take a month at the most. I am not really sure. As I said, I have never even witnessed a dragonblood egg being laid nor ever seen a brood hatching."

"A month to see the most perfect children to ever walk the earth. I hope I am a worthy mother to be blessed by them." Lilith was unable to take her eyes off the egg as it grew to the size of a watermelon and then stopped.

"Oh, the next egg is ready sooner than expected. Lilith, please hold her arms again." The white dragon sang out her words again as Rebecca screamed out curse words.

"May the fucken' gods take my life now and end my suffering," she cried out as she pushed.

* * *

"These were the longest two days of my life. Lilith, I am going to lie here and die now. If you wake me up, I will kill you." Rebecca passed out and started snoring.

Lilith stared at the eggs, never taking her eyes off them, not even to blink. "All five are here and safe. I cannot wait to see my babies. This will be the longest month of my life. I have never been more excited about something. I hope I will be a good mommy."

"Young one, just be ready for when they hatch. You might be a little depressed until they get older." The white dragon walked next to her.

"Dragonbloods still have our instincts. The hatchlings are more dragon than human. They are purely instinctual, and they know whom their mother and father are by smell. They will not enjoy your company until they are a little older and more aware of things." Lilith nodded at the white dragon while she inspected the eggs carefully.

"None of them are runts. Consider it lucky... as the mother is a runt." She said that in a way that made Lilith a little upset.

"I am fine with them not needing me at first. I can still watch over the brood. I will be their protector." She looked around and noticed that the dragon was back into her dragon form and was staring at her.

"It will take us both to keep the eggs safe. If there is even a single mishap, one can die. Notice how warm the fire is? It must stay lit the entire time. They can get a little cold when you are adding more wood to the fire but not for very long. I need you to gather wood while I nap. When you come back, I will watch them as you nap." The dragon laid her head down and closed her eyes.

* * *

Lilith's eyes widened as one of the eggs wiggled. She tried to shout at the others but was worried she would scare the little one. So she decided to toss a rock at Rebecca and the dragon.

They quickly ran over as little legs popped out of the egg. Arms and a head followed as the baby stretched. Shortly, they heard crying as other eggs began to wiggle.

"They are the most perfect things I have ever seen!" Lilith could hardly contain herself as all her emotions came out.

"I'm glad that the white dragon helped teach you how to express your emotions, but now you are always a little noisy." Out of natural instinct, Rebecca picked up the baby and rubbed her nose to the baby's as it stopped crying. She did it one by one as each one popped out.

"Well, more girls to listen to. I just hope they do not cause me problems like I did to my mother." She let out a grunt as she had flashbacks of her youth.

"Rebecca, three of them are boys. I am sure I know that is a penis." Lilith pointed at one of them.

The white dragon took a closer look while in her dragon form. "I thought you said the father was a human."

"He was, I'm sure he was—he thought he was. How am I to know every race and sub-race?" She scoffed a little and looked closer. There were three boys with yellow hair and eyes.

"I think you are the first dragonblood to give birth to boys by a human mate." The dragon whistled songs at them.

"I do not understand. Why is everyone surprised?" Lilith stood there staring at the babies.

Rebecca carefully covered them with blankets as she tried to explain. "Dragonbloods only have girls unless they mate with another dragonblood. That is the only time they have males."

Lilith lowered her face close to one as it was sleeping and whispered, "I think they are all perfect. I will be a great mommy."

A male voice softly echoed in the cave. It sounded a bit childish but had a deep tone. "I am now a great uncle."

They turned around and saw a man standing there. His skin was dark gray. He had no eyes, except for the one on his forehead. His clothing was that of a noble, and he grinned as he stood at the entryway.

The white dragon growled at him as she said, "Who are you?"

He bowed politely. "I am Apophis. I am Lilith's uncle."

Lilith jumped back a little and said in a worried voice, "How did you break free? I checked on you—"

"Over a year ago. You have not checked on my prison for over a year. I was able to see you each time you paid me a little visit. I pretended to be in a slumber so you would give false reports to my darling sister. It became easier to gain power once you stopped visiting." His grin became a frown.

"I hate to bother you at this time of great joy but I must take you. I decided it is time we bonded and got to know your uncle. If you come with me, I promise I will not harm any of the new babies." He took small and shallow breaths. "I am learning how to show compassion. I do think my love wishes to have one of these things, so I must show that I am no longer a monster."

The white dragon let out a beam of bright light. It burned the rocks as it passed over and hit Apophis. He just stood there, unaware that anything hit him. Rebecca charged at him with her breath attack ready and punched the side of his head. He still just stood there.

"You must be the love." He looked at Rebecca with his one eye and grabbed her arm. She tried to kick and punch him but all she managed to do was break her skin and bleed on him.

Lilith attacked with her sword. He moved his head slightly to dodge her and grabbed her with his other hand. "Did my sister tell you my skin is the hardest substance to exist? If you keep on resisting, I will snap this little dragon's neck." They both stopped struggling and Lilith nodded her head.

He grinned as he let Rebecca go and held onto Lilith's shoulders. "See, I can be a kind god. I will even tell you some exciting news. I know you had a run in with Aeron. You shall be glad to know that he died over a month ago. Now, we will be off. I will even allow you to say parting words."

Tears fell from both Lilith and Rebecca's eyes as they held hands. "I only agreed because he would kill the babies, and I cannot allow that. Father will save me. Just find him." They tried to kiss but Lilith disappeared along with Apophis.

"He used a teleportation spell. It would kill mortals to use such magic." The dragon looked at Rebecca. "Little one, you must stay and protect your broodlings. They can only be taken care of properly by the mother or the father."

"If I tell you where their father is, can you bring him here?" Rebecca was barely able to hold back her anger.

"I can. I also know of some spells to make milk for the babies. However, that man withstood even my attack. What will you do?"

"When he held onto my arm, it was like he was holding a twig. There is only one other person who has made me feel that helpless. She is the only one I know that can help me. I must find Aluxes." She rubbed the tears from her eyes as she looked at the white dragon. She clenched her fists tightly, turning her knuckles white as the veins in her face bulged.

CHAPTER 35

ASSAULT ON THE AMAZONS

The stars danced in the night sky. The light from the torches barely broke the canopy of the thick tree line. In the center of the forest was a large city, the place of the Amazonian people. In the center of the city was a large fire pit. Many children sat around as an elder told stories about their legends and laws. The elder would time the blinking of one of the stars with his story. Therefore, when a tragedy would occur in the story, the star would vanish. He would clap his hands and the star would return, marking the end of the story.

Parents walked their children home for the night. They went to their little houses which all seemed to be connected, forming a maze. A few of the families walked into the forest since they did not live in the city. As one of the guards watched the last family walk into the thick forest, a loud scream echoed.

A handful of guards ran into the forest, each holding a spear. A man holding a torch that had a brighter light then regular torches followed the girls. One of the guards let out a light gasp as she fell onto a large web.

The man with the torch waved it around and noticed that the entire area was covered in webs. They tried their best not to utter a word out of fear something would hear them.

Screams echoed out in the distance. The group tried to free their stuck comrade by hitting the web with spears and swords, but the material was too strong.

The man with the torch heard a wiggling noise and moved the torch to see a person wrapped up in the webbing. It was hard to tell if it was a man or women. The small hole they were breathing out of was too narrow to see anything properly.

A giant spider quickly lowered from a nearby tree and snatched the body faster than the man could blink. Screams followed shortly after.

The man looked up and let out a loud scream that startled the girls. They all also looked and saw a spider the size of three horses looking down at them. On its back was an old man. The spider leaped down and the group jumped in different directions to avoid getting squashed.

One of the guards quickly swung her sword but it bounced off the leg of the spider and they heard the sound of metal hitting metal. Another tried a spear but the weapon's shaft snapped.

The spider raised its two front legs, exposing its dagger-sized fangs. It bit one of the girls and stabbed two more with its front legs. Their screams filled the others with fear, and they ran off towards the city. One of the guards looked behind her as she reached the city and noticed that she was the only one left.

In the distance, she could still see the light that the man held. It slowly faded out as he screamed.

The guard quickly rang a large bell by her post, which was followed by other bells. Every abled Amazon rushed out and was ready to fight. Some of the men equipped themselves with swords and stayed in their houses to protect their family.

The surviving guard screamed out "*Moasa!*" and tried making the shape of a spider with her hands.

They quickly broke out into squads and each group made a double spear wall line. They stood there ready, waiting for something to jump out of the deep dark jungle.

A large spider leaped out into the spear wall and crushed a handful of soldiers. It scurried off as the archers tried to hit it. Another spider climbed up one of the towers and pulled the archer off. Her screams stopped when she hit the ground. Eleven spiders rushed into the city, causing utter chaos.

The twelfth spider with the man on its back went straight for the large pyramid and barged into the throne room. The rider laughed as he saw the Amazon king sitting on the throne, quietly looking at the spider.

"I am sorry to barge in like this but I wish to see your queen. Her uncle wishes to see her." The old man stood on top of the spider and bowed.

The king stood up. He was a large, muscular man, and his skin was almost the color of bronze. His thick black beard came barely below his chin, and he had an odd smile on his face as he moved his hands to gesture.

His voice was deep and powerful. He was a man that sounded like he was raised by grace. "She is not here at the moment. Her grandfather is having words with her. I am her husband. I demand you leave her kingdom at once." He slowly walked down the steps towards the spider while popping his knuckles.

"I am sorry, sir. I have no idea who you are. I pride myself in knowing everything, but you—I have never heard of." The old man raised his hand, exposing his twelve fingers as he held his head and pondered.

"I am a hero from a long-forgotten age who is now dead to the world outside of this kingdom. I pride myself in not being known." He stood in a fighting stance, ready to battle the spider.

"You wish to fight my spider with your bare hands? I have seen many fools try to take them out with every weapon you can think of. You are the first moron to try with your hands." The old man tried his best to hold in his laughter.

The spider tried to stab the king with his mandible but the man grabbed it and held it in place. The spider struggled as it attempted to pull away but the grip was strong.

"Now, I shall show you why I am the king to my beloved." The king pulled back, causing the spider to fall over. The old elf managed to leap off before he hit the ground.

The spider leaped back up and charged at the king. Then it stopped short. Curving its abdomen, it shot webbing at the king. It knocked him over and he became stuck to the ground. The spider rushed over but was halted by the elf.

"I still do not remember who you are. I have never heard of a human with your strength." The elf stood over him, deep in thought.

"As I said, I am forgotten. Even by an eternal like you. I am fully aware of who you are, and I remember seeing you." The king grunted as he struggled to break free from the web.

The elf waved his hand. He looked strangely sad. "Well, I would love to bring you back to my library, but sadly, I must kill you and inform my lord that we need to capture the queen's sister." He waved his hand and the spider slowly approached.

It lowered its fangs and was ready to strike when the king let out a laugh. "I guess playtime is over." His fist broke from the web and went into the spider's head, killing it.

The elf screamed in pain as the man stood up and popped his knuckles. "I hate to use this to win a battle but it seems that you are very powerful. I shall tell you my name, young man."

The king stood still and whispered in a low voice that only the elf could hear. "But how can you know my name and not die?" The elf let out another painful scream and fell to the ground.

"I take it they found out how to kill your little spiders." He stood over the elf like a giant and grinned.

"You have the energy of a human but the power of the gods." Out of fear, the elf quickly raised his hands and shot out a bolt of lightning. The king flew and hit the ground.

"That blood, I know the smell of that blood! You are one of the three children. Tell me, have you seen your father, Turiacus, lately? My Mast—" He let out another scream as one more spider died.

"I have not seen my father since the death of my older brother." The king rubbed his face. "I went through great pains to get rid of the blasted curse that his blood gave me."

The elf screamed some more and laid there, unable to move. The king stood up and slowly walked towards him.

He was unable to hide his joy. "If I remember, once your last spider dies, you also die. Such is the curse of the Fallen eternal."

The elf howled and one of the remaining spiders rushed in and grabbed the elf as they ran away.

One of the soldiers rushed in to check on the king. He held up his hand and smiled. "The royal family is fine. There is a reason why your queen married me." The guard noticed the dead spider and looked around for a weapon.

The spiders rushed for two days until they reached a beach. They gently lowered the elf, and he cried as he counted his spiders. He raised his hands and noticed that he had four missing fingers.

He grunted through his pain and pulled out an orb from his robe. "Sir, I have to inform you that the queen has been taken to the holy realm. We must go after the sister."

"Ah, the little spy, I remember you. My love granted you the gift to regain youth every time a spider ate someone."

The elf fell back as he spoke. "Lord Apophis, I did not expect to hear from you so soon."

"Tell me what your shadow has learned. Where is the sister?"

"Yes lord. Well, she has made a home in a cave. Her wife is a pregnant dragonblood and is ready to lay her eggs." His voice trembled a little as he talked.

"I think it is time she had some one-on-one time with her uncle. I would like to congratulate her on expanding our family. I am sure Father would be happy."

"Yes, my lord. I shall tell you how to find her."

CHAPTER 36

BATTLE FOR THE BODY

Taranis paced back and fourth from his desk to the table. He pondered as he slowly waved his hand and moved a chess piece.

Albert let out a soft breath and moved his rook. He smiled. "Checkmate."

Taranis laughed. "Good work, my boy. You have learned the art very quickly. As a reward, I will allow you to help me plan our attack."

Albert carefully removed the board while Taranis placed a map on the table. "We have around two thousand dark elves and maybe five hundred nal and nox."

"And their own numbers, Father?"

"Maybe three thousand, more on the way. After the spy was discovered, they have figured out that we will come back for the body." They both looked at the map carefully.

"Do we know the route that the reinforcements are arriving from?" Albert put his face closer to the map.

Taranis used charcoal to draw a line. "The elf kingdom is arriving from this direction. There is another group of elves coming from this direction." He drew another line.

"During the day, the only real army we have is the dark elves. The nal and the nox are useless during the day. If we attack at night, the larger part of our forces will be targeted by the nal and nox. We need more that are allied to us besides the dark elves." The confidence in Albert's tone made him sound older.

"You are correct, my boy, which is why I decided to make a pact with the trolls. It was easy since they are eager to rise above the orcs. I do not know how many troops they will send, so I did not count it in our roster." Taranis placed stones on the map to represent forces.

"What do you think would be best, son?"

"I think we should use the trolls to attack that smaller group of reinforcements. Both are unknown in numbers. If we send the dark elves to attack the other reinforcements, it may draw out some of the forces in the outpost to aid. We then get the others into the outpost to cause chaos, and then use that to bring in the trolls and dark elves to finish the rest off—that is—assuming any of the groups win." Albert looked up with a smile on his face.

"That is indeed a risky yet a good plan. It leaves too much to chance. You only looked at the map and came up with a good plan, but there is a lot that the map does not show." He stood there, waiting for Albert to figure it out.

"What is there to see here?" Albert tried to look more closely but was still confused.

"There is the underground. One area many fail to protect them- selves from is underground. We will use sappers to dig a tunnel and collapse one of the towers from underneath, while another group digs a hole to inside the outpost." He drew more lines to show the areas they will tunnel.

"Why dig to the tower?"

"It will distract them. They will focus on the one spot, while our men ambush them. They had already started digging a week ago and shall reach it by today." Taranis readied his sword and armor.

Albert tried to get ready as well but was stopped. "No, you must stay here, for if we fail, you must run back to Master and let her know. Tell her everything you know, even about my lord's condition to his awakening."

Taranis approached a small encampment where the tunnel entrance started. "We must take the post before the reinforcements arrive. How much longer till they knock the tower?"

A dark elf wearing gold-plated armor smiled. "The ghoul lords that they chased out have been great allies. They are able to dig much faster with their army."

"It is the first time that ghouls have joined any force to fight in a battle. I promised them they could live in their home once we take it back for them." Taranis checked his armor and sword to make sure everything was connected properly.

"I shall lead the charge. We need to make sure we get the body back no matter the cost." He pulled out his sword and shouted as the elves followed him into the tunnel.

* * *

"Sir Verus, some of the men swear they can hear sounds." An elf ran up and bowed in front of him.

"Where is this sound coming from?" Verus raised his head as the elf pointed to one of the guard towers.

Verus walked towards the tower and placed his ear next to the ground. "Get off the tower at once!" He quickly jumped back as the tower began to shake.

The elves on the top tried to quickly rush down the steps as the walls began to crumble. It collapsed before any could make it out. The elves screamed as it crushed them.

"Ghouls are digging through!" Verus got into a battle stance as others formed up with him.

"I have never heard of ghouls attacking an outpost before," one of the elf officers said as he stood next to him.

"It is rare, but when ghoul lords really like a place, they would do anything to take it back, and this group has three." The ground rumbled a little and then suddenly stopped.

Everyone stood in battle formation, ready for the ghouls to swarm out but they never came. Some of the men started to lower their weapons as they mumbled amongst each other.

"Stay ready, soldiers. This is one of their tactics." Verus stayed focused on the tower.

Then, the ground behind them exploded as a fireball erupted out. Before the troops had time to turn, Taranis charged forward and cut down five troops.

Dark elves stormed in from behind and charged. When the elves turned to deal with the ambush, a large log from the tower flew into the formation, killing three as it slammed into them. A ghoul lord stood there snickering as lower ghouls rushed from behind him.

The fighting was intense but the ambush was a bit too successful and the elves were unable to recover. None of them could match Taranis or the ghoul lord.

Arrows from outside the post began to rain in. The dark elf archers had an easy time picking off the defenders as they became more surrounded.

"Men, stay strong. The queen will be here with reinforcements soon!" Verus tried his best to encourage the troops to raise their spirits but it was mostly in vain as they barely made a dent to the enemy.

Verus found a small gap in the encirclement and used his shield to push his way through, making it bigger. Other elves quickly followed. They managed to attack the ghoul side from the rear and make the weak point wider.

The ghoul lord let out a loud growl and pointed at Verus. The other ghouls backed off and made noises that sounded like chanting. As the ghouls broke from the fight, the encirclement became weaker and the defenders had a better chance of fighting off the dark elves.

The ghoul lord charged at Verus, swinging the large stone blade at him wildly. Its speed surprised everyone and Verus barely had time to block it.

The ghoul kept swinging wildly and rapidly, not allowing him to focus on the beast. He tried his best to dodge but the beast's speed was too much. His shield became more dented and cracked with each block.

When it tried to kick him, he managed to swing his sword and cut its leg. The ghoul cried in pain and backhanded Verus at the same time, knocking him off his feet.

Verus used the momentum to roll back onto his feet. His helmet was cracked; a piece was blocking his sight so he was forced to take it off. "You know of my ability. Not allowing me to focus on you." The ghoul attacked like a wild animal, barely giving him time to prepare for a block.

He was pushed back and tripped over a stone. The beast leaped at him, trying to take the advantage but was unable to avoid his blade as he raised it up.

It pierced the ghoul's shoulder, causing it to back off a little and giving Verus the time to get back up. The beast tried to attack again but the wound made his swing weaker. It was deflected with little effort.

"I have already won this, you foul beast. I do have actual talent as a fighter." Verus stood in a stance behind his shield. He slanted it upwards slightly. "I also had time to focus on you."

The ghoul gripped the blade with both hands and used all his might to swing. The very moment it touched his shield, Verus let go and ducked as the angle made it go above his head. He lunged from his squatted position towards the beast and plunged his blade deep into its chest. The ghoul yelped loudly and fell over dead. The elves cheered as one ran up to him to congratulate him.

Verus held his arm close to his body. "I was a little slow, I broke my fucken' arm."

The cheering slowly died down as they noticed that the ghouls did not run. The sound of swords clashing on the other side ended. Taranis stood there with his sword pointed at Verus as they were now surrounded.

"You are a remarkable soldier. I would hate to end you here. I would also like to add—the other two ghoul lords do not look very happy that you killed one of their brothers." He nodded his head towards the hole. The ghoul lords stood ready to fight Verus.

"I will be a fair general and request you to surrender this post. I will gladly allow you to run to the reinforcements that should arrive by the end of the day." Verus nodded and Taranis lowered his sword.

"Ah, I see the other party went well." Taranis smiled as Verus turned his head towards the opened gate and saw trolls strolling in with corpses of elves slung over their shoulders.

"Mark my words, I will be back. The queen and I will retake this mine." Verus sounded confident but he was terrified on the inside. He counted over a thousand trolls.

Taranis whispered in his ear, "You can have this fucken' shaft if you want. I will only need this area until your daughter arrives. I am sure I can hold out long enough for that." Verus tried to lash out in anger with his sword but Taranis pummeled his broken arm.

Some of the elves quickly dragged him as he tried to fight them. He screamed, "I will kill you if you harm her, you fucken' monster!"

As if to taunt him, Taranis waved at him with a smirk before the gates closed. The cheering from the inside drowned out the commotion of their retreat.

"Let go of me. I can walk!" Verus looked at the wall with anger blazing in his heart. "We need to be smart. We shall set up a camp before the queen shows up. I will starve out his entire army if I must." He looked around at the men. "We need to make a pact with the dwarves."

An elf officer looked at him and tried to speak. "*Iayati hummao*" He then pointed to his head.

"No, my friend. Their is no honor in King Loux. He is allied to this monster—he can go to hell!" Verus spit on the ground. "After I stop this bloody mess, I will kill the king myself."